THE RUIN OF SOULS

Michael Carlon

ISBN-13:978-1-7321846-7-1

For the memory of Sam Witryol, Ph.D. I learned so much from the wisdom he shared on our walks between the Psychology building at the University of Connecticut and Monteith Hall.

The Prayer to St. Michael

St. Michael the Archangel,
defend us in battle.
Be our defense against the wickedness and snares of the Devil.
May God rebuke him, we humbly pray,
and do thou,
O Prince of the heavenly hosts,
by the power of God,
thrust into hell Satan,
and all the evil spirits,
who prowl about the world
seeking the ruin of souls.

CHAPTER ONE

A Coded Message

I walked briskly across the University of Connecticut campus towards the psychology building, and the early April sky looked as if it was going to open up at any minute. *Screw the May flowers*, I thought to myself. The last thing I wanted to do was start off the most important presentation of my life self-conscious over being soaking wet. I made a note to myself to buy a damn raincoat, even if it would make me look like Columbo.

I stopped for a moment in front of St. Thomas Aquinas Church on campus. While I was once a man of strong faith, a series of events eroded my belief in a loving God, including the death of my son and the clergy sexual abuse scandal. That an all-powerful being could let such tragedy befall his children was a laughable notion. Still, there was something about that building that seemed to call to me every time I passed by and I often found myself stopping in front of it and staring at it. The clouds seemed to be getting darker, so I ended that brief meditation and continued towards my ultimate destination.

As I walked in front of the university's auditorium, I had

to evade some protestors who used signs and bullhorns to proclaim their utter outrage that Marie Charcot was coming to campus that night to perform her show, *Opening the Mind's Eye.* Charcot, who adopted the stage name Madame Charcot even though she wasn't French, was part stage hypnotist and part motivational speaker. She was bringing her stage show to the University of Connecticut tonight and historically the show had been a hit with college-aged students as they got to see their fellow classmates perform outrageous acts at her suggestion.

Recently, through her motivational speaking business, she'd developed professional ties to a former Republican president of the United States—a fact that had outraged a far-left campus group. Although she identified as female, some of their signs compared her to Adolf Hitler and it was clear from their chants that they wouldn't leave until the administration cancelled the event—so much for free speech on college campuses! I once had the naïve notion that part of higher education involved having meaningful dialogue with people who share opinions different than yours, but that was squashed when I entered a doctoral program five years ago. If there's one thing I learned in academia, it's that it's more acceptable to be a Communist than a Republican, forcing any non-left leaning students and faculty into the closet for fear of reprisals.

I got through the protest unscathed and made it to the psych building just before the thunder rolled and the rain started to fall. The building itself is one big maze and most psych students joke that all who enter are part of a learning experiment to see how quickly they find learn their way around—like a mouse hunting for a piece of cheese.

After a series of left and right turns, I made my way to my dissertation advisor's office, which was immediately to the right of the department chair's. The symbolism was clear.

Although retired, Sam Shoah was the right-hand man to whoever was in charge of his former department. Evie Rotter might technically run the department, but nothing of any consequence happened without Sam's blessing.

Shoah is the Hebrew term for Holocaust, and it wasn't the last name he was born with. Sam changed his name as his own personal promise to never forget the horrors that he and millions of others experienced during World War II. It was his outward sign of an inner promise, if you will.

As a young boy, he was sent to Auschwitz along with his twin brother Saul, and the fact that he was a twin undoubtedly saved his life as it qualified the boys for participation in some of the barbaric twin studies overseen by the wicked Josef Mengele—most kids were killed upon arrival as their captors reasoned they had little to offer the war effort, but twins weren't killed immediately as they were considered valuable research subjects.

Fortunately for Sam, he wasn't chosen to be the test subject in the experiments they were forced to participate in. The Nazis would poke, prod, and poison Saul while doing nothing to him, who played the role of control subject. While he wasn't hurt physically, the mental anguish he suffered by seeing his brother experimented upon was just as bad.

As a rule, if one twin died as a result of an experiment, the other was immediately killed, and the two bodies were then examined to measure the impact of experimentation. Sam was convinced that Saul's ability to hold on was rooted in the fact that he had to in order for his brother to live. The notion that having a purpose can fuel a will to survive greatly impacted Sam's approach to psychotherapy, as it did another Holocaust survivor, famed neurologist and psychiatrist Viktor Frankl.

While Saul was strong, he wasn't immortal. Sam's twin eventually died in January of 1945, the day before the Soviet army liberated Auschwitz. By then, the boys' tormentors had fled and Sam was safe—as safe as he could be in Hell.

When I walked into Sam's office, he was cleaning out the bowl of his pipe and dumping the spent tobacco into the waste basket.

"Not a word from you on this," he said as I walked in. "I'm 82 and it's the only vice I have left."

It struck me how much he'd aged in the past five years. When I met him, he was just shorter than my five-foot-eleven-inch frame, but now he barely came up to my shoulders. He had more age spots now than he did back then; while he was a believer in the benefits of being out in the sun, he wasn't a big believer in sunscreen. The one thing that hadn't changed, though, was his combover. He was clearly bald but pushed over the long strands of hair on the side of his head to give the appearance that he had some left on top. In this way he reminded me of Don Rickles, though I believed Sam was funnier.

"I'm too nervous to give you hell about that, Sam."

"Good. Nerves are good, they are a reminder that you are still alive." He then walked over to me and put both of his hands on my shoulders and looked me directly in the eyes, "You will do fine, blue eyes."

Sam was fascinated that I had dark hair but blue eyes and often joked that had I been blond, he would never have taken me on as a student as I'd have reminded him too much of his captors.

"Your written dissertation is the best to come through any of our desks in a quarter century. Today is just a formality."

At forty-six, I'd be the oldest person to graduate from the University of Connecticut's doctoral program in clinical psychology. I entered the program five years ago primarily because Sam championed my application. Very few universities would take on a forty-one-year-old doctoral candidate, but something in my application story stood out to Sam and, considering his input was given a disproportionate amount of weight, I was offered one of the six spots they would fill that year.

I had a career in big tech before entering the grad program, and gave my fair share of presentations, but this was one of the most meaningful I'd ever give and I didn't want to screw it up. "I just want to do well."

He then squinted and smiled. "Is that grey hair I see around your temples? I guess after today we can call you Dr. Salt and Pepper."

It felt as if the grey appeared overnight, an outward testament to the stress building in my body.

"I appreciate your saying that."

"About your hair? No problem."

"No, about my work. Regarding the hair, I'm just stressed out about defending the dissertation."

"Michael, it's already slated for publication in a peer-reviewed journal. Just watch the politics in the room and you'll sail on through."

I thought the tech sector was as political as they come, and then I entered academia. Tech's got nothing on a university when it comes to back stabbing, strategic rumors, and infighting.

I looked over at the whiteboard on Sam's wall and saw a series of shapes, some with dots and some without. Sam caught me staring at it.

"Are you a Kappa Sigma?" I asked.

"Why do you ask?"

"My college fraternity used a cipher like this so that brothers could send coded messages to each other." I almost laughed as I said it, thinking how silly it sounded. I went to school in the early 1990s, not the 1790s.

"No, I didn't have time for such things when I was in

school."

That's right, to hear Sam talk about his college days in the mid-fifties you'd have thought his alma mater, Syracuse, where he earned his undergraduate, master's, and doctoral degrees, was about as fun as summer school. He'd always mutter something about the Cold War when pushed further, but I knew not to push further today because doing so would inevitably lead to a lecture, and I didn't have time for that.

"This pigpen cipher was used by both the Freemasons and Knights Templar to send coded messages to their members. Actually, it is believed to have been created by a Jewish rabbi; just another of our forgotten claims to fame."

"Hey, you still have pastrami on rye."

Sam smiled. "They can't take that away from us. Want to take a guess at what this says?"

As a software developer fluent in multiple computer languages, I was always up for a challenge to unscramble a code. I picked up a dry erase marker and drew a three-by-three table with an X next to it. I then put two letters of the alphabet in each square on the table and in each of the four angles in the X. While I was the Grand Master of Ceremonies for my fraternity and had to commit this silliness to memory and present it to new members, I was amazed at how quickly creating the cipher key came back to me.

Now that I had the cipher key, I then looked at each of the shapes Sam had on the board and wrote the corresponding letter from the key underneath; if any shape had a dot in it, I knew to use the second letter in the square or angle. The message spelled out, *Good luck Michael.*

"Nice job, but that was a softball because the cipher key was in alphabetical order. Try this one."

I watched as Sam wrote down another coded message from memory on his whiteboard.

"Try to use the cipher key you created before."

I did and got a nonsense word.

He then erased each of the letters in the table and X that I created and put SY and MB and OL across the top row of the table.

"This is a substitution cipher. Knowing the word *symbol* is key to solving the code. So in the cell under SY, you would put in the next letters in the alphabet following each of those, which are T and Z. In the cell under BO you would write CP, etcetera. Sam then completed the cipher key.

"Now decode the message."

I did and it read, *Defend us in battle.*

I recognized it as a line from the prayer to St. Michael, one I was familiar with from my Catholic school days.

"Patron saint of the military," I observed.

"The enemy of Satan and the fallen angels. He ejected Satan from paradise, so the story goes. I'm guessing the Devil didn't take that lightly."

"My mother named me Michael after him, so the story goes."

"My my, you have a lot to live up to with your name," Sam quipped.

"For a Jew, you know a lot about Christian saints."

"At one point, your people persecuted mine. We Jews thought it wise to know our enemy."

I wanted to ask Sam why he had a pigpen cipher on his whiteboard in the first place but looked at my watch and saw that I only had fifteen minutes to go before my presentation was supposed to begin and wanted to make sure I had no issues connecting my laptop to the projector. If there's one thing I learned working half my adult life in the tech space it's that if something is going to go wrong in a presentation it's going to have to do with the audio/video system.

"I'm going to head down to the conference room and set up. Want to join me or are you going to take a few hits off of that cancer delivery vehicle?"

"You couldn't help yourself, could you?"

"Nope."

I put my bag over my shoulders and Sam picked up a heavy canvas bag of books off his floor and handed it to me.

"Mind carrying these for me?"

When I took Sam's class on psychological tests and measurements, I always met him in his office beforehand and offered to take his bag for him so that he could enjoy his pipe on the walk between the psych building and the building our class was in. It struck me that, given my coursework was all done and all I had left to do was defend my dissertation, this might be one of the last times I got to carry his bag.

"Of course not. I'm going to miss this, you know."

"I am too, Michael," Sam said.

He locked the door behind him after we stepped into the hallway, and I'm certain he whispered it again.

"I am too."

CHAPTER TWO

Defending My Life

Thankfully there were no tech issues, and I had a few minutes to review my slides before people would start coming in. Fortunately for me, it was an associate professor's birthday and many of the attendees for my presentation were enjoying pizza and cake in a conference room on the third floor and would most certainly be a few minutes late to the presentation. Nothing attracts an underpaid academic like the temptation of free food.

As a former tech entrepreneur, I had to make countless high-pressure pitches to potential investors. Being raked over the coals comes with the territory when asking rich people to part with their money, or, as the case may be, other people's money. At that moment, though, it struck me that I was more nervous about the presentation I was about to give than anything I'd done in my past life. Perhaps it was because they had the power to give me something more valuable than money: credibility, prestige, and the ability to use my degree to help others in the way that I should have helped my son.

I felt myself going down a mental rabbit hole of how I got to this point in my life, when my attention was called to Dr.

Evelyn Rotter, Evie to her friends, who was walking into the room. I walked out from behind the podium and greeted her in the doorway. Her pin-straight silver hair rested just on top of her neckline and she looked tired, as if the weight of the world were on her shoulders. Being a department chairperson isn't an easy gig; due to funding cuts, she had to take on some teaching responsibilities as well as oversee a staff of twenty-five full and associate professors, not to mention fifteen teaching assistants. It wasn't uncommon for her to pull eighteen-hour days, a fact betrayed by dark circles around her eyes.

"Dr. Rotter, welcome," I said and extended my hand, which I knew had some perspiration on it due to my nerves.

"I don't think I've ever seen you nervous, Michael. Not even during the Socratic hours in my History of Counseling course."

Dr. Rotter was fond of using the Socratic Method as part of her approach to teaching. While unnerving to many of my fellow students, I found it to be a captivating method.

"One of my favorite courses," I replied.

"Break a leg," she said and walked over to chat with Sam.

Next to arrive were two of my fellow clinical students, Gianna Mazzone and David Breeze, both of whom were on track to defend their dissertations next spring, just one year from now.

"Thanks for coming. It's nice to see some friendly faces."

Gianna looked me up and down and couldn't help but take a jab at the suit I was wearing. "Look at you, old man. You look like you're about to offer me a toaster if I open an account at your branch."

She entered the graduate program immediately after earning her undergraduate degree and I had a good twenty years on her.

"You are too young to know about banks offering toasters

as incentives for accounts," I quipped.

"I know. My mom says that all the time when she sees a dude in a suit."

It was rumored that Gianna's grandfather was high up in one of New York's infamous crime families, but I'd never asked her about it directly. Besides, didn't Giuliani get rid of the mob?

"The tie really brings out those blue daggers," David said. "I'm sure the ladies in the room will be melting."

Gianna then punched him in the arm.

"What's that for?" he asked.

"As if women are so weak-minded they can't see past a handsome man? Go grab us a few seats in the back," she said, and David did as she commanded. Yeah, she was totally mobbed up.

"You really broke his heart when he found out you weren't gay," she said.

"I drove one significant other into the arms of another man," I quipped. "No doubt I'd do the same to him."

"Self-deprecating humor doesn't work for you. Now stop deflecting. You got this, okay?"

"Thanks."

Gianna left to take a seat next to David and I greeted the remainder of the invited attendees, which included the three additional faculty members on my dissertation committee and a first-year clinical student looking to get a glimpse of what she was in for in another four years.

I walked back to the podium and was about to welcome everyone to the presentation when the door to the room opened and Dr. Anton Levy, the chair of the university's biology department, walked in. As a famed virologist known for working with novel viruses, he was well known on campus and I was taken aback at his presence. It wasn't just that he was about as far away from the biology building as he could possibly be, but because his long hair, pale skin, and thin frame made him look like a vampire. I hoped he didn't come to siphon some of my blood.

While dissertations were open to the public, it was rare that someone from outside the psych department would attend a dissertation defense. Those from the hard sciences, like Dr. Levy, tended to look down on our field as being soft and felt as if attending a dissertation defense wasn't worth their valuable time. Microbes, to them, were much more interesting.

Sam perked up when Dr. Levy took a seat next to him and asked, "To what do we owe the honor of your visit, Dr. Levy? Should you be busy studying amoebas?"

He was the kind of guy who had an inability to whisper and I heard him reply, "I just happened to be passing by."

Sam then nodded towards me, indicating I should begin my presentation, which I did by welcoming everyone to the session and thanking Dr. Rotter and my entire dissertation committee for coming.

I made the mistake of glancing over at Dr. Levy, who seemed uninterested judging by the fact that he was scrolling through something on his smartphone. *Asshole,* I thought myself.

Dr. Rotter was clear that the entire presentation should not exceed sixty minutes and at least thirty of those should be carved out for questions and answers, so I only had thirty minutes to distill five years of research.

The purpose of a dissertation is for a student to demonstrate his or her capacities as a researcher. To do so, one has to identify an area of interest and be able to research it in depth by employing appropriate research tools and then communicating findings clearly. In addition to the output, the student is also evaluated on their ability to complete work on a specific timeline and take direction from their committee.

It's also understood that the work should be original in nature and advance thinking in the field.

Initially, I planned on starting off by discussing why I had an interest in the topic of social media and its potential consequences on mental health amongst at-risk youth, but my committee members advised against it. My story was too personal, they argued, and might distract attendees from the research itself, which had to be the star of the show. Instead, I spent five or so minutes summarizing the literature review which helped inform my hypothesis and then dove into how I structured my experiment and the outcomes.

While I did, I noticed that Dr. Levy had put his phone down and was taking vigorous notes.

Time seemed to fly by as I walked everyone through my slides. Every now and then, I'd glance over at Sam who, like a conductor, would use hand gestures to tell me to either slow down or pick up my pace. Once I got to my final slide, I took a deep breath and summarized my key findings into three sentences.

"While social media allows teens to create online identities, communicate with others, and build social networks, many of which are positive, it can negatively affect teens by distracting them, exposing them to bullying, and providing unrealistic views of other people's lives. Additionally, for youth who are shown to be prone to depression and anxiety, higher levels of social media use are significant predictors of suicidal thoughts. More research amongst a clinical sample of subjects is recommended."

Five years of work summarized by three sentences. I advanced to the next slide, which simply said Q&A, and waited for the trial to begin.

Dr. Rotter asked the first question. "Can you discuss any limitations of your research, Mr. Corrigan?"

My committee prepared me for this one, as it is a universal

one at any dissertation. The fact that it came early, though, was a good sign as it suggested that I didn't leave the department chair wondering why I chose the topic, what my project was all about, or anything to do with the mechanics of the study. I'd seen Dr. Rotter dig into some of my fellow students with these basic questions when their answers weren't apparent during the presentation.

"As mentioned, my sample size for this research was three hundred teens aged thirteen to eighteen. Most of the subjects for this study were from what I would call a 'non-clinical sample,' meaning they did not score high on tests of depression and anxiety that I administered as part of the research. I had a subset of thirty subjects from our university clinic who we know suffer from anxiety or depression, but I'd like to see this repeated with a larger sample size."

"That's a big conclusion to base off of thirty people," Dr. Levy's voice cut through the room like a sharp spear through flesh.

"The conclusions aren't just based on the thirty people from our clinical subgroup, Dr. Levy. We did find that even amongst our non-clinical sample, higher levels of social media use were related to thoughts of self-harm."

"Of course, correlations do not establish cause and effect," Dr. Levy said dismissively.

Sam spoke up, "While we do allow questions from observers, it is customary that the bulk of questions in a psychology dissertation come from our own faculty and staff."

"What's the matter, your protege can't take the heat from a real scientist?" Dr. Levy snickered.

It's fair to say that I have an ego and am not afraid of verbal sparring, but I was eager to get to some questions from people in my own department. I was surprised when Gianna raised her hand to ask a question as we agreed that no questions would come from friends during the presentation. As no one else had a hand up, I nodded towards her.

"I thought your presentation was excellent, but can you tell me why this research was so important to you?"

I recognized what she was trying to do—have me tell a personal story that would eat up the remaining time and spare me from any more questions from Dr. Levy.

"Thank you for your question, Gianna. Many of you might know that before I was a graduate student here, I was in the tech space. During my time in that area, I launched a social media app called MyLife, which allowed users to build a profile and share video and images with others. It became very popular with teens."

"What's the point?" Dr. Levy rudely blurted out.

"As popularity with our app grew, we heard complaints from parents' groups that kids were spending too much time on the app, causing them to stay up late. Teachers' organizations also reached out complaining that some students had become so obsessed that they were actually using the app in class, instead of paying attention. At the time my management team and I believed that it was a matter of free will and that parents and teachers simply had to do a better job at vying for their kids' attention. We remained thick-headed even after a group of mental health counselors approached us with an alarming story that they saw an increased number of cases of self-harm attributed to usage of MyLife."

I took a sip of water from the bottle next to me before continuing.

"It wasn't until I lost my own son to suicide that I started taking any of this seriously."

"So, it's possible that the research question at the center of your dissertation was influenced by bias. Is that right?" Dr. Levy said without any hint of emotion. I even looked to see if he had pointy ears, the telltale signs of a Vulcan.

"I beg your pardon?"

"Certainly you are smart enough to know that confirmation bias is a big no-no in research, even psychological research," Dr. Levy said condescendingly.

"Maybe you drew conclusions because they confirm your existing beliefs or theories. That's called confirmation bias, or didn't you learn that over your five years in this program? What kind of program are you running here, Rotter?"

The department chair took offense at the accusation, but Sam grabbed her arm and whispered in her ear. I wasn't close enough to hear what he said, but whatever it is she was placated.

While extremely insensitive, Dr. Levy's criticism was valid, and I had to address it.

"While it's true that my son's death influenced my interest in this topic, I've cited evidence not just from my own research but from studies conducted around the world that social media can have an adverse effect on youth, particularly those prone to depression and anxiety. I stand by my research and hope to do more in the area. Should you want to audit my dataset, I'd be happy to make it available to you, Dr. Levy."

"No need to get so defensive, Mr. Corrigan. This is a dissertation defense, not tee ball. Someone has to ask the tough questions."

"To that end, does anyone have any more questions before I let the committee adjourn to decide my fate?"

"I do," Dr. Levy said. "How do you think you will feel being characterized as the tech world's Benedict Arnold after your research is published?"

While his question had nothing to do with the defense of my dissertation, he did have a point—my research put a massive target on a billion-dollar industry that I helped to create. I suppose I was a traitor of sorts.

"Big tech will be just fine," I replied. "It's humanity I'm worried about."

"I think that's a good one to end on," Dr. Rotter said. "Now would anyone not on Mr. Corrigan's dissertation committee please leave the room so that we may talk about him?"

I unplugged my laptop from the projector and thrust it into my bag and left the room before anyone else. My pulse was racing, my blood was boiling, and I was in desperate need of some fresh air. I navigated the maze of the psych building and exited through a side door that led to a patio, where I'd often find Sam toking on his pipe. The rain had stopped, and I saw patches of blue sky and the sun breaking through the remaining clouds. I took it as a good sign.

CHAPTER THREE

A Gift

I spent the next forty-five minutes on that patio doing anything I could do to keep my mind occupied, a task that was made more difficult by the fact that I didn't have a smartphone. I swore off them after leaving the tech industry as I had first-hand knowledge of how truly invasive they are.

During my first year in tech after graduating from Stanford, I worked for a company called Modulation Media, which billed itself as the world's first interactive marketing agency. Led by a brilliant and eccentric entrepreneur named Bob Ahlers, or BA to his friends, that company's mission was to create advertising so good that people would view it as a service. The vision was that ads would be so well targeted they would no longer be seen as an intrusion, but rather something of value as they gave people an opportunity to learn about products that were relevant to their needs.

I got to work on tracking technology that was eventually embedded into smartphones and other devices that would literally listen in on people's conversations and then predict what ad they should see based on what it learned. So if you've ever been talking to someone about going on a trip and then were barraged with travel ads, it's not a coincidence.

The trouble was that some companies took the technology too far and started experimenting with ways to use it for social engineering. It's one thing to use targeting to improve the return on investment for advertising spending, but it's another to use it to influence public opinion and elections, particularly with false information disguised as news. So when I said goodbye to tech, I also eighty-sixed any smart devices I owned, including my phone. Now I only use a good old-fashioned flip phone which I affectionally call a dumb phone.

Since texting on my antique communications device was beyond annoying, I actually used it to make calls and I spent that forty-five minutes calling friends and family to pass the time. Just to show how desperate I was to get my mind off what was happening in the conference room, I even called my ex-wife, Anna.

Statistically, many marriages have difficulty surviving the tragedy of losing a child, and mine was no different in that regard. Compounding matters, though, was my desire to do a complete about face professionally and go back to school for a doctorate in psychology. Anna met and married a hard-charging tech entrepreneur and was attracted to that guy. Once I changed, so did the nature of our relationship. She tried to stick with me through my first year of graduate school, but found living in the Connecticut countryside not nearly stimulating enough compared to the Manhattan pace she was accustomed to. Plus, as it turned out, she'd been carrying on an affair for years with a journalist and that was much harder to do two hundred miles away from Manhattan.

When we decided to call it quits, I didn't balk at giving her just over half of the money I banked in tech because I considered it blood money. I kept enough in cash to live off of during my graduate studies, used some to purchase a modest home on Lake Coventry near the university, and put the rest in conservative investments.

I looked at my watch and saw that it was a quarter to five and wondered if Thursdays were still her tennis days. I supposed not, because she picked up on the third ring.

"Hey," she said. "How did it go?"

"Did I even tell you I was defending my dissertation today?"

"No. Sam did and asked if I might come, but I couldn't make it."

I introduced her to Sam when I was a first-year grad student and they seemed to hit it off. I had no idea they kept in touch after our divorce. Sam hadn't mentioned anything to me about it—he was funny like that.

"How did you do?"

"It was going great until some asshole from the bio department stared asking obnoxious questions."

"I'm sure you rocked it. You always did whenever I saw you on stage."

Her saying that reminded me of the times when things were good between us. Part of me missed those days, and missed her. We made a good team at one point.

"How are things in New York?"

"Fine. I'm in the middle of redoing the kitchen."

"Again?" I asked.

"Mike, we did that ten years ago. Plus, Philip loves to cook."

Her response filled me with mixed emotions; she was the only one I ever allowed to call me Mike and it made me happy to hear her use such a familiar term, but she invoked the name Phillip who, for all intents and purposes, was my replacement. Apparently, he was one big story away from becoming the editor of *The Times'* science section but had yet to find a scoop big enough to get him that gig. Anna said he reminded her of a young me. I guess that's a compliment, right?

Before I could snap back a snarky reply, I spotted Sam out of the corner of my eye walking towards me, pipe in hand.

"I'm being called back into the room."

"Text me their decision," she said.

"You know I don't text."

"Then send a smoke signal," she replied and hung up.

"You have another one of those things?" I asked Sam, referring to his pipe. Maybe tobacco would calm my nerves.

"Haven't you heard, these things cause cancer," he said after taking a puff. "I'm here to tell you that your fate has been decided. Come with me to see if it's thumbs up or thumbs down."

"It sounds like I could be fed to the lions."

"It's feeding time at the zoo," he said and then held the door open for me. "Age before beauty."

After navigating back to the conference room, I walked in to the sounds of cheers from Dr. Rotter, the other members of my committee, as well as Gianna and David. There was champagne on a table in the corner as well as a cake. At that moment, I knew I had successfully defended my dissertation and could breathe easy.

Gianna handed me a piece of cake and other faculty members started entering the room; I liked to think that they were there to congratulate me but knew that the pull of free food and drink is too much to pass up.

"Don't fill up on that," Sam said. "I'm taking you to dinner to celebrate."

"Hey there, Dr. Corrigan," I heard Gianna say, "don't forget I promised to take you to the Madame Charcot event tonight if you successfully defended your dissertation."

"Don't worry, Gianna. Sam is eighty-two. I can guarantee

that we will be hitting the early-bird special, which will leave me more than enough time to make it to see the controversial Madame Charcot." I underscored the statement by placing my hands in front of my face and wiggling my fingers to poke fun at going to see a hypnotist.

"Good, because I have a surprise waiting for you there."

I was curious as to what kind of surprise she had in store. It also made me wonder what she would have done if the dissertation went the other way.

"Dinner is at six," Sam said. "And you are driving."

At eighty-two, Sam was quite independent behind the wheel, except after the sun went down. Plus, he did enjoy a cocktail or two which meant it was safer for everyone if Sam had a chauffeur.

"Bitterman at your service," I replied, referencing the movie *Arthur*, for which Sam and I shared a fondness.

Sam's favorite restaurant near campus was an Australian-themed steakhouse known for its overly seasoned steaks and fried onion appetizer, which Sam ordered.

"This thing should come with a coupon for a coffin," I remarked while grabbing one of the onion straws.

"First you chastise me for my pipe and now my blooming onion. I'm well into the back nine of my life, Michael, with only a hole or two to go. Life's better with a little fun in it. Which reminds me to ask, what do you plan on doing with yours now that you've earned your doctorate?"

"Evie approached me during the reception about the open associate professor position."

"You don't want to do that," Sam said curtly.

"I don't?" I replied.

"You aren't a teacher, Michael. You are a doer."

Sam had an uncanny ability to call it like it is and deep down inside I knew he was right about this opportunity.

"Don't get me wrong, you are an expert researcher, but you don't have the patience for academia. It moves at a snail's pace and you are a sprinter."

"I also have the chance to do a post-doc at…"

Before I could finish my sentence, Sam had started shaking his head.

"You don't need more training. You are a solid clinician, all of your past supervisors in the clinic said so."

Throughout the clinical program, I had to work at least a thousand supervised hours at our university's mental health clinic performing mental health assessments and therapy for patients from our community. At first I would get a lot of feedback and guidance from my supervisors, but over time I was able to work more independently.

"You are ready for a career as a clinician, if that's what you want to do."

Sam was quiet for a moment and his silence was deafening.

"Is there anything you suggest?" I asked.

"You need to find something that will provide you with meaning."

Here we go, I thought to myself. Sam's lecture on the importance of meaning.

"Don't look at me like that," he scolded. "Let me ask you something, when you were making a mint in the tech industry, were you happy?"

Happy? Who said anything about having to be happy when it comes to work?

"There were times when I enjoyed what I did."

"Ah, but you eventually left. Right?"

"Yes. When I felt I was losing my soul."

"Think about the good times, though. Did you feel as if your work had real meaning?"

I thought back to the various phases of my career. While I

helped invent technology that helped advertisers get their sales pitches in front of consumers more efficiently than they could before and also helped people connect with each other through social media, I can't honestly say that I derived any meaning from those accomplishments.

"Maybe it did for the people I was working for, but it didn't for me personally."

"You keep telling yourself you pursued this new calling because of your son's death, but did you ever stop to think about what you really want to do with your life?"

At that moment I recalled a memory that I had suppressed.

"When I was in college, I thought that I wanted to live a life of adventure and work for the Central Intelligence Agency but abandoned that plan."

"Why?" Sam asked after taking a sip of his cocktail, a vodka gimlet.

"I was dating a girl and things got very serious. I told her about my thoughts about the agency and she clammed up. She said it would ruin our future plans."

"What did you do?"

"Obviously, I walked away from that plan."

"How old were you at the time?"

I wasn't up for a game of twenty questions, but given I owed a lot to the octogenarian in front of me, I continued to play along.

"Twenty."

"Why did you listen to her?"

"I was in love. I thought she was the one."

"She's a lovely woman, but was she the one?"

"Well, we divorced four years ago. What's the point of all this?"

"The point is, you were never truly satisfied in your career because you made too many compromises. It cost you your happiness and even your marriage. You have an opportunity now to write the next half of your story, so don't waste it doing something that isn't personally meaningful to you."

Wise words from a wise man, but out of all the questions I've been asked in my life, the one I always had the hardest time answering was, what do you want?

"And another thing," Sam said while putting his finger up and doing his best Columbo impersonation, "purposeful work isn't the only key to finding meaning. We also find meaning in love and in having courage in the face of difficulty."

"You remind me of Peter Falk."

"You know, most people think he was Italian," Sam said, "but he was a Jew from Westchester. But enough with the deflection, are you listening to what I'm saying?"

"Yes. I need to find meaning in work, love, and in being able to stand up for myself when the going gets tough."

"If you remember these things, then I have nothing more to teach you."

The waiter came back with our meals and we dug in like two people who hadn't eaten in weeks.

The ride back to his house was a silent one as Sam was dozing off; a combination of the vodka as well as the proximity to his bedtime of eight pm.

While driving by the park that's about a mile away from his house, Sam opened his eyes and yawned.

"That's funny," I observed while we were about to drive by a mailbox."

"What's that?" he asked.

"That mailbox has graffiti on it. I passed by it earlier and could have sworn it wasn't there."

I wondered what kind of gang uses a butterfly to tag their territory. Hell, what kind of gangs does rural north eastern Connecticut even have?

Sam put on his glasses just in time to see it and I could tell that his whole demeanor changed; I chalked it up to his being annoyed at vandalism in his neighborhood.

Once we pulled into his driveway, I got out of the car while leaving it running and walked around to the passenger side to help him out, as was my custom.

I walked him to his front door and was about to say goodbye when he told me to wait for a moment on the porch.

"I have something for you. I'll just be a minute."

He came back a few minutes later and handed me a book. After looking at the cover I immediately knew just how sentimental a gift this was.

"*Man's Search for Meaning* by Viktor Frankl. Is this a first edition?"

Sam nodded. "Signed by the author as well. He and I have a lot in common beyond psychology. We both survived the Holocaust."

I got choked up thinking just how special this gift was. "I don't know what to say."

"You don't have to say anything. Words are cheap. Do something! Find meaning in your life. Promise me that you will."

"I promise."

"Michael, you are like the son I always wanted. It was an honor advising you over these past five years."

After he said those words, I had a sinking feeling in my stomach that I'd never see him again.

"I can't thank you enough for all you did for me."

"I'd do it all again. Working with you gave great meaning to my life. Now you better get going if you are going to make it in time for that hypnosis show."

"You sound skeptical."

"I have no issue with hypnosis as a vehicle to help with therapy but am not fond of it for entertainment purposes. You know, that woman called me recently?"

"Marie Charcot?"

Sam nodded. "She wanted to pick my brain on something, but wouldn't say what it was over the phone. She even offered VIP tickets to the event so long as I'd meet with her while she's on campus."

"And you didn't want to meet the great Madame Charcot?"

"Madame," Sam said dismissively. "She isn't even French, she's Eastern European! Besides, I had better things to do today, like watch you defend your dissertation."

I smiled and then looked at my watch and realized I had to get moving if I was going to get Gianna in time for the event.

We hugged and I turned around to walk away and then realized we left Sam's car back at the psych building.

"Want me to pick you up tomorrow morning?"

"For what?"

"To get your car. We left it on campus?"

"That's a good idea. Enjoy the book. It's very insightful, especially the end. And remember, a rose by any other name…"

"Would smell as sweet," I finished the quote from *Romeo and Juliet* for him. It was an odd exchange to end on given he and I never discussed Shakespeare before.

I waved back at him after getting back into my car. I then looked behind me while backing up and when I turned to wave one more time at him, Sam was gone, as if he simply vanished into the night.

CHAPTER FOUR

Future Life Progression

I parked in the lot adjacent to Hale Hall, the residence hall where Gianna lived. Nathan Hale regretted that he only had one life to give for his country and I regretted that I didn't use the restroom before leaving Sam's house. I called to let her know I had arrived, and she said she'd be down in a few.

While I was waiting, I picked up the copy of *Man's Search for Meaning* that Sam gave me and opened the cover to examine Dr. Frankl's signature. Along with it was an inscription which read, "Sam, remember, everything can be taken from a man but one thing: the last of the human freedoms—to choose one's attitude in any given set of circumstances, to choose one's own way."

Sam echoed this sentiment to me countless times in the past, though I'm not sure why he felt the need to and I made a mental note to ask him about it one day. I then flipped to the back of the book to see if Sam had captured any notes on the pages that were intentionally blank and was surprised to see another pigpen cipher; this one with many more letters to decode than the ones we did in his office. I didn't have time to try and solve it for two reasons: I had to figure out what the codeword was in order to create the cipher key and Gianna was banging on my window. I put the book in my glove compartment and got out of the car.

"I still can't get over the fact that you have a flip phone," she said. "My dad had one up until a couple of years ago and then he too joined the twenty-first century."

"I hate to tell you this, but I'm old enough to be your father."

"You actually have a year on him," she replied and then let out a trademark cackle. "You ready to get mesmerized tonight?"

All psych students learn about German doctor Franz Anton Mesmer and the relationship between his belief in animal magnetism and what would later be called hypnosis, though he was eventually debunked as a charlatan. However, people still use the term mesmerized as a synonym for hypnotized.

"I plan on observing, not participating," I replied.

"Keep telling yourself that," she snickered as we made our way down the hill that led to Jorgensen Auditorium, the twenty-six-hundred-seat theatre located near the heart of campus. While I'd been on campus for five years, I've never stepped foot in the place. I know, all work and no play makes Michael a dull boy.

"I mean it. I will not be getting on that stage."

"Well, you are no fun."

"That is well documented."

We had to make our way through some remaining protesters, but thankfully their numbers dropped off on account of it being colder than usual and the fact that the campus bar was offering a drink special. Nothing will tempt college students away from a protest like cold weather and dollar pitchers of domestic light beer.

We entered through one of the pair of large glass doors and

walked into a vestibule with high chandeliers and a red carpet that, given the wear and tear, looked to be the original that was set down in 1955 when the facility opened. There were ads for upcoming performances, including one by comedian Nick Di Paolo. I didn't know much about him but figured he must not be a leftist comedian since someone drew a small Hitler mustache on the picture promoting his show.

The tickets were on Gianna's phone and an undergraduate with more metal in his face than Pinhead from those *Hellraiser* films scanned them.

"You seaths are in thirteenth row. It's best to go down the centher aisle."

I'll never understand why people get tongue rings. To me they add nothing to one's life but a self-inflicted speech impediment.

"I have to take a quick detour before we sit," I said to Gianna.

"I told you to go before we left the house," she joked.

I found my way to the restroom and by the time I came out the house lights started blinking, suggesting that patrons should make their way to their seats.

I approached Pinhead again and smiled as I attempted to walk by.

"Not so fasth. I need to sthee your ticket."

"I was just here a moment ago," I protested. "My friend has it on her phone."

"Then your friend needs to come here to get you," he replied. "No excepthons to the rules."

I pulled out my cell phone and Pinhead started laughing.

"Sthally, look, this funeral director looking dude hath a flip phone."

I then realized I still had my suit on from my dissertation presentation earlier. I was, by far, the most overdressed person in the place.

"Stop being such a dick, Tristan. He came in with my Psych TA, Gianna. Let him go."

Tristan? I pictured him growing up in some wealthy Connecticut town like Greenwich or Darien and wondered what his blue-blooded pop-pop thought of the facial jewelry.

I made my way to Gianna and got to my seat right as the house lights went down for good.

"What took you so long? You got IBS or something?"

"I'll tell you later," I replied and then focused my attention to the stage.

Suddenly, loud music started coming from the speakers which I can only describe as new age meets electronic dance music. Lights started flashing and smoke started billowing up from below the stage. After a moment of this spectacle, the lights went out and everything got eerily quiet. Seductively, a woman's soft-spoken voice came over the speakers and cut through the darkness of the room.

"Welcome to tonight's journey into the mind's eye. Over the next two hours you will be taken on a journey into the mysteries of the subconscious mind. To begin, everyone take a deep breath and hold it until I start counting back from ten."

I closed my eyes, inhaled and waited until I heard her start counting to exhale.

"Ten, nine, just sit back, nothing bad will happen to you here. Eight, seven, relax your neck, shoulders, and back. Feel the tension leaving your body as you exhale. Six, five, relax your legs, your backside, and your feet. Four, three, take another deep breath and hold it until I finish counting. Two, one. Now exhale slowly."

Marie then snapped her fingers and asked us all to open our eyes. When we did, a spotlight came on her and I feasted my eyes on one of the most beautiful women I'd ever seen. I felt as if I'd been hit by a thunderbolt just as Michael

Corleone was when he first laid eyes on Appolonia in *The Godfather*. His Sicilian bodyguards described it as a longing in a man for a particular woman and right now Marie Charcot was my Appolonia.

She had long wavy blonde hair cut just below her shoulders and I was close enough to see her crystal blue eyes. She was slender, but not a waif, like some of the models Johnny Depp would date in the nineties. She was dressed in a flattering red top and dark, form-fitting jeans and I found that I just couldn't take my eyes off of her.

"It's okay to blink," Gianna whispered when she caught me staring at Marie. "Wait, are you salivating?"

Wait? Was I? Maybe I was having a Pavlovian response to seeing such a beautiful woman.

"Anyone who has been to my show before, please pay special attention to what I'm about to do," Marie said and then grabbed a lime off the table and bit into it.

"What the what?" Gianna whispered.

"That's different," I replied.

A moment later, I heard the sound of people running towards the stage and saw a few people in front of me stood up and bolted towards it. Each of them sat in one of the chairs on stage in a trance-like manner.

"And so, we begin," Marie said in a soft voice, and then addressed the twenty or so students who had joined her on stage.

"You are all in a safe space. I want you all to just focus on the sound of my voice. While you are listening to the sound of my voice, your body will continue to relax. As you relax and listen to the sound of my voice, breathe deeply and slowly."

Her tone was so soft, I found myself relaxing as well.

"I'm going to snap my fingers and when I do you will all be deeply relaxed."

She then snapped her fingers into the microphone and all of those assembled on stage looked to be in a very deep sleep.

Marie then addressed the audience.

"All of the people on the stage have been to my show before. If you stay till the end, and I hope you do, you will see that I will plant a hypnotic suggestion that will be triggered if you ever see me bite into a lime. In technical terms, this is called an anchor. I used to use lemons but found that too many lemons can lead to heartburn, nausea, vomiting, and other gastroesophageal reflux symptoms. Try saying that three times fast."

This earned some laughs from the audience.

"Should we have some fun with these volunteers?"

The room erupted with encouragement.

"Alright. First things first, I need to make sure everyone who's up here wants to remain up here. I wouldn't want to be unethical, even though I have been accused of working with Republicans in my private practice.

This comment earned her some more laughs.

She then turned her attention to the people on stage who still appeared to be in a deep sleep.

"I'm going to count from one to ten now and when I reach ten and stomp my foot, you will all be wide awake."

Marie counted, stomped, and everyone on stage opened their eyes, and some began laughing immediately while others look confused.

"Welcome to the show. We upgraded your seats. You've all seen my show before and have a choice to make, do you want to be part of the show or go back to your seats? No hard feelings if you do. If so, you are free to leave right now."

The students all looked at each other and about five of the twenty decided to head back while the rest stayed on stage.

"Alright you brave souls. I want to remind you that I'm not going to ask you to do anything that might be harmful to you, but I can't promise that you won't be embarrassed. Raise your hand to show me that you understand and that you are here of your own free will and accord."

Everyone did.

"Now, keep your hands up as you go back to sleep." Marie snapped her fingers again and everyone on stage closed their eyes and kept their hands up. She then turned her attention back to the crowd.

"Hypnosis is a state of deep relaxation. None of these people are really asleep. If they were, they couldn't hear anything I say nor would they be able to move their limbs as the body is technically paralyzed when someone is in a deep sleep."

"You may put your arms down now," she said to those on stage. Everyone complied.

"In hypnosis, I am speaking to the unconscious mind and bypassing all critical faculties." Marie snapped her fingers again.

"I want you all to imagine that you are holding a big balloon full of helium in your right hand. It's the biggest balloon you have ever seen."

As she said this, the right arms of everyone on the stage started to rise.

"Now imagine that you are holding a twenty-pound weight in your left hand."

Immediately, their left arms went directly to the floor. This earned applause from the crowd.

After removing the suggestion about the weight and the balloon, she then called on her volunteers to imagine that, after she claps her hands, they are all aliens who landed on Earth but could only communicate by coughing. When they did, the audience couldn't help but laugh.

In between suggestions, Marie would put her volunteers back into a relaxed state while she taught us about how hypnosis can be used to treat phobias, eliminate addictions, and uncover very early memories in detail.

"We are going to try something new tonight," Marie said. "As many of you know, in addition to entertaining audiences around the world, I help senior executives and other people in leadership positions excel in their work. I used to close each of my shows with past-life regression, but tonight I'm going to try something new. A lot of what I do with my executive clients, which as some of you know include people very high up in politics, is something I call future-life progression. Under deep hypnosis, I have them visualize an ideal life for themselves and then have them verbalize it to me. I then spend time with them analyzing what their story means. It's been a very powerful way to reveal what their subconscious mind is craving and help them overcome barriers for leading a more fulfilling life."

"That actually sounds interesting," I whispered to Gianna.

"It's about to become more interesting," Gianna replied.

"How do you know?"

"Is there a Michael Corrigan in the show tonight?" Marie said.

My stomach dropped when I heard my name. I looked over at Gianna. "You didn't."

"Oh, I did, Dr. Corrigan," she replied and then stood up and pointed at me. "He's over here."

Everyone around me started clapping, it was so loud I could barely hear Marie say, "Come on up to the stage, Michael."

I turned to Gianna and said, "I'll never forgive you for this." I then stood up and reluctantly approached the stage. After ascending the five stairs leading to the stage, I approached Marie and shook her hand.

"Are you a professor here at the university?" She asked.

"Actually, I'm a doctoral student. I just defended my

dissertation today."

"Congratulations. Was it successful?"

I nodded.

Marie turned to the crowd. "How about a big round of applause for the future Dr. Corrigan." The audience complied with her request.

"What field are you in?"

"Clinical psychology."

"So, I bet you are either all in on this show or think it's a bunch of mumbo-jumbo."

"More the latter," I admitted, and Marie laughed.

"I just need you to keep an open mind about this. Can you do that for me?"

"Absolutely," I replied. Actually, I'd do anything for her. After replying, I heard the sound of applause coming from everyone seated in front of us.

"Just have a seat and listen to the sound of my voice. Don't think about everyone here in the crowd, just pay attention to me."

Her voice became quite soft and I heard what sounded like a metronome start ticking.

"That's it. Relax your body. Take a deep breath and hold it. Good. Exhale. Feel any tension in your muscles release. Good. Keep breathing deeply. Great.

I felt myself beginning to relax and heard her start to count backwards, a moment later, I was out.

CHAPTER FIVE

Silver Alert

Gianna and I exited the auditorium and walked into the crisp April air. By all accounts, I had quite the day and should have been exhausted but found that I wasn't the least bit tired. Not ready to go back home, I had a thought.

"Are you in a rush to get back?"

Gianna looked at me quizzically. "Don't tell me Doctor No Fun wants to go out for drinks."

I wasn't a huge drinker and certainly couldn't keep up with my fellow graduate students who could still put them away as if they were undergrads. I preferred to nurse a glass or two of wine at most in the peace and serenity of my own home.

"No. Sam left his car on campus and I have his spare key. If you were up for it, I'd ask you to follow me to his house in my car and then I'll give you a ride back to campus."

"I've always wanted to drive a Tesla," she replied.

There aren't many doctoral students who can afford a high-end electric vehicle, but I loved the damn thing and couldn't part with it after I began my graduate studies. There had to be some benefits to being a tech pioneer.

Once we got back to my car, I handed her my key fob and she drove me back to the psych building where Sam's car was parked. The engine of his hunter green '98 Buick was stubborn for a moment, but eventually turned over. Gianna then followed me to Sam's house and after pulling into his driveway, I could immediately tell that something was wrong. All the lights were on and his front door was ajar.

Sam Shoah was, quite possibly, the most frugal person I'd ever met. He'd never leave a light on after retiring for the evening, let alone all of the ones in his home. Additionally, he was like a trained seal when it came to locking up for the night. Something was definitely off here.

"What's going on?" Gianna asked.

"I'm worried about a break-in. Do me a favor and wait in the car while I check it out?"

"Oh, look, Prince Valiant trying to protect a poor defenseless woman from danger. Listen, if there's trouble in there, I grew up in the Bronx and whipped more ass in my life than you. How about you stay in the car and I'll check things out?"

As someone who'd never been in a fist fight, I had to admit that Gianna's courage put me at ease. "Fine, come along."

Before we even entered the house I could tell that something was very wrong. The door looked to have been forced given damage to the hinges. I pushed it open and shouted, "Sam," but there wasn't a response. I turned to Gianna, "He's a light sleeper. If he's here, he would have heard me."

"Not if he's dead," Gianna quipped. I gave her a dirty look to which she replied, "Hey, that's how it happens on TV."

"This isn't TV," I reminded her.

His usually tidy foyer was littered with mail and we followed it like a trail to the kitchen which contained evidence of a struggle. Sam must have tried to defend himself by throwing plates, as shards of porcelain covered the floor like new fallen snow. As we walked to his study, it crunched underneath us.

Sam's small study was completely turned over, as if someone had been looking for some buried treasure. But what could Sam have that anyone would go through this trouble to find? The man spent his entire career in academia. While he supplemented his modest income from the university by working as a therapist, it didn't make him a rich man. His supplemental income mainly funded his summer travels and a modest condo in Pompano Beach, where he'd spend his winter and spring breaks. To my knowledge, there was nothing worth stealing in his home.

After reaching his bedroom, I prayed that I wouldn't find his body pooling with blood on the floor and was relieved to find his room empty, save for an uncharacteristic mess on the floor.

"He's not here."

"What do you think this means?" Gianna asked, pointing to a sheet of paper on his nightstand with the word *rose* printed on it in what appeared to be his hastily written handwriting.

"No idea." My mind was racing, fearing for Sam's safety, and I couldn't process Gianna's question. "I better call the police."

I took out my phone and dialed 911 to report a break-in and potential kidnapping. I was assured by the dispatcher that someone would be out within five minutes. Sometimes it pays to live in a slow town.

The two of us were distracted by the sound of a vehicle pulling into the driveway.

"That was less than five minutes. I'm surprised they didn't turn the lights on."

"That's not an emergency vehicle," I said while looking out

the window. "It's a black SUV and you'll never believe who just got out."

A moment later Marie Charcot walked through the door.

"Is this Sam Shoah's residence?" she asked in a confused tone after entering the room.

Wearing a hoodie and sweatpants, she was dressed more casually than she was for the show, but looked no less beautiful even though she had a Boston Red Sox baseball cap covering her hair. If circumstances had been different, I'd have made a crack about the '86 World Series when my NY Mets bested them. But Sam's home was a mess and my friend and mentor was missing, so I held my tongue.

"Yes. We just got here a minute ago and found it like this."

I then stared at her in silence for a moment, partly mesmerized by her beauty and partly because I was trying to figure out why she was standing in Sam's living room.

"I'm Marie…hey, I remember you from the show tonight."

"Yeah, thanks to this one," I said and pointed at Gianna.

"Guilty as charged. I'm Gianna Mazzone, doctoral student. I arranged for Michael to participate in your show as a surprise gift for defending his dissertation earlier."

"Your last name sounds familiar. Any relation to Patsy Mazzone?"

"He's my grandfather."

"His restaurant Puzzo's is the best on Arthur Ave," Marie said. "How's he doing?"

"Great, now that he's been out of college for a year."

"I didn't know your grandpa went back for a degree. And I thought I was too old to go back to school."

Gianna clarified. "Where he comes from, college is another word for prison."

While I was curious to know more about why Gianna's grandfather was in prison, I was more eager to uncover why Marie was standing in Sam's house.

"If you don't mind me asking," I said, "why are you here?"

"I had reached out to Dr. Shoah a week ago to arrange a meeting with him while I was on campus. I'm putting together a live event for some of my elite clients and thought his Holocaust story would be inspiring for them to hear first-hand. I wanted to see if he'd be willing to participate in the event but he turned down my offer to meet. I just wanted another at bat before leaving campus to head back to Washington."

"Mookie Wilson didn't hit a single every time he went to bat," I said, hoping that she would catch the reference to his walk off single in game 6 that forced a game 7 for the Mets. Since she used a baseball term, I couldn't help myself.

"We've never forgiven Buckner," she retorted. "I have to admit I didn't expect to find his place ransacked. What's your relationship to Sam?"

"Sam was my dissertation advisor and friend," I replied.

The three of us were distracted at the sign of flashing blue lights reflecting off a tree in the front yard. A few seconds later, the SUV which those lights belonged to was parked in the driveway, blocking both my car and Marie's in.

Officer Donald Dickerson entered Sam's home and we went through the introduction process again.

"So why are you all at an eighty-two-year-old man's house after his bedtime?"

"I drove him to dinner earlier and he wasn't up to picking up his car from campus afterwards, so I told him I'd bring it back. Gianna and I were at an event on campus tonight and she was kind enough to follow me in my car so I could bring his back tonight instead of tomorrow morning. When we arrived, we found his house like this."

I'm not sure how Officer Dickerson captured all of that on one page in his very small notepad, but he did. When he was done writing he stared at Marie.

"And you?"

"I was the event on campus tonight."

"Oh year, the lady from the posters. You look different with the hat on. So why are you here?"

At the time, I wondered if Officer Dickerson knew just how much he was channeling Peter Falk's Columbo with his disheveled look and mannerisms.

Marie explained to the cop what she had told us, that she wanted to invite Sam to participate in a motivational speaking event for people who'd be interested in his story of being a Holocaust survivor.

"Any idea if Dr. Shoah had any enemies?"

"Nazis," I said, and Gianna chuckled.

"Run that by me again?" Dickerson asked.

"He was a Holocaust survivor," Marie added for context. "It's one of the reasons I wanted to chat with him."

"Assuming there hasn't been a sudden influx of Nazis here in rural Connecticut, any other ideas?"

"No. He was semi-retired and well liked. Didn't have any trouble with drugs or alcohol. He eschewed gambling, lived as frugally as they come, and honestly never had a bad word to say about anybody."

"Except Nazis," Gianna said under her breath.

"Any family? Maybe a disgruntled grandson looking for some cash?"

"Sam never married," I said. "His job was his life. Psychology was his first and only love."

Dickerson took a moment to write that down.

"Is every room like this?"

Gianna and I nodded.

"I'm just going to walk around for a moment. Stay here."

"So you were with him before the show?" Marie asked.

"Yes. Funny enough, he mentioned that you reached out and wanted to meet with him earlier."

"I wish he came to the show, then we wouldn't all be standing here."

Dickerson came back into the room.

"Well, whoever did this was clearly looking for something. Any of you have an idea of what that could be?"

"Sam's books were his most prized possession," I said. As the words left my mouth I remembered the one that Sam gave me earlier and the pigpen cipher I uncovered in the back while waiting for Gianna before the show.

"What?" Marie asked, looking directly at me.

"I didn't say anything," I protested.

"My mistake," she replied. I could tell by the way she said it and how she looked at me that something registered inside her.

"Well, unfortunately, there's not much I can do. I'll look into having someone back at the department call his bank and credit card companies to see if there's any activity on his accounts. Maybe we can narrow down where he might be that way."

"No waiting twenty-four hours before considering him a missing person?" Gianna asked.

"This isn't TV," Dickerson replied. "Let me grab all of your phone numbers in case we have more questions later."

After giving him our numbers he said, "I'm going to have our crime scene unit come out here to photograph the place and see if they can find anything of interest. You guys are free to go."

"Not exactly," Marie said.

"Why's that?" the officer asked.

"You are blocking us in."

"Oh, sorry."

Dickerson put his notebook back into his pocket and then walked out and moved his vehicle.

"I need to call it a night," Gianna said. "I have clinical

hours early tomorrow."

"I'll take you back to campus," I said as the three of us walked outside.

"Are you heading back to Washington tonight?" I asked Marie, who looked at her watch.

"It doesn't look like it. I'm told Bradley airport has a 10 pm curfew and it's already 10:30. I'll never make it."

"You'd never make it to Bradley by then, let alone through security," I offered.

"That's not an issue, I fly private."

"That's it, if reincarnation is real, I definitely want to come back as a motivational speaker," Gianna muttered.

"What's that?" Marie asked.

"Never mind," Gianna said.

"You have any hotel recommendations around here, or should I stay at the airport?"

"Michael here has plenty of room at his fancy lake house," Gianna said and then offered a sly smile. I knew her catching me staring at Marie would eventually bite me in the butt. I responded by coughing.

"You are probably better off by…"

"I hate hotels and can be out of your hair first thing. The noise abatement is over by seven am. You won't even know that I'm there."

I could kill Gianna for offering up my house but then realized I just might be the only red-blooded straight male who could get upset at the prospect of having a stunning woman like Marie Charcot at my place for a sleepover. The truth is, I'd avoided intimacy—both physical and emotional—since the end of my marriage and was nervous at the idea of hosting Marie at my place.

"I just have to bring Gigi here back to her dorm. Just follow me there and then we'll go to mine."

Gianna flashed me a look of anger. She hated being called

Gigi, almost as much as I hated having other people offer my house as refuge.

"How about I just grab my bag out of the SUV and tell my driver to take off? Then I'll ride with you. That's easier, right?"

Well, it's easier for someone. I suppose that's why she gets paid the big bucks.

"Fine," I said.

Marie walked back to the SUV, had a quick chat with the driver, and then removed her roller bag from the back. She then slung her laptop bag over her shoulder and met me back at my car.

"Fancy car for a grad student."

"I wasn't always a grad student," I said while holding the passenger side door open for her.

"How come you never hold the door open for me?" Gianna asked.

"Because you would mistake that act of courtesy as a sign of male power and dominance and then you'd chastise me citing your disdain for the patriarchy."

"That's about right," Gianna replied. "Now take me home, but don't you dare walk me to the door!"

CHAPTER SIX

Houseguest

I dropped Gianna back at Hale Hall and Marie was glued to her phone while I drove to my house on Lake Coventry. Since my passenger was giving her thumbs a workout, I had some time to reflect on all that happened today; I successfully defended my dissertation, had what may have been my final meal with my friend and mentor who's currently missing, and was entertained by a woman I was captivated by from the moment I first set eyes on her who, amazingly and not insignificantly, was sitting in the passenger seat of my car. Talk about a strange day.

I passed my favorite local restaurant, The Bidwell Tavern, on the way and remembered that establishment was the primary reason I lived on the lake to begin with. The real estate agent I was working with treated me to lunch there and drove me around some of the nearby neighborhoods. Initially, I wanted to be closer to campus, as I imagined long days in the classroom or library studying and didn't like the thought of driving farther than necessary to get home but sensed a calmness by the lake that felt right in my soul. She showed me a few houses for sale and I made an offer slightly above asking price to ensure I got it and it served me well over the past five years.

It had three bedrooms, which was certainly bigger than I needed and turned one into my writing room, selected because of the magnificent view of the lake from the center window. The master bedroom was obscenely big for one person and the third bedroom down the hall was set up as a guest room. To date, it had never been slept in. It hit me that I needed to decide what I was going to do with the house, assuming I left the area after graduation. I better get to work on finding meaning in my life.

"Fancy place for a grad student," Marie said after I pulled into the driveway. "Hale Hall not your speed?"

"I'm forty-six. Living with a bunch of young adults in their early twenties isn't my idea of a good time. I needed something more peaceful."

"We're the same age. I couldn't imagine having to keep up with someone twenty years younger. Hey, this is quite the kitchen for a single guy. I'm sure you entertain all the ladies in here."

I chose not to tell her that she was the first woman I'd had in my house since moving in five years prior. Hell, I hadn't been on a date since getting divorced. I buried myself in the pursuit of my degree to take my mind off the trauma of losing my son and the end of my marriage. Deflection, I found, was a great defense mechanism.

"Can I get you something to eat or drink, or would you prefer to see your accommodations for the evening?"

"No need to be so formal with me, Mike," Marie said while smiling and staring into my eyes. How the hell were her eyes that blue? And why did she smell so good? Normally I'd correct anyone who called me Mike instead of Michael, but I gave Marie a pass. Hell, she could call me Peter for all I cared.

"How about I drop these bags off, freshen up, and then join

you for a glass of wine?"

"Red or white?"

"Surprise me."

Marie grabbed her bags and walked towards the staircase.

"Don't you want to know which room is yours?"

"I'll just choose one that feels right," she replied.

She apparently felt me staring at her as she walked away and said, "That wine isn't going to open itself."

I walked over to the wine fridge and realized my heart rate was above normal. My hand slipped as it grabbed the handle to the small fridge and realized I was sweating. Why was my nervous system in overdrive? Of course I knew the answer—there was a mesmerizing blonde creeping around my bedrooms upstairs.

I looked over some of the reds I had stored in the fridge—while many store them at room temperature, I preferred them a little chilled. Given it was spring, I thought a cabernet would be too heavy and I wasn't feeling white, so selected a pinot noir from Oregon. Hopefully Madame Charcot wouldn't object.

I opened the bottle and poured two glasses. No need to go through the decanting ritual for an eighteen-dollar bottle of red.

Marie came back downstairs as I was setting the glasses down on the island. She had ditched the Sox cap and looked to have touched up her lipstick. I pulled out a stool for her and then sat down next to her.

"You just might be the last gentleman on earth," she said softly while holding eye contact. She then playfully tapped my wrist with the backside of her fingers and then put the wine stem to her nose.

"Pinot noir?"

I nodded.

"Good choice for this time of year. So, do you come here

often?" she asked and giggled.

I could honestly say I had never met a woman like her, then again I never had my twenties, as the kids say these days. The only girl I dated before my ex-wife was my high school girlfriend. After my divorce, I didn't exactly make up for lost time so, in many ways, I was very inexperienced with women. I took a sip, hoping it would fuel an inspired comeback.

"Some days I feel as if I never leave this house."

"Really? Handsome guy like you, clearly with a few bucks. I'm sure you clean up in this town."

She tapped my wrist again with the back of her hand and giggled. It was an odd trait, but not one that was altogether unpleasant.

"I haven't made much time for socializing since moving up here."

"All work and no play…"

"Makes Michael a dull boy. I know. I just haven't made my personal life a priority."

"Well, that's a shame," she said. "Let me guess, divorced. Former finance guy who was tired of selling his soul to Wall Street so decided to become a therapist and save the world. Close?"

"Almost. Not finance; tech."

"What did you do in tech?" she asked while playfully playing an air keyboard.

All she needed to do was Google my name and she'd find out who I was, so it didn't make any sense to mislead her. "You ever go onto social media and see an ad for something you were talking about earlier in the day and wonder, is my phone listening?"

"Yes, all the time?"

"Well, it is, and I helped create that technology, among other things."

"What kind of other things?"

"Ever hear of MyLife?"

"Who hasn't? I use it every day."

"That was my baby," I said, but left out the part of how it cost me my son.

"I sense there's a story there," she said, and did that thing with her hand again, not that I minded. It was the most physical contact I'd had with a member of the opposite sex since getting divorced.

"One that I'm not interested in sharing at the moment," I replied. Thankfully, she didn't pursue it any further. I was about to ask her a question about herself when she hit me with another about me.

"So, why clinical psychology? Why go back to school at all after having a big career in tech?"

My choice of clinical psychology as a profession was significantly impacted by my son's death, but admitting as much would involve a level of intimacy that I'm just not ready for, so I shared the sanitized version.

"I became convinced that the work I had done in tech could be harmful and wanted to prove it. A doctorate in clinical psychology offered me a path to do so."

"A penance of sorts," she observed.

"Not that I'm religious anymore, but you could put it that way."

"And have you been absolved of your sins?" she said playfully, while flirting with her eyes.

No amount of repentance could ever bring my son back, I thought to myself. "Time will tell," I replied. "Now tell me something about you."

"What do you want to know?"

"How does a stage hypnotist motivational speaker become friends with a who's who of people in politics and business?"

Her expression suddenly went from all smiles to all

business. "I could tell you, but then I'd have to kill you."

Her words hung in the air for a moment and her icy expression sent a chill down my spine. Who the hell was this woman? Her stony expression broke and offered a laugh after tapping my hand again.

"Got ya!" she said. "Like you, I had a different life before reinventing myself. Made a ton of money in the market and my success on Wall Street helped me build a solid network of powerful friends. I felt as if something was missing in life so took a year off and went to Europe. My mother was from East Germany, when there was such a place, and my father's family came from France and I spent a year immersing myself in both cultures. While in France I learned about relative who pioneered the use of hypnosis to treat hysteria and I became obsessed with the topic. I found a guild in Paris that agreed to train me, and my planned year off turned into five. I came back to the States with a new profession and a new *joie de vivre*, as the French say."

I then thought of what Sam had pushed me on earlier. "Do you find meaning in what you do?"

"That's a big question. We are going to need more wine."

I poured us each another glass, emptying the bottle.

"Well, I know I'm impacting people's lives for the better, if that's what you are asking."

"I bet the protestors outside of your event tonight might beg to differ."

"Whenever I go to a college it's the same. The current president and I go way back before he was into politics. I'm not even a registered Republican."

"It doesn't matter. Guilt by association."

Marie laughed and then smiled at me. "There's something I've been meaning to ask you since Sam's house."

I guess we are done talking about her. "What's that?"

"Do you know that you have a tell?"

"What, have you seen me play poker or something?"

"Tells aren't just in poker. You had a flash of inspiration back at the house but held back. When you did, your left eye twitched."

For the last hour, I had forgotten that Sam had gone missing and that his house was ransacked. Her comment brought me out of the fantasy I had been enjoying and right back to reality.

"Do you know what I'm talking about?" she pressed.

I thought back on being at Sam's and remembered talking about his books being his most valued possessions.

"When I told the officer about how important Sam's books were to him, I remembered that he had given me one just before I said goodbye to him earlier."

She looked at my quizzically. "Why hold back on the officer?"

"Because I found something in it."

"Words?" she joked.

"No, not yet anyway."

"Well, now I'm curious."

I debated whether I should show her the code or just keep it to myself but rationalized it might be helpful to have another brain working on the riddle of the codeword so threw caution to the wind.

"I'll be right back," I said and then left the room and headed to the garage to retrieve the book from my car.

"This book meant a lot to Sam and I was touched when he gave it to me after defending my dissertation."

Marie reached her hand out and I gave it to her.

"I can see why. First edition and signed by the author with a personal inscription."

"Yes, but skip to the back."

She did and saw the pigpen code and the look on her face betrayed the fact she had no idea what it was.

"Is this some form of hieroglyphics?"

"It's a code," I said and then gave her a primer on how pigpen codes work.

"So you need a six-character word to decode it?"

Her eyes went wide as she said this, I could tell she was interested.

"Yes, but do you know how many six-letter words there are?"

"We are going to need another bottle and I'm going to need a couch to get comfy on."

My kitchen was an open concept and Marie walked over to the sectional in front of the TV while I opened another bottle and refilled our glasses. She made herself comfortable and I did the same.

"Think back to your conversation with Sam. Maybe he gave you a clue."

I closed my eyes and tried to remember if he had, but so much had happened that day, I found myself not remembering specific details.

"Nothing comes to mind."

"Maybe I can help," she said.

"How?"

"You are the same Michael Corrigan who participated in my show tonight, right?"

And then it clicked; she wanted to hypnotize me.

CHAPTER SEVEN

What's in a Name?

I looked skeptically over at Marie and wondered how hypnosis was going to lead me to the codeword needed to build a cipher key to decode Sam's message.

"Are you going to make me cluck like a chicken?"

"Very funny. No, but I can relax you and get your subconscious mind to remember whatever Sam told you."

"It's worth a shot, I suppose."

"I just need three things from you."

"Okay."

"First, I need you to light one of those candles on the coffee table."

I walked over to the fireplace where I kept some matches and then lit a candle. "What else do you need?"

Marie took out her smartphone and tapped the screen a few times until a steady clicking sound emanated from its speaker. It reminded me of the click tracks my old guitar teacher had me play to when I was taking lessons.

"Next, I need you to focus your visual attention on the flame of the candle and focus your listening on the sound of the clicks coming out of my phone."

Her voice had become remarkably soothing, just like it was when I was on stage.

"Now, take in a big, deep breath, and hold it. Good. Now exhale and as you exhale, I want you to imagine all the tension and all of your worries leaving your body. Imagine that these tensions and worries are the color red and as you exhale your breath is red. As you inhale, imagine the color blue flowing into your nose and entering your lungs. Now imagine it spreading through your entire body, helping to relax. Big breath in. That's great."

I kept my stare on the candle's flame and felt my entire body start to relax. I heard Marie counting down from ten to one and the next thing I knew, Marie was guiding me through my dinner with Sam and our subsequent conversation. I saw and heard everything as clear as if I were watching a filmed version of it.

"Did Sam say anything out of the ordinary to you before you left?"

"I remember he wanted me to promise him that I'd find meaning in my life."

"You are doing so good. Just continue to listen to my voice and stay relaxed. I'm going to take you a bit deeper now. Tell me, Michael, where do you feel most relaxed?"

"Harding's beach in Chatham, Massachusetts."

My wife and I would take our son there every summer and it was the one place I felt I could truly let my guard down and relax.

"Good. What do you find relaxing about Harding's beach?"

"The sound of the waves hitting the shore. The sounds of the seagulls circling overhead. The sound of my son laughing."

I didn't intend to tell her anything about my son, but it just slipped out. She paused for a moment and then continued.

"Now imagine you are standing on the edge of the beach, where the water meets the sand. Imagine immersing yourself into the water and as the water envelops your body, that part of your body becomes all the more relaxed. You are now up to your knees in the water and your legs are becoming lighter and lighter. The water is up to your stomach and now your chest. Now your entire body is in the water and you are as light as a feather, so light that you are now floating on the water and are moving up and down with the gentle waves. Take a deep breath and fall deeper into relaxation."

I was conscious of nothing except that I felt more relaxed than I'd ever been in my entire life. I knew that I wasn't asleep, but I wasn't awake either.

"Now Michael, try and remember anything Sam may have said to you that felt out of the ordinary."

In my mind, I was still floating on the water. I looked around and saw something floating next to me. As my eyes focused, I realized it was a rose, and that's when I remembered what Sam said to me just before I left his place earlier.

"A rose by any other name."

"What's the significance of that?"

"I don't know, but it's the only thing he said to me today that was out of the ordinary."

As I stared at the rose floating next to me I saw something else next to it. A sheet of paper with the word *rose* on it, written in Sam's handwriting.

"Rose," I said.

"What's the significance of the word *rose*?"

"I don't know"

"Is there anything else you can remember about your interactions with Sam today that might give a clue as to what the codeword might be?"

I replayed all my interactions with Sam today in my mind

and couldn't come up with anything.

"No."

"Okay, Michael, I'm going to bring you out of this state now. As I count from one to ten you will slowly start to wake. When you hear me snap my fingers, you will be wide awake."

She counted from one to ten and snapped her fingers. I was awake and felt well rested, as if I'd been asleep for hours. In actuality, it was only about twenty minutes.

"What do you remember from that experience?"

"Everything," I said.

"So, what's the significance of the rose?"

"I don't know, but clearly it was important to Sam. Why else would he have written that?"

"He must have known you would find it."

"Wait a minute," I said. "*Flower* is a six-letter word. Maybe that's it."

I sprang from the couch and went to my writing room and got a notebook and pencil. I created the cipher key using the word "flower" and attempted to solve the code.

"That can't be it," I said.

"How do you know?"

I showed her the notepad with nonsense words on it.

"Dammit."

The wine had taken its toll on my bladder and I needed to excuse myself for a moment. When I came back, Marie had her nose buried in *Man's Search for Meaning*.

"What's in a name?" she asked while thumbing through the book.

"Huh?"

"That's the question that precedes the line spoken by Juliet in Shakespeare's play. She's lamenting the fact that if Romeo had any other last name, her parents wouldn't have a problem with their being together."

"Juliet has six letters!" I shouted and quickly tried to solve the cipher using her name as a the codeword, but it didn't work.

"Christ."

"Maybe I missed a clue in the book," I said and held my hand out. Marie gave me the book and I examined every page for some clue written in the margins, to no avail. I lay down on the couch and put the book over my head hoping the answer would come through osmosis.

That's when it hit me. What's in a name? The author's last name had six letters. Frankl. I started to laugh.

"Have you officially lost it? Maybe we should call it a night."

"Toss me that notebook," I said, and Marie complied.

I went to work like a man possessed and created my third cipher key of the evening and went about solving the code.

I looked back and smiled, although my smile didn't last long.

"What does it say."

I had to re-read the words a few times before finding the strength to say them aloud.

"I was in prison once and I refuse to die there. Seven three one N. Ocean Blvd Pompano Beach. Fridays. Four pm."

"Pompano Beach?" Marie said quizzically.

"He has a place down there, but that's not his address."

I then typed it into my phone and was surprised to see search results listings for St. Gabriel Roman Catholic Church.

"I thought you said he was Jewish."

"He is." That didn't make any sense.

"It sounds like he wants you to go there, and tomorrow is Friday."

"That's crazy, I just can't fly down to Florida on a whim."

"Whim? His life could be at stake," Marie protested.

"I should give this to the police."

"I don't think so."

"Why not?"

"Because he clearly didn't want anyone but you to have this, or else why write it in a coded message? You've got to be the one to go there. Aren't you the least bit curious?"

I was beyond curious, but since I'd buried my head in books and psychology over the past five years, I hadn't been the least bit adventurous.

"Yes, but…"

"No buts, Michael. Your friend and mentor needs your help and you are the only one who he trusts. You have to go, and you know what? I'm going with you."

This kept getting better. Now this woman who I lusted over earlier in the evening is demanding to accompany me on some potential wild goose chase to Florida.

"Why would you want to do that?"

"It's clear that you need me," she said and smiled, breaking down whatever weak barrier I had put up. "Plus, I haven't given up on asking him to participate in my event. So, if I help find him, he won't be able to turn me down."

"I guess I'll call to make some travel plans," I said while grabbing my phone.

"Don't be silly." She touched my wrist again and replied, "I have a perfectly good private jet waiting to take me anywhere I want to go."

All of a sudden, I felt a wave of fatigue come over me and looked at my watch. It was well after midnight and we killed over a bottle and a half of wine.

"I think it's about that time," I said to Marie.

"You look very tired," she observed. "We've both had long days. We can pick this up in the morning."

Her voice was soft, almost a whisper. My arms and legs began to feel so heavy, I felt as if I didn't have the strength to even make it up the stairs.

"Why don't you just make yourself comfortable right here?" she said. If I didn't know any better, I'd have thought she was trying to seduce me.

"Close your eyes and rest. We have a big day tomorrow."

I don't think I could have gotten up from my couch if I wanted to, so I did as she suggested and drifted off to sleep. I slept soundly until mid-morning the following day.

CHAPTER EIGHT

An IOI

I normally woke up before dawn and never required the assistance of an alarm, but that morning I slept until almost ten, something I hadn't done since my college days. At the time, I chalked it up to the wine from the night before combined with the stressors I faced earlier in the day.

I looked around the kitchen and all evidence of having a house guest was erased. The wine glasses we used had been cleaned and put away and the empty bottle had been placed in the recycling. The remaining half-full bottle of pinot noir was placed back in my wine fridge.

"Marie?" I called upstairs, but no one answered. "Did she leave?" I wondered. So much for going to Florida with me.

I walked upstairs to pack a bag and take a shower when I heard the water running, though the sound wasn't coming from the guest bathroom, it was coming from the master.

I felt odd knocking on the door of my own bedroom but wanted to respect my guest's privacy.

"Oh good, you are awake," she said. "I was debating waking you up but you looked so peaceful, so I let you sleep. I had to shower in here as there was no soap or shampoo in the guest bath. Hope that's okay."

Okay? Of course it's okay! If I were more of an alpha male, I might have invited myself in to join her, but I wasn't. Hell, I'm not sure what I'd even do if she invited me in seeing as I hadn't been with another woman since my marriage fell apart, and even then I was, at best, a clueless lover.

"Do you want me to keep the water on for you?"

I have a friend named Joe who, if here, would inform me that what she just said was an IOI or indicator of interest. He continually chastised me for not picking up on them.

"That's okay," I said nervously. "I'll wait until you are done."

I heard the squeak of the shower's knobs being turned and the clunk my pipes make when the water is turned off. A moment later Marie opened my bathroom door clad only in a towel. "I'm glad to hear there's at least one gentleman left in the world. It's all yours."

I stepped into my bathroom fully dressed as I felt self-conscious about undressing in front of my guest. As I disrobed, I caught the scent of Marie's perfume lingering in the air. It was a light and clean scent that sent a charge akin to loose electricity running throughout my circulatory system. What was happening to me?

Once I was done, I got dressed and took my small roller bag out of my closet. I used to travel quite a bit for business but hadn't been on a plane in the past five years. As such, a fair amount of dust had accumulated on it and I sneezed three times in rapid fire.

"Everything okay in there?" Marie asked through the door.

"Dust allergy," I said. "It's been a while since I've needed a suitcase."

"Are you decent? Can I come in?"

"Sure."

Marie entered and was dressed casually in jeans and a

white blouse; purely radiant.

Is that all you are bringing?" she asked, looking over the contents of my suitcase, which had been placed on top of my bed.

"I like to travel light," I replied. Even when I was traveling weekly for work I'd take the bare minimum amount of clothes needed for a trip. Not only did it make the bag lighter to carry, but it meant I had fewer decisions to make when getting dressed.

"You've got to anticipate being away longer than just overnight. What if what you learn in Pompano takes you somewhere else?"

"Where could it possibly take me?" I asked. Apparently five years in academia had turned me into a less critical thinker.

"Just plan for a few more days. And maybe pack a bathing suit, we're going to the beach after all."

Leisure had not been on my mind at all, but to appease her I went to my dresser, pulled out my trunks, and put them in the bag.

"Do you need to do anything else before leaving here?"

Given that all my coursework was complete and that I successfully defended my dissertation, I really had nothing more to do on campus except attend commencement next month.

"Nope. Good to go."

"Alright. I'll call ahead to let Captain Schilling know we'll be ready to go wheels up in an hour. Want me to call an Uber? I doubt you can on your antiquated communications device."

"I was just going to call a cab."

"I'll take care of it," Marie said and tapped away at the screen on her phone.

"Our ride will be here in five minutes. I guess that's one of the good things about living in a college town, there's no shortage of rideshare drivers. I imagine that most of the town's Uber and Lyft drivers were students from the university. Beats having to dance at a strip club for extra cash."

"You didn't?" I asked.

"Just seeing if you are paying attention."

"Out of curiosity, what is the driver's name?"

"What, you want to see if you know him?"

"Humor me."

"Tristan, and he's got 4.5 stars."

"Oh great, Pinhead," I said under my breath.

"Huh?"

"You'll see."

A Range Rover pulled up in front of my house and it confirmed my suspicion that Tristan was from a wealthy Connecticut family. Why else would he be driving a car that retails for eighty-thousand dollars? But if that was the case, why was he driving for Uber? Then it hit me, weed money.

I watched as Pinhead got out but realized it wasn't to help us with my bags but to tuck in his shirt and zip up his fly. I really didn't want to know what he was doing before picking us up.

"Tsay, I remember you from last night," he said while I walked towards him. "No fuckin' way," he said when he saw Marie exit my house.

"Some show last night, huh?" I said and winked at him.

The ride to the airport was quiet; given the nature of what was bringing us down to Florida in the first place—a coded message sent to me by a now missing octogenarian—we didn't want to discuss what we were doing, especially in front of Pinhead. For all I knew he'd blab about it to everyone he knows on campus. Instead, Marie was busy on her phone and since that wasn't an option for me and I had no interest in talking to Pinhead, I just stared out the window as we made our way to Bradley Airport in Windsor Locks, not far from the Massachusetts border. Pinhead didn't seem to mind, he was engrossed with some band called the Dead Milkmen, who I thought sucked way back when I was an undergrad.

"What airline?" Pinhead asked after passing the welcome sign for the airport.

"We are flying private, just bring us to Terminal B," Marie said.

"No sit," he said while bearing right and driving towards the terminal. He had a hard time pronouncing the letter H because of that silly tongue ring.

"If you need a ride when you get back, hereth my card. You can just bypath Uber and Venmo me."

"Thanks," I said while taking the card from him. He popped the trunk for us but didn't offer to help us with our bags. After closing the trunk, I tapped on it twice and he pulled away from the curb.

I followed Marie into the terminal, and she walked towards a sign saying *Charters and Private Travel*. We then walked into a small office where we showed our ID and were lightly screened by their own private security. We were on board her plane shortly thereafter and sat directly across from each other.

I used to hob nob with Silicon Valley financiers who never flew commercial, so this wasn't my first rodeo. However, I was curious as to how a consultant who spent part of her time on the motivational speaker circuit and the other half of her time doing stage hypnosis shows could afford such a luxury.

"Do you always travel private?" I asked.

"There was a time when I was putting on a show or speaking at a private engagement at least four times per week. Sometimes, I'd have multiple engagements in a day. I could be talking to a group of executives in New York at lunchtime and putting on a show in California at night. My business manager recommended I look into a plane share, but I found I needed something with more flexibility, so we bought this plane and I put Captain Schilling on salary."

"Not a cheap proposition," I observed.

"I'm worth it," she countered.

A moment later Captain Schilling's voice filled the cabin.

"Pre-flight check is complete. We'll be wheels up in fifteen minutes. Estimated flying time to Pompano Beach Executive Airport is three hours and twelve minutes. Weather down south is eighty-four and sunny. Perfect beach day."

I looked at my watch and saw that it was close to eleven, so based on these figures we'd arrive by about two fifteen, giving us forty-five minutes to make it to the church on time.

"We have plenty of time," Marie said and touched my wrist with the back of her hand. She then whispered the word, "Relax," into my ear and I started to do so, as if on command. My eyes felt heavy and the last thing I remember was the scent of her perfume penetrating my nose.

CHAPTER NINE

Tyler's Story

Someone once told me that God doesn't punish you for your sins; your sins punish you. I've found this to be true.

At one point in time, I was married to my career. I made code my family and spent more time in front of a screen than in front of my ex-wife and child. I wanted to make a name for myself in the tech space and that's what drove me to start MyLife.

I was obsessed with managing every detail of the service, from the initial wireframe design concepts all the way through product launch and subsequent releases. I was involved in every aspect of that product to the point where my investors had to sit me down and tell me I'd be no good to them if I were burnt out or, worse, dead. I didn't listen and continued to work eighty-hour weeks and didn't see the toll it had taken on my family. I had no idea my wife had been cheating on me or that my son, Tyler, was suffering from depression.

Reality came at me like a punch in the face seven years ago on April 16, 2013, when I found my son's lifeless body hanging in his closet. He was only 14.

Yes, your sins punish you and I'm continually punished by a recurring nightmare of walking into my son's room only to find that I was always too late to save him.

Thankfully, I was awoken from this nightmare by the sound of Marie's voice.

"Wake up, sleepy head," she said while tapping me on the shoulder. I opened my eyes and felt confused. I looked out the window and saw that we were high above the clouds.

"How long was I out for?"

Marie looked at her watch. "About ninety minutes."

Ninety minutes? I guess yesterday's stress was still catching up with me.

"Who's Tyler?"

I was just dreaming about my son and must have been talking in my sleep and wondered how often I do that. There'd be no way of knowing until I started sharing my bed with someone else, and I didn't see that happening anytime soon.

I had a decision to make, either have a very intimate conversation with someone I barely knew or just brush it off as if I don't know what she's talking about. I opted for the latter. While I fantasized about being physically intimate with her earlier, I was in no way, shape, or form ready to open myself up to her emotionally. What can I say? Men are from Mars and women are from Venus.

"You don't trust me, do you?" she asked.

"What do you mean?"

"It's okay. I know we only just met, but like you, I help people for a living. We just go about it differently."

"How do you figure?"

"Well, when I'm not doing stage shows for entertainment, I help executives reach their full potential. You are about to embark on a career helping people through therapy. Both of us, though, are really just trying to help people live better lives, aren't we?"

She had a point. At least she left out the part where she will make one thousand times the income I ever well.

"You are never going to reach your own potential, Michael, until you let go of whatever is holding you back."

I knew she was right, but there was one problem; I didn't want to let go of that pain. I deserved it.

"Noted," I replied and saw that she was drinking coffee. "Where'd you get that?"

"There's a small galley in the front. It's self-serve. I don't spring for the flight attendant."

I got up to pour a cup of salvation and had to admit it felt good to stretch my legs. I sat back down across from Marie and tried my best to turn the conversation back towards her.

"When's your next gig?"

"I'm giving a keynote speech to some market research group at their annual conference next Tuesday."

"Where's that?"

"Thousand Oaks, California."

While my company was based in New York, my investors were in Northern California. Before Tyler was born, my wife would accompany me on business trips out there and one year we decided to explore Southern California a bit and spent a weekend in Westlake Village, which is adjacent to Thousand Oaks.

"You smiled when I said that. Why?"

"My ex-wife and I spent a weekend near there once. It was a happy time."

"Care to share any more about that?"

I shook my head.

"Where is she now?"

"Remarried, living in our old co-op in Manhattan."

"Does it bother you that she started a new life in the home you bought?"

"Not at all. I offered it to her as part of our settlement. There's nothing but ghosts there for me."

Captain Schilling's voice cut through the silence than hung in the air after I said that. "We've begun our initial descent to Pompano Beach. Please make sure your seatbelts are fastened. We'll be landing shortly."

I stared out the window and watched as we descended through the atmosphere and slowly approached land. We flew parallel to the coast, providing a nice view of the high-rise apartments that lined the beach. After flying over a fishing pier, we banked west and flew for about ten minutes before making a wide U-turn and flew towards a small airfield next to a golf course.

"Welcome to Pompano Beach," the pilot said after the wheels touched down. "You'll be off this bird in no time."

Marie and I sat in silence as the plane taxied to a small terminal. Once we were parked and the engines were shut off, Captain Schilling came out of the cockpit to shake our hands.

"Any idea how long we'll be down here for?"

"At least overnight," Marie replied, "so feel free to let loose."

"Copy that," the pilot said.

"That reminds me, I didn't think to make a hotel reservation."

"I've got that covered. We're staying at the Ritz Carlton in Ft. Lauderdale.

"That beats the Bali Hai Hotel."

"Never heard of it."

I pointed to a small hotel about two hundred yards from the airport.

"I bet they have an hourly rate," she remarked.

"And I bet it doubles if you ask for a room without bed bugs."

We walked into the terminal and I arranged for a rental car at the Hertz counter as I didn't want to put my fate in the hands of South Florida's rideshare drivers. Florida is only second to Massachusetts when it comes to bad driving, and if I was going to meet my demise in a motor vehicle accident, at least I'd be behind the wheel.

After pounding a keyboard for what seemed to be an eternity, Marco, the assistant manager of Hertz Rent a Car looked up and said, "For an extra forty dollars a day, I can upgrade you to a convertible, Mr. Corrigan."

I looked outside and saw that there was only one car in the lot, and it was a convertible.

"How much of that has to do with the fact that you have no other cars available?"

Marco laughed, "Everything."

"Come on, Corrigan," Marie said. "Live a little. Plus, it's a ragtop day."

"Looks like you just made a deal." Cue the Jimmy Buffett tunes.

CHAPTER TEN

The Souls of Purgatory

We used the GPS app in Marie's phone to navigate us to St. Gabriel Church as it wasn't a feature on my archaic flip phone.

"For a former tech guy, you have a shitty phone."

"I have a shitty phone because I'm a former tech guy."

Marie didn't push the issue. Instead, she took a call which sounded like it had something to do with a schedule change for the weekend. I tried not to eavesdrop in order to give her some privacy.

Our route took us north on state road A1A, which paralleled the beach, and, given that it was a beautiful day, the sand was packed with the post-school crowd getting a jumpstart on their weekend. On the left side of the car, we passed some modest homes which all had one thing in common, kids playing in the front yard. It was almost like we entered a world where smartphones and tablets didn't exist. It brought me back to my own childhood in the days before the Information Age. I couldn't help but feel a twinge of guilt at my role in the digital revolution.

Screen addiction is real. My own research showed that

positive interactions on social media, such as receiving a like on a post, trigger a chemical reaction in the brain. This reaction floods the brain with a neurotransmitter called dopamine, providing feelings of elation throughout the body. To put this in greater context, dopamine is also linked to sex, gambling, and drugs. Given that it's so easy to seek this reward through a screen, it's no wonder why kids are glued to their phones. They are getting high, but it's on such a small scale that they don't really realize it—but that doesn't mean they aren't becoming dependent.

Some might chalk this up to being a victimless crime. Surely, it's better for people to increase dopamine through social media than, say, ingesting illicit drugs. It's hard to argue with that; however, just as with drugs, the brain builds up a tolerance to dopamine uptake and needs more of it to feel normal, and that leads to more screen time and less real socialization.

It's also important to consider what happens when the likes go away. The brain, which has become so dependent on this reward pathway, can't get its dopamine fix unless it has more stimulation and therefore depressive symptoms set in. Compound that with what happens when other users start criticizing one's posts, depression and anxiety, the toxic twins of mental health, take up residence, leading to disastrous consequences for some people, particularly adolescents who have a hard enough time dealing with all the changes their bodies throw at them even without the added pressures of social media.

I paid this no attention when I was building up my own little social media empire with MyLife. In fact, I didn't even begin to take these concerns seriously until my own son died. Now, I can't forgive myself for the role my work played in his death.

We pulled up to St. Gabriel Church with fifteen minutes to

go before 4 pm. The church itself was located directly across the beach and I wondered if, in addition to being God's great messenger, St. Gabriel the Archangel was into surfing. Maybe the bishop who opened this parish knew something about good old Gabe that the rest of us didn't.

A sign out front displayed the mass times and just below them it advertised confessions, Fridays 4-5. So that's it, Sam wanted me to talk to a priest. But why?

"You look nervous," Marie said after I put the car in park.

"I'm not what you might call a good Catholic."

It's not that anything bad happened to me at the hands of a priest, let me be very clear about that. In fact, the only thing I found offensive about my catholic upbringing was the overabundance of acoustic folk music that was popular in the church when I was a kid in the seventies and early eighties. My problem with the Church was how it played musical chairs with pedophiles and then worked like hell to cover it up.

"I believe the term the Church uses is 'practicing Catholic,'" Marie clarified

"I'm not one of those either and Sam knew that. Why the heck would he have me come down here?"

"Only one way to find out," Marie said.

The minute I walked into the church I was hit with the scent of votive candles burning. Their flickering gave their presence away on the far wall underneath a statue of the Virgin Mother. A printed sign recommended a donation of $1 for a small candle and $3 for a large one, as if God was some kind of Coke machine and your prayers would get to Him faster after donating some legal tender.

Marie reached into her wallet and fished out a five-dollar bill and lit one of the big candles.

"What?" she asked. "It can't hurt."

I was in my fair share of churches as a kid and young adult

and knew how to spot a confessional. In this one it was midway down the nave and had a mural depicting a story from the Gospel of John that involves a woman caught in the act of adultery and a group of men who wanted to stone her for it. As the story goes, Jesus intervened and challenged anyone without sin to cast the first stone. One by one her accusers departed and Jesus offered her absolution, commanding that she go forth and lead a life free of sin.

The light above the door to the confessional was illuminated, signifying that a penitent was in with the confessor.

"Must have a big one to confess if they are here that early," Marie observed. "I'm going to check out the artwork."

Receiving the sacrament of reconciliation is a pre-requisite for making one's first holy communion and I remember being told as a child that the time before making a confession should be spent examining one's conscience. Even though I was no longer religious, it wasn't like there was anything else to do in the church, so I sat in silence and thought about my life while I waited for the penitent to finish his or her confession.

While I sat in the pew, I had this memory of a time when I was younger and went to my mother after my girlfriend had broken up with me. My mother's response wasn't to try and give me a pep talk or to give me the ole "plenty of fish in the sea" line. Instead, she told me to offer my suffering up for the souls of Purgatory.

In the Catholic faith, Purgatory is this intermediary place a soul must visit after physical death for further purification of earthly sins. We were called to pray for these souls which, apparently, benefit from the prayers and pious duties that the living do for them. In other words, my own suffering didn't matter, and I should give it up for the sake of someone who was already dead. Maybe that's why I had a tendency to put myself last in life.

I learned a hard lesson though; recommending that one offer suffering up for the souls of Purgatory wasn't a two-way street. My second semester in college was a particularly difficult one for me and I brought home a less than stellar report card. When my mother expressed her disappointment, my recommendation to offer it up for the souls of Purgatory was not met with, how shall I say, an open mind. My room became my own earthly Purgatory for the next week.

I was whisked away from this memory after hearing the door to the confessional open. I watched as an older woman exited and knelt in a pew towards the back of the church, Rosary in hand, presumably to offer her penance.

It's now or never, I thought to myself, and stood up and did something I hadn't done in twenty years—walk into a confessional.

CHAPTER ELEVEN

For I Have Sinned

I walked into the small booth, which was divided down the middle by a makeshift wall with a latticed opening. There was a door on the wall that the priest would use to enter and exit from his side of the confessional.

I instinctively knelt down and offered the customary, "Bless me, Father, for I have sinned," which was drilled into me by the nuns from my Catholic school when I was preparing for my first holy communion.

"We are all sinners, my son," he replied with an accent I pegged to be Eastern European. "And how long has it been since your last confession?"

"About twenty years," I replied.

"Welcome home," he said, without a hint of judgment. How refreshing.

"And what sins would you like to confess today?"

"I know this might sound odd, Father, but does the name Sam Shoah mean anything to you?"

The priest paused for a few beats and then replied, "Indeed it does. What is your name, my son?"

"Michael Corrigan. I was his student."

After saying that, the door on the inside of the confessional leading to the priest's chambers opened and a middle-aged-looking man appeared in the doorway. He had dark hair which was grey at the temples and a clean-shaven face which didn't hide the long scar running from his chin up unto his forehead.

"Come here," he said quietly. I did as I was told and closed the door behind me once I entered his side of the booth. There were two chairs; he sat in one and I the other.

"Some people prefer to make their confession face to face which is why this setup is here. But clearly you aren't here to confess your sins. Given the circumstances, I need to confirm that you are who you say you are. First off, how did you find me?

I told him the story about how Sam left a coded message for me in his copy of *Man's Search for Meaning*.

"Just like he said he would," the priest muttered.

"Father, I'm sorry, but what is going on here?"

"I met Sam a few years ago, let's say we share a similar past."

Similar past, what does that mean? How much of a past can an old devout Jew like Sam possibly have in common with a Catholic priest fifty years his junior?

"Like what?"

"As you know Sam Shoah survived the Holocaust that claimed everyone else in his family. My people faced a Holocaust of their own, though on a much smaller scale."

Given his accent and presumed age I asked, "Bosnia?"

The priest nodded

"Most of the men and boys in my family were victims of ethnic cleansing, though I fled into the night and was found by relief workers the following day. They smuggled me over the border to Croatia where they left me at a Catholic church, and I stayed there until the war was over. After the fighting ceased, I went back home and my worst fears were confirmed, my entire family was gone. I returned to Croatia and sought refuge in the Church, where I was welcomed back with open arms. I never forgot the kindness I was shown and eventually felt the calling to convert to Catholicism. Later on, I felt called to the priesthood and was ordained ten years ago. I was sent to America three years ago as your country is in desperate need of priests."

"So, you were both exposed to the worst humanity has to offer."

He nodded again. "It's why he trusted me. There's an unspoken bond amongst survivors of such atrocities."

"But how did he find you and how did my name come up?"

"He was down here on vacation one winter break and passed by the Church. Being the good Jew that he was, Sam knew that St. Gabriel the Archangel was considered the guardian angel of Israel, known to defend the Israelites against the angels of other nations. He knocked on the door to the rectory and asked what I knew about the namesake of my parish."

I had to admit, that sounded like something Sam would do.

"When he asked about my background, I shared my story, and then he shared his."

While that brought me up to speed on what Sam and the priest had in common, it didn't do much to help me understand why I was there.

"Where do I come into all of this?"

"You are here because Sam is in trouble."

"What kind of trouble?" I asked in a tone that betrayed my rising level of frustration. It didn't seem to faze him.

"What's really going on here?" I asked and emphasized my question by clenching my hand into a fist and punching my knee.

"Your friend and mentor needs your help, but I can't tell you where he is because I don't know. It's safer that way."

I was thoroughly confused. "If you don't know where he is, then why am I here?"

"As to why Sam chose you, that's a question only he can answer. I can tell you, however, that many lives are in danger unless you can find Sam and continue his work."

Continue his work? What the hell was this guy talking about?

"He's a psychologist!" I protested. "What do you mean 'many lives are in danger'?"

"Both Sam and I made promises to ourselves that we would do anything in our power to prevent another genocide. I don't know the specifics, but since he had you come to me and not someone else, he must have uncovered something big."

"If you don't know where he is or what this is really all about, how the hell am I going to find him?"

"He gave me something to give to you."

The priest dove into a bag he kept in the corner and pulled out a tablet computer.

"Don't judge me. Oftentimes I spend an hour alone in this box and my iPad helps me stay productive. I received this email from him last night but have no idea what it means."

I looked at the timestamp and surmised that it must have been sent immediately after I dropped him off, just before he disappeared.

He double-clicked an attachment and lo and behold there was another pigpen cipher drawn in Sam's handwriting.

"Not this again," I said. "I need a six-letter word to decode it. Let me read the body of the email, maybe he put a clue in his note."

"I'm not sure that will be much help. The only thing his

note said was, 'how do we pray?'"

I began to mutter. "How do we pray? How do we pray? Silently? Reverently? No, too many letters in reach of those."

"I should say a prayer to St. Anthony, patron Saint of lost things," the priest joked.

"I don't think that will do any good. We haven't lost anything because we haven't found it yet."

That's when I remembered one of the puzzles I solved the day before in Sam's office. The phrase was *defend us in battle,* which came from the Prayer to St. Michael. Something clicked in my head.

"Father, do you have a copy of the prayer to St. Michael?"

The priest searched his bag for a prayer book and then flipped through it until he found the prayer. He handed it to me.

"This has to be it!" I said with excitement.

"What?"

And then I read the second sentence. "May God rebuke him, we humbly pray. The code word is 'humbly.'"

I then went about drawing a cipher key and decoded the message as *one Corinthians thirteen thirteen.*

"I need a bible."

"No, you don't," the priest said. "I've done enough weddings to know that one from heart. 'But now faith, hope, love, abide these three; but the greatest of these is love.'"

"What's love got to do with this?" I asked, inadvertently channeling my inner Tina Turner.

"The code you used to find me was placed in a copy of Frankl's *Man's Search for Meaning,* right?"

I nodded.

"And what are the three ways Frankl suggested a person could lead a meaningful life?"

Oh great, a pop quiz. It's a good thing that Sam drilled this into me over the past five years.

"Fulfilling work, loving relationships, and the ability to have courage in the face of danger."

"Where do you stand on all three?"

Like Ray Knight during game one of the 1986 World Series, I had to admit I was 0 for 3.

"Well, you've got a start on finding fulfilling work as you've left one career for another, so how about we give you that one. That leaves love and courage in the face of danger. Given the message you decoded, I'd say your next step has something to do with love."

"I haven't made time for love since my divorce."

"Interesting," the priest said.

"Interesting? I thought you people eschewed divorce."

"While unpopular with many of my brother priests, I firmly believe that not all marriages are meant to be. Tell me, how did your marriage end?"

"My wife and I had a son named Tyler who took his own life." I normally wouldn't tell this to a perfect stranger, but given it might help in finding Sam I went against my tendency to keep that part of my life hidden from view.

"Not many marriages can survive such a tragedy."

I gave the priest an overview about my past career and how I felt the tool I built contributed to my son's death.

"My son suffered from anxiety and depression and I didn't even know it. When I looked into his MyLife account, I saw that he was being bullied and ridiculed by some other kids. I can't help but think that, had I not created that stupid platform, Tyler would be alive today."

"How long after Tyler's death did you and your wife stay together?"

"She tried to support me when I went back to school and even lived with me for a bit, but there was nothing there. To be honest, our marriage had started to crumble before Tyler's death. That, too, was my fault."

"You carry a lot of guilt on your shoulders. You need to release yourself of those weights."

Now he sounded like Marie. Speaking of whom, I wondered what she was doing at the moment.

"So, Sam wants me to find love in order to find him? I'm not exactly big on the dating scene, Father."

"Maybe he doesn't want you to find love. Maybe he wants you to reconnect with the last woman you loved. Did he know your ex-wife at all?"

"Yes. As a matter of fact, he called her the other day to invite her to my dissertation defense."

"Maybe that's not all he reached out to her about."

"Great. So now I have to go up to New York."

"It seems that way. But keep in mind that, at some point, you will also need to demonstrate courage in the face of danger."

"Are you saying I will have to channel my inner St. Michael?"

The priest nodded. "And what was St. Michael the Archangel most known for."

"Booting Satan from paradise," I said. "But you don't mean to suggest I'm going up against the Devil?" I joked.

"To quote Baudelaire, the greatest trick the Devil ever pulled is convincing the world that he doesn't exist. Evil is real, Michael, and it may be up to you to stand up to it."

Let me get this straight, an eighty-two-year-old retired psychologist apparently has uncovered something, though there's no telling what that is, that may ignite a holocaust here in the States. He's in trouble and has chosen me to help him with that task and, if what I've learned in this confessional is right, my ex-wife holds some key as to how I can find him. Furthermore, I will, at some point in the near future, have to go to battle against evil incarnate. Did I understand all of that correctly? It's an understatement to say that this didn't turn out exactly how I expected it would.

I looked at my watch and it was ten minutes after five. "I hope no one's out there, Father, because your office hours are over."

"That's my problem to worry about."

It dawned on me that I'd been with the priest for over forty minutes and I had no idea what his name was, so I asked him.

"Amar."

"Thank you, Father Amar. Shall I call you with an update on Sam?"

The priest shook his head. "It's best that I don't know. That way, no one can torture it out of me."

Did he just say torture? I had forgotten where he was from and what his frame of reference was.

I nodded to acknowledge what he said and, out of respect for the priest, I crossed myself before leaving the confessional. When I was back into the church, I found Marie waiting for me with an eager look on her face.

"So?"

"I don't even know where to begin, but I am starving so it's going to have to wait until we eat."

CHAPTER TWELVE

The Girl with the Butterfly Tattoo

After we exited the church, I handed the keys over to Marie as a way of asking her to drive. My head was pounding, and I didn't want to endanger either of us by driving.

"I have an idea," she said. "How about we head over to the hotel and get settled? You can take a hot shower and we can order room service."

I thought that sounded glorious. "Deal."

"Want some help with your headache?" Marie asked after I buckled my seatbelt.

"You have any pills?"

"No, something better."

She tapped my wrist and encouraged me to close my eyes and take a few deep breaths, which I did. She must have leaned towards me because I smelled her perfume and the combination of that scent, my deep breathing, and her calming voice put me right at ease. Before I knew it, all the tension I felt before was leaving my body and I drifted off into a relaxed state.

I don't remember anything about the drive to Ft. Lauderdale as I must have been asleep the whole time. I do remember dreaming about the conversation I had in the confessional but chalked it up to being on so fresh in my mind when I dozed off. I've often noticed that I'll dream of things that are fresh on my mind just before going to bed, as if my subconscious works out problems even though I'm asleep. Before I knew it, Marie was tapping me on the shoulder encouraging me to wake up after pulling up to the Ritz.

"You can stay in the car and sleep, but the valet might think that's weird," she joked.

I smiled, got out of the car, and waited for a bellman to retrieve our bags from the car. Five-star service at its best.

"How do you feel?" Marie asked.

"A thousand times better than when we left the church," I admitted.

The bellman followed us inside with our bags and waited as we checked in.

"I got us a two-bedroom suite. I hope that's okay."

Okay? Yes, it's okay! In fact, do they have any one-bedroom rooms available? Though I thought it but didn't say it. I just nodded my approval.

Across from the front desk was something I had never seen in a hotel before—a vending machine for champagne. The woman at the front desk caught me staring and said, "We are part of a pilot program for Moët and Chandon."

"How do you prevent minors from getting any?"

"Everyone has to scan their license, but we know that isn't foolproof since kids can snag someone else's ID, so those of us behind the desk here keep an eye out. We've only had it a few weeks and haven't had any issues yet."

"Will you folks need help getting these bags to the room?" the bellmen asked.

I was tempted to brush him off, but Marie, who was clearly more accustomed to luxury hotels, took him up on his offer. I hoped she had tip money, because I had no cash on me.

After she checked us in, I walked over to the champagne vending machine and bought a bottle.

"You have big ideas tonight?" Marie asked.

"I just wanted to see that it worked," I replied.

"It worked," she said with a wink. "And it would be terrible for it to go to waste, don't you think?"

Now both my mind and heart were racing. Was my five-year dry spell about to come to an end?

We took the elevator up to the eighth floor and entered room 841, which had a stunning view of the Atlantic Ocean. The sun was on its way down and out in the distance I spotted several cruise ships lit up on the horizon waiting for their turn to come into Port Everglades to the south of us. Also, out along the horizon were a bunch of container ships with goodies likely from South America.

Marie must have tipped the bellman because he was gone and now we were alone.

"How's the tension?" she asked.

Raging, I thought to myself regarding the sexual tension I was experiencing, but figured she meant my headache.

"Better now," I replied. I was happy that she wasn't in a rush to talk about what happened back at the church as I was afraid it would lead to another headache.

She pulled out a chair from the round table in the corner. "Have a seat," she said. "I want to check something out."

She didn't have to tell me twice. I sat down and a moment later felt her hands on my shoulders; her thumbs were putting pressure on the base of my neck, rubbing it shiatsu style.

"When was the last time you had a massage?"

I had to think. "I guess my honeymoon," I replied.

"So how long ago was that?"

"Twenty-one years ago."

"You mean to tell me you haven't had a massage since you were twenty-four years old? I'm going to call the concierge and book you one for tonight."

I've never had a woman take this kind of interest in my personal health before. My ex-wife wasn't exactly what you'd call a giver.

"You're pretty good at that," I said. Jesus, I must have been relaxed because normally I wouldn't say something so forward to a woman I barely knew. At best, I could be described as being awkward around women, but what I just blurted out felt confident.

"The amount of tension you have in you requires professional attention."

The way she whispered that into my ear ignited a spark that traveled with light speed from my ear canal down to just below my waist.

"I'm hungry. How about I order us some dinner? I assume you are still fine with staying in?"

"Yes," I replied. Not like I could actually stand up at the moment in case she wanted to go out. Talk about a tell.

"How about a few salads and then some steak and fish? We can split everything up."

Fish? I hated fish, but I didn't challenge her suggestion.

"Sounds good."

I watched as she placed the order, and hearing her talk about food was enough of a distraction to get the blood flowing above my waist once again.

"Sounds like the kitchen is backed up and it will take a while, but I have an idea," she said and then got up from the couch she was sitting on when she was talking to room service. She walked into one of the bedrooms and a moment later I heard water running.

"You need to do something about that tension. I'm going to run you a bath. How about you just relax and I'll catch up on some work? Then we'll eat dinner whenever it arrives. Maybe even watch some TV and live the wild life in Ft. Lauderdale on a Friday night."

My head was spinning, but why the hell not treat myself to a bath?

"I like the way you think."

Marie walked over to where I was sitting, extended her arm for me to grab, and then tugged on it until I was out of the chair. She then guided me to the bathroom where the jacuzzi tub was almost half full.

"The temperature controls are here," she said while pointing them out. "And the jets are here. And I'll be waiting for you right over there," she said while pointing to the bedroom.

I didn't need my friend Joe to tell me whether this was an indicator of interest. Of course it was and I needed to take the risk. I'm sure this isn't what Frankl meant when he said courage in the face of danger, but here went nothing.

She pulled her hand away, thereby breaking contact between us, and I immediately grabbed it back. Our eyes met and I'll never forget how she bit her lip just before closing her eyes. I pulled her close, put my hands around her waist, and kissed her.

Our lips connecting sent a bolt of electricity running through my body. Her hands pushed against my chest, separating us just enough so she could stare deeply into my eyes. "What were you waiting for?" she asked, before placing both of her hands on my face and joining my lips with hers.

I paused kissing her only to catch my breath and looked down to see that she had already started to unbutton her jeans. She then placed my hands on her blouse and I went to work unbuttoning it and we left a goodie trail of clothes between the bathroom and the bedroom. Once on the bed, I looked over the most perfect body I'd ever seen and was intent on exploring every inch of it. While kissing down the center of her body, I noticed a tattoo of a butterfly on her hip and made a mental note to ask her about its significance.

I'm not sure how long the first time lasted, but I can tell you it was unlike any sexual experience I'd had up until that point. She was the most attentive lover I'd ever been with, telling me what she liked and asking me what I wanted and didn't balk at anything I asked for. I felt love, passion, safety, and excitement and couldn't believe what I had found myself in the middle of. My sex life with Anna was vanilla; she wasn't all that interested in anything other than five minutes of missionary and I was too timid sexually to ask for anything else, Marie, though, was what can best be described as an awakening.

After the first time, I collapsed on top of her and slid off to rest on my back. After a few moments, she turned towards me and whispered into my ear, "That was perfect, but I'm not done with you yet," and she slithered on top of me for a second round and, when that was over, a third.

Eat your heart out, Tony Robbins. As far as motivational speakers are concerned, Marie Charcot had just awakened the giant within.

Neither of us heard room service knocking at the door; I can only imagine what they heard coming from the other side of the door. Eventually I got up, put on a robe, and retrieved the now cold food from the cart in the hallway. I brought it to the bedroom where Marie and I took turns feeding each other like two young newlyweds on our honeymoon.

"Feel better?" she asked.

"Much," I replied.

After we finished eating she turned to me and said, "Why don't you get some rest. I have some work to do."

I stood up and walked around to massage her shoulders. "I have an idea…"

"I like the way you think, but let's table that for later," she said while gently massaging my wrist. You should rest."

Her tone was soft, like a mother encouraging a newborn to sleep. "You are going to need to save some strength for later."

As excited as I was at the prospect of being with Marie again, I had to admit that I was tired and that some rest would do me good. I walked over to the bed, which was damp with sweat and smelled of sex, and rested my head on the pillow. When I woke up, it was morning and Marie was gone.

CHAPTER THIRTEEN

A Murder in Pompano

I looked around the room and took stock of just how much my life had changed in the past day. I successfully defended my dissertation, my advisor, friend, and mentor went missing under mysterious circumstances, potential doom and gloom was on the horizon, and I spent the night with a woman who, to put it mildly, had rocked my world. Talk about a wild twenty-four hours.

Where the hell was she, anyway? Did she even come back last night? I got out of bed and walked over to the desk in the corner expecting to find a Dear John letter, but there was none. I fished my phone out of the pocket of my jeans, which were still on the floor of the bathroom, and didn't see any missed calls. Did I dream the entire night?

I walked into the other bedroom and didn't see her Louis Vuitton luggage anywhere. Was I just the victim of a one-night stand? Maybe I was so bad a lover that she had to cut her losses and run away. Whatever the case, I remembered that I came down to Florida for a reason, and it turns out it was to meet with a priest who was befriended by my mentor years ago over their shared experiences with genocide and, oh yeah, I was likely the key to stopping another one provided that I could find Sam and learn just what the hell was going on. This would be a hell of a lot easier if the man could just be direct with me. I had to remind myself that he was a psychologist and being indirect comes with the territory.

I knew that I had to make my way to New York and talk with my ex-wife and, to put it mildly, that was something I wanted to avoid like the plague. There was a lot of pain there for me; I failed her so badly as a husband that she found solace in another man's arms. But if she holds some clue as to where I can find Sam, who can give me some real answers, I needed to suck it up, swallow my pride, and talk to Anna.

I took a shower to wash the night off of me, got dressed, and went down to the lobby.

"Checking out of room 841," I said to the cheery agent behind the counter. Her name tag stated that her name was Nicole and that she was from Oklahoma.

"Mr. Charcot?" Nicole asked.

"Corrigan, but the room was under Charcot."

"My apologies, sir, I see that here. All room charges have been paid for, but you can stay up until 1pm if you like."

"No thanks, I have to make my way back north," I said.

"Very good, sir. I do have a note for you."

Nicole handed me an envelope. I thanked her for her time and walked over to the corner where I opened the note. It was from Marie.

Thank you for a wonderful evening. I had a client emergency and need to head back to Washington. Best of luck finding Sam. Keep me in the loop.

So that's it? Why not just tell that to me in person? I was curious as to when she left the note so went back to see Nicole.

"Is there something I can help you with, Mr. Corrigan?"

"I'm just curious, do you have any idea when Ms. Charcot left this note for me?"

"Well, I came on at seven this morning and it was already here, so it must have been before then. I can call the team member who worked overnight to check, though."

I decided it wasn't worth the trouble of waking someone who was up all night. "Never mind," I said and added, "do you offer transportation to the airport?"

"Yes. We have a complimentary Suburban that shuttles guests to and from shopping destinations as well as the airport. Would you like me to arrange a ride for you?"

"That would be great."

"What time does your flight leave?"

And that's when I remembered that I didn't have a return flight booked. I spotted a computer terminal in the lobby, presumably for guests to use to print boarding passes. If I had to wait for the Suburban, I might as well try to use the computer to book a ticket.

"I don't have one yet but leaving ASAP would be great."

Nicole picked up the phone and dialed the number for guest transport and found out the driver could take me in thirty minutes, which would give me more than enough time to book a ticket to New York.

"Thanks, Nicole."

"No problem, Mr. Corrigan."

I was able to get myself on an 11 am JetBlue flight to LaGuardia airport in New York, which would put me at Anna's place around mid-afternoon, which reminded me to call her and let her know that I was coming over. She picked up on the third ring.

"You never told me how it went on Thursday."

Not hello, how are you, just straight to business. That's the way it always was with my ex.

"I got a bit distracted," I said, offering the understatement of the year. "Are you going to be around later? I'm coming to New York and there's something I'd like to talk about."

"You have me now. What's up?"

This wasn't exactly the kind of conversation I wanted to have on the phone.

"I'm leaving for the airport in a few minutes. I'd rather just talk in person."

"Airport? You could drive to New York in the time it would take you to fly from Hartford."

I was distracted by the sight of Nicole trying to get my attention to tell me the Suburban was ready to take me to Ft. Lauderdale International Airport.

"I'm in Florida. Look, I'll explain later. I should be there between three and four. Is that okay?"

"It's fine but what's going on? You were just in Storrs on Thursday. It's not like you to take a random trip these days, certainly not a quick overnighter."

"I'll tell you later," I said and hung up. I grabbed my bag and stepped outside into the humid South Florida air where a luxurious black Suburban was parked out front.

"Señor Corrigan?" the driver asked as I walked towards the vehicle. He was dressed in a form-fitting grey suit and his name tag read Elian. I assumed that by his physical features and name that he was of Cuban descent, a suspicion confirmed after he introduced himself.

"My name is Elian and I understand we are going to Ft. Lauderdale Airport. What airline, sir?"

"JetBlue. And there's no rush, I have some time."

"Very well, sir. It should take us about a half hour. Traffic isn't too bad."

I took a seat in the second row of the oversized vehicle, where there were copies of both the *Sun Sentinel* and the *Miami Herald* waiting. Since I tended to experience motion sickness whenever I read in a moving vehicle, I took a pass on reading.

"Anything you want to listen to on the way, sir?"

"Maybe just the news," I replied while pulling my seatbelt over my shoulder. As I did, a familiar scent came across my nose—Marie's perfume.

"Say, you didn't drive an attractive blonde to the Pompano airport this morning, did you, Elian?"

"No, not this morning," he replied.

"Oh," I said. Maybe it's a popular perfume.

"I mean, sir, that I drove a blonde woman to the Pompano airport last night."

"Really. About what time?"

"Probably around 9 pm. She seemed to be in a hurry, but oh *Dios mio*, was she *caliente*."

Nine pm? I can't remember what time I feel asleep and estimated it must have been between 8 and 9 pm. She must have left for the airport right after I fell asleep, but why?

"Did you know her, señor?"

"She's a friend of mine."

"I wish I had some friends like that," Elian replied, and then laughed. "*Mi esposa* doesn't look like that."

Elian made a left onto Federal Highway, which leads straight to the airport. Traffic was flowing at a brisk pace when a news story came on that caught my attention. "Can you turn this up, Elian?"

"Sure, señor."

"In local news, the parish secretary for St. Gabriel parish in Pompano Beach got the shock of her life today when she came to work to find the pastor, Father Amar Tomasavic, who survived the war in Bosnia, shot to death in his bedroom at the rectory sometime last night. Police are searching for leads but some parishioners believe it was anti-Catholic sentiment from the area's growing Muslim population. Father Amar converted to Catholicism from Islam when he was a young man. For more on this story follow us on…"

The radio went silent as we entered the Kinney Tunnel.

"People are *loco*, señor," Elian said to break the silence and then he crossed himself and kissed his knuckle.

I just stared out the window and felt my stomach drop. While I had only met the priest yesterday, I could tell that he was a kind soul and, given all he lived through, deserved much longer life. His death also reminded me that Sam's life, and my own for that matter, was in grave danger. The stakes just got higher.

It couldn't be a coincidence that the priest who believed that Sam had some information about some catastrophic event was now dead. What was it he said yesterday, it's better that he didn't know where Sam was so no one could torture it out of him? The lapsed Catholic in me was tempted to say a prayer not just for the repose of Father Amar's soul, but for my own safety as well. What the hell had I gotten myself into?

I wondered if I should go to the police but realized I had nothing concrete to give them. Plus, Sam was the key to all of this, and I had to find him; going to the cops would just tie me up. As we made our way south towards the airport, I became preoccupied with the frightening thought that I was heading into some real danger. Somewhere I knew that I needed to find the courage to face that; although I was becoming increasingly scared about my safety, I had to push on.

Elian dropped me off at the curb right under a sign for JetBlue departures. I handed him a twenty-dollar tip and then walked into the terminal, which was full of families making their way back home from their April vacations. I still had plenty of time to make my flight so took it as an opportunity to people watch.

I saw one father lose his temper at what appeared to be a

set of triplets as one of them kept dropping a stuffed animal on the floor. I saw a mother who had an expression on her face suggesting the need for a chardonnay. Every parent I saw looked exasperated and I just wanted to tell them all that, even though they didn't know it, these would be the finest years of their lives. Kids grow up to fast, and then they leave.

Finally, it was my turn to hand my credentials over to the TSA agent who took my boarding pass and ID with the same level of enthusiasm a teenager has to go to back school on a Tuesday after a long weekend. This guy couldn't pass a personality test to work at a Wendy's, yet here he was making sure air travel is safe.

After walking through the body scanner, I was bestowed with the knowledge that I had been randomly selected for additional screening and enjoyed a thorough patting down by a blue-gloved agent. Whoa buddy, at least buy me dinner first.

With that unpleasant business behind me, I made my way to the gate. Forty minutes later I was on board, crammed in an impossibly small window seat in the back of the plane. A young couple with one son took the row behind me. The kid's name was Eric, and I knew this because his mother was shouting his name every two minutes. It took all my strength not to do the same because his favorite game apparently was kick the back of Corrigan's seat. Thankfully, Eric fell asleep halfway through the flight to New York and I was able to get some peace.

We arrived at LaGuardia just after 3 pm and given how full the flight was and far back I was sitting, I didn't deplane until just after 3:30. I stepped into the terminal looking for the closest men's room, and that's when I sensed that I was being followed.

CHAPTER FOURTEEN

Losing My Tail

A man with olive skin and a thick beard was following me just a little too closely as I made my way through the terminal. Was it just paranoia? Had I read too many spy novels? Maybe, but I was keenly aware that I'd gotten involved in something big and dangerous and had to keep my guard up, lest I wind up like Father Amar.

My advisor Sam, who apparently led a secret life, was missing and just as a handler does to one of his agents in a spy novel, sent me a coded message directing me to meet with someone who was now dead. I was now on my way to see my ex-wife under the assumption that Sam may have told her something that would help me find him and then it hit me, by doing so, he may have placed her in danger. Time was of the essence and I needed to get to her ASAP.

Having spotted a men's room, I ducked into it to relieve my bladder and see if the man, whom I had now nicknamed Mustafa, had followed me in. I looked over my shoulder while standing in front of the urinal and saw that he had. Now, it was all entirely possible that he had to go too, another traveler who felt the call of nature, but I was uneasy about him from the moment I spotted him after I left the gate. Only the paranoid survive, right?

I pushed my kidneys to their limit to hasten my stream, finished up, washed my hands, and high-tailed it out of the bathroom. I had a friend in college named Dave who used to walk impossibly fast when he'd been drinking; we called it six-pack speed. At the moment, I was in twelve-pack speed, though I looked like another traveler running to catch a flight.

My original plan was to jump in a yellow cab and head straight to my old brownstone on the Upper West Side. Instead, I decided to take the M60 bus to 125th Street and take the 4 train to Eighty-sixth and then walk west through Central Park to my old neighborhood. While it would be a pain in the ass with my roller board, I thought it would be the best way to lose my tail. Plus, it's not like I had a lot in my bag, I could always ditch it and replace its contents later.

I headed downstairs to arrivals and was happy I didn't have to wait for a checked bag as baggage claim looked like Shea Stadium when the Beatles played in '65. I headed to a MetroCard machine as I needed one to pay for the bus and my eventual subway fare. While I was making my transaction, I looked over my shoulder, didn't see Mustafa, and headed out to wait for the bus.

While Florida was hot and humid when I left, New York didn't get the memo that it was springtime and a blast of cool air hit me in the face. Unfortunately, it was mixed with the exhaust from a rental car shuttle bus that had just passed by and I coughed a little after inhaling the smog. Still no sign of Mustafa.

I only had to wait five minutes for an M60 to arrive and, thankfully, it was only half full. I knew that would change as it made its way through the other terminals, but at least I wouldn't have to wait for another one. I got on, took a seat, and then noticed some commotion around one of the doors to the terminal. A moment later, Mustafa ran out of the doorway and waved at the bus driver, who was just about to pull away from the curb.

"You're lucky I'm feeling nice today, pal," he said while opening the door.

"Thank you vedy much," Mustafa said with an accent I couldn't pinpoint as he entered. He swiped his MetroCard and then took a seat on the other side of the bus, a few rows behind me. All the better to see me with, I suppose.

I had a choice to make: get off the bus at another terminal and find another way into Manhattan or stay on the bus and continue with my current plan. If I got off, and Mustafa followed, I'd know for sure that he was after me but I'd also have a problem—I'd be cornered at the airport with limited options to hide and then get into the city. If I waited to try and ditch him after arriving in Manhattan, I'd have more options to flee to. I decided to wait.

It was an agonizing thirty-five-minute ride from Queens to Manhattan. I'd glance over at Mustafa occasionally, but never caught him looking my way. He seemed to always be glued to his phone.

As we pulled up to the Lexington Avenue stop along 125th Street, I stood up and grabbed my bag in preparation to exit. Out of the corner of my eye, I noticed that Mustafa had done the same. This unnerved me as, on the way, I'd convinced myself that it was just a coincidence that he made his way onto my bus. Survey says, nope!

I exited the bus and walked towards 125th Street station to grab the subway, hoping I could lose him, but if Mustafa was trying to be inconspicuous, he was doing a poor job of it. I wished it were a Friday because rush hour would have been in full swing and I'd have had an easier time hiding from him, but it was a Saturday, and the station was sparsely populated. I swiped my MetroCard at a turnstile and made my way to the platform for a downtown four train. Mustafa was right behind me.

I made the decision to get on the next downtown train and then get immediately off to try and lose him. The train arrived and I got on but found it packed to the gills with a bunch of people wearing NY Rangers jerseys. Just my luck, the blue shirts made it to the post season. Already inebriated, one of the fans pulled me in and his compatriots then blocked the door, making it impossible for me to hop off. I looked to my right and saw that Mustafa was on as well. I'd have to lose him while getting off at Eighty-sixth Street.

As the train approached my stop, I said to the group of fans who'd adopted me as one of their own, "I hope Hank's glove is on fire tonight," referencing goalie Henrik Lundqvist, who was nearing the end of his playing prime. That comment earned me some goodwill and my new friends stepped aside, giving me a clear path to the door.

I stepped onto the platform and noticed that Mustafa had done the same. Part of me wanted to confront him and ask why he was following me while the other part wanted to run like hell. Given that courage wasn't one of my traits, I opted to walk briskly up the stairs to the station exit and made my way to the southwest corner of the Eighty-sixth Street exit. My shadow followed.

As an avid runner, and former Manhattanite, I knew Central Park as well as anyone could and decided it would be there where I'd make a break for it. I walked one block south to Eighty-fifth Street and then made a right and crossed over both Park and Madison Avenues until I reached Fifth, and entered the park. I spotted a homeless man about my size with a sign that read, *I'm being hunted by ninjas and need money for Karate lessons.* Only in New York.

"I don't have any cash, but how'd you like a nicer bag for your belongings?" I asked while stretching my quads.

He responded with a puzzled look on his face.

"The suitcase is yours and you can keep the clothes inside," I said and then sprinted off as Mustafa approached.

When I was halfway down the southern part of the Jackie Kennedy Onassis reservoir, I made a left towards the Great Lawn softball fields, but there were games being played, so I veered towards West Drive and made a left towards Hunter's Gate. Later in the spring I might have found a jazz quartet playing, but there was none today. I looked over my shoulder and saw no sign of Mustafa.

I thought of entering the Museum of Natural History to further try and hide from the mysterious mustached man who was following me but opted to take my chances and run north along Central Park West until I reached Eighty-seventh street.

I arrived at my old brownstone out of breath and must have looked like shit because when Anna answered after I knocked on the door all she said was, "You look like shit."

I darted inside, slammed the door behind me, and looked out the peephole to see if Mustafa was in sight. He wasn't.

"Michael, what the hell is going on?"

"I'm being followed," I said and then locked the door and walked to the kitchen, as if I still lived there.

"Followed? By whom, the dissertation police?"

The kitchen was in shambles and then I remembered that Anna said she was redoing it again as her new husband, Phillip, loved to cook.

"Is Phil here?"

"You know he prefers Phillip and no, he's on assignment in California doing a piece on social media and election interference. I told him he should talk to you but I think I insulted him."

"Mind if I have some water?"

Anna reached into the refrigerator and pulled out a bottle

of Amstel Light instead. After popping the top she said, "You look like you could use this more."

I took a long pull on the beer and guzzled it down. My heart rate had started to slow back to normal and I took a moment to admire how pretty my ex-wife was. A lot of shit had gone down between us, but we had a past, and it wasn't all bad.

"Where's your bag? I thought you said you were coming here from Florida?"

"I donated it to a man who has to fight off ninjas," I remarked.

She looked at me with a raised eyebrow. "I see you rediscovered your sense of humor," Anna replied. "Now are you going to tell me what this is about or not?"

"It's about Sam, and a dead priest."

"What?"

"Let me start from the beginning."

I recounted everything that had happened after I defended my dissertation and Anna was clearly stunned.

"I need something stronger than a beer," she replied.

She left the room for a few minutes and came back with two mixed drinks. "You still like gin and tonics?"

I nodded and then she handed me one.

We both took a sip of our drinks and then she looked up and said, "Come to think of it, Sam did mention something out of the ordinary when he invited me to come to your dissertation defense. I didn't think anything of it as I rationalized that I was talking to an eighty-two-year-old man who was losing his marbles."

"What did he say?" I asked.

"He said that I needed to help take a weight off of your shoulders."

Sam had frequently mentioned that he was worried about the guilt I carried over my son's death and the subsequent end of my marriage. At the time, I thought he was just playing therapist with me, but I had to be open to the possibility that he had an ulterior motive.

"He also said that we should look to Freud for guidance."

Freud? Neither Sam nor I subscribed to the psychoanalytic school for our approach to therapy. What did Freud have to do with anything?"

"Did he say anything else?"

"Yes, and this is why I thought he was slipping mentally. He said that if you were confused, to look to my name as a hint."

"Anna," I said.

"What?" She replied.

"Sorry, I was saying it out loud to try and think through something."

"I must say, you are more interesting as a psychologist than you ever were as a computer scientist."

I didn't pay her backhanded compliment much attention. I just went back to trying to put this puzzle together. "Anna Freud was the youngest daughter of Sigmund Freud, and also a psychoanalyst. But what does she have to do with us?"

"Would you like to lay on the couch as you free associate?" My ex-wife joked.

"That's it! Anna, you are brilliant."

"I am?" she asked and raised her glass to take another sip.

"Anna O was the pseudonym of a one of Josef Breuer's patients, a woman he was treating for hysteria. Breuer was a contemporary of Freud and together they pioneered what became known as the talking cure, which was the beginning of the practice of using free association as a form of therapy."

"So, what does that mean?" she asked.

I looked at her in the eyes as a feeling of extreme nervousness came over me. "It means we need to talk."

CHAPTER FIFTEEN

Scenes from an Italian Restaurant

When it comes to phrases in the English language, there are few that strike terror in someone more than *we need to talk*. When a sibling says them, it's typically followed by a request for money. When a parent says them, it often means someone is sick. When a romantic partner says them, though, it typically only means one of two things; they want to know where the relationship is going, or they want to break up. Of course, Anna and I had already ended our marriage, but that didn't mean we weren't about to have a deep conversation, and perhaps one more intimate than any we'd ever had. I had a problem, though, I was very hungry and a little tipsy from the alcohol. I needed to eat.

"Do you have anything to eat?"

Anna laughed. "Look around, I'm at the threshold of hell."

I had to give her props for making a *Christmas Vacation* reference. It was our favorite holiday movie when times were good. You can have your George Baileys and Ebenezer Scrooges, but I'll take my Clark Griswold whenever I can get him.

"We've been eating out every night, and I wasn't exactly

expecting you for dinner."

I had two problems with going out tonight: I looked like hell and didn't have a change of clothes, and Mustafa could be lurking around waiting to grab me or, worse, us. I explained as much to Anna.

"If he were still outside, he'd have tried to get in by now. It's probably just your overactive imagination playing tricks on you. With regards to the clothes, you and Philip are about the same size, I'm sure we can find something that fits. I'll call Scalinatella."

That restaurant on the Upper East Side was our favorite when we were a couple.

"How about a place less sentimental?" I asked.

"It's a Saturday night in New York and I know I can get a table there. You're welcome to try the Olive Garden in Times Square if you prefer.

"Scalinatella will be fine," I said. "Mind if I shower?"

"I was hoping you would. Feel free to use the master and take whatever you want out of Philip's closet."

When I was done showering I found a pair of jeans and a black mock turtleneck that transformed me from shabby-looking academic to Steve Jobs wannabe and met Anna downstairs.

After exiting the brownstone, I looked up and down the street praying that I wouldn't spot Mustafa. Since everything looked clear, I hailed a cab and we headed across town to Sixty-first and Third.

Anna and I discovered Scalinatella when we first moved to New York. It's quite unassuming from the outside as it's in the basement of a residential building and there's nothing that gives away the dark elegance on the inside.

We walked into the romantically lit dining room after being gone for six years and I immediately had the feeling as if I were home. Marco, the host, greeted us with a warm welcome and showed us to our table in the corner, which was alongside the interior rustic brick wall. Unlike other restaurants in Manhattan, they don't shoehorn you in at Scalinatella; there's enough breathing room to have a comfortable, dare I say intimate, meal.

I ordered a bottle of Brunello and Anna and I made small talk while we waited for it to be brought to the table. Once the waiter came back with the bottle, I sampled it, offered a nod of approval, and our glasses were filled. He then went through a list of no fewer than thirty specials from which Anna and I selected. We had learned early on never to order off the menu, the specials were where it's at. Realizing we had an hour to go before our meals would be served, I decided it was time to begin the session, so to speak.

"Do you remember the first time we came here?"

Anna nodded. "Must have been twenty years ago. We were so young."

"Our lives were in front of us."

Anna reached out and grabbed my hand as a gesture of kindness; one which I did not mistake for love. Our marriage was over, neither one of us wanted to resurrect it, but neither of us hated the other. She was trying to offer me an olive branch of sorts, and I accepted.

"When did I lose you?" I asked.

Anna withdrew her hand, perhaps put off by the gravity of the question. She took a sip of wine as if to build up some courage to respond.

"It's okay," I replied. "I won't hold anything against you."

She took another sip.

"I can't pinpoint a date. We just drifted apart. You were so wrapped up in work and I felt so alone. I heard from my girlfriends who were, for all intents and purposes, finance widows that they all felt lonely and started flirting with guys just for the attention. I vowed I wouldn't give into that temptation, but you were just gone so much and when you were home you weren't really there."

She was right, I was wrapped up in work, but in my mind I was doing it to help secure our future. No doubt those finance widows' husbands were doing the same.

Now it was my turn to have a sip. "So, before Tyler?"

Our son came along five years into our marriage, yet I had been an absentee husband before that.

"Yes, I felt that way before Tyler, but after he was born I had him to distract me. Plus, for a while, you were very involved, always taking over at night and spending all weekends with him. Of course, that was before you started MyLife."

"Believe me, if I could go back in time and do anything, I wouldn't have started that company."

"Why?"

"You know why."

"If you didn't start that company, you would have started another. You were so smart, so driven. You were meant to do big things. Great things. It's part of what attracted me to you in the first place."

"What, my devilish good looks weren't enough?"

Anna laughed. "They didn't hurt, but I guess I didn't realize that your drive came at a price."

She took a pull on her wine and then asked me, "When did you know about Philip?"

"I had my suspicions when you started going on all those weekend girls' trips. It was so unlike you. I had tried for years to get you to go away with your friends because I knew you needed the break after Tyler came along, but you always refused and said that you wanted to go away with me instead."

"It was the truth. I did. I wanted to re-connect with my husband."

"So when you started going out of town, I got suspicious. Once I was going over the Amex bill and saw that on most of your trips when you paid for dinner it was always for a party of two. It didn't take me long to figure it out."

Anna looked me in the eyes, and I detected more than just a hint of anger.

"That was three years before our marriage ended. If you suspected anything, why the hell didn't you say something?"

I didn't expect that from her.

"You know I'm no good at confrontation…"

Before I could firmly mount my defense, Anna cut me off.

"Don't give me that horse shit about confrontation, Mike. If you love someone and suspect them stepping out on you, you call them on it. Did I ever not call you out on something?"

During the course of our marriage, if there was an argument to be had, Anna would be the one to start it. She'd later admit that she would get me angry because she knew how much I held inside and that it was better if I just let it all out.

"No, you called me on stuff. But I'm not you," I protested.

"One of our biggest problems was that you just couldn't communicate. It's almost like you spoke computer code fluently but got all flustered when it came to English."

"What would you have done if I had called you on the affair?"

Anna took another sip. "I'll tell you it would have sucked, but I would have respected you."

That stung. To hear that the woman you loved, the woman you did everything for lost her respect for you was like a punch below the belt.

"I would have called it off with Philip and suggested that we get counseling."

Well, we did get counseling, but not until after our son's

death. At that point, we were past the point of no return.

"To be honest, I never felt as if I deserved you. You were everything I ever wanted in a woman and part of me never accepted that I was good enough for you. That's why I worked so much, I wanted to give you a fairytale life. When I suspected you of cheating, it only confirmed my suspicions that I was right all along, I was living a fantasy."

"We were in couples therapy for six months and you never said that."

"I know. I only had that realization about thirty seconds ago."

We paused to let our emotions regroup. I got our waiter's attention and ordered another bottle.

"Are you happy with Philip?"

"I am. He's a good man. It's the second time around for both of us. We've both learned a lot about what can go wrong and are very proactive in addressing how we are feeling."

"That's good," I said. It wasn't a lie; I was happy for her.

"What about you? Not that you have to tell me, but has there been anyone in your life?"

"No one serious," I replied. I held back on telling Anna about the porn star experience I had the night before. There's a fine line when it comes to having an intimate conversation with one's ex and boasting about sexual conquests.

"I do hope you find someone. I always felt as if you had a tremendous capacity to love, and that is something that shouldn't be wasted."

"I'll drink to that," I replied.

"There's one more thing I want to say before the end of the night, and I may as well say it now before the food comes."

"What's that?'

"You have to stop blaming yourself for Tyler's death. It wasn't your fault."

"I don't think I'll ever believe that," I replied.

After my son died, I always had the feeling that Anna blamed me for his death. I was the absentee father who for heaven's sake didn't even suspect he suffered from any form of mental illness. On top of that, it was his use of the MyLife platform that served as kindling for his anxiety and depression. If I never created that stupid thing, he might still be here.

"Listen to me, Mike, you've got to let it go. I miss him so much, I can't even begin to describe it, but it wasn't your fault, and it wasn't my fault. Tyler was sick."

"And I didn't even know!" I said, a little too loudly based on the stares coming from the other patrons.

"I know it's easier said than done, but you have to forgive yourself."

I nodded and the silence that came between us was interrupted by the waiter bringing us our food: lemon sole oreganata for Anna and chicken Sorrentino for me.

We made light conversation and enjoyed our food at a casual pace, as was our custom when we were a couple—we wanted to savor every moment.

We decided not to split a dessert like we used to but did take the waiter up on the complimentary limoncello. Anna paid the bill, we said goodbye to Marco, and ascended the stairs back to reality. On the way out I could have sworn I saw the self-proclaimed King of all Media himself, Howard Stern, at a table in the corner with his much younger wife.

"Where are you staying tonight?" Anna asked and that's when I realized I hadn't made any reservations. I certainly didn't want to impose and invite myself over.

"I'd offer you the guest room, but it's got the new kitchen cabinets in it."

"I'll take a car service to New Rochelle," I said. Tyler was buried next to my parents at a cemetery in that Westchester County town and there were plenty of hotels to choose from.

I decided I'd book a room there en route and go visit his grave in the morning. From there, though, I had no idea what my next step would be to find Sam.

"If that's the case, I'm going to flag a cab and head back home."

"Sounds good," I said.

She leaned in and I offered her a kiss on the cheek and whispered, "Thank you."

"It was good to talk," she replied. "Remember not to be so hard on yourself."

I stayed with her until she hailed a cab and then took out my flip phone to call the usual limo company I use in New York. I walked one block up to Sixty-second Street and turned right so that I'd be walking in the right direction for a car to come and easily get on the FDR. I had to admit that this was certainly a time when I missed having a smartphone.

As I was walking east, a town car pulled up next to me and I assumed it was a livery driver looking for a fare. My phone was pressed to my ear and I didn't hear the sound of a car door open and close or the sounds of footsteps behind me. I did, however, feel two sets of hands grab me from either side and practically lift me off the ground. Next thing I knew I was in the back of the town car that had pulled over and heard an accented voice say, "Mr. Corrigan, you are a very slippery person."

The driver turned around and, to my surprise, it was Mustafa.

"Time to go night night," he said, and then I felt a pinch in my neck and saw one of the goons who had thrown me into the car remove a needle.

My vision went blurry and all sound became muffled as if I were being spoken to underwater by someone with an impossibly low voice. A brief feeling of elation was followed by a heaviness in my head that I'd never experienced before.

My world went dark.

When I came to, my mouth was as dry as a desert and my head was on fire. I opened my eyes and found that my vision was still a bit blurry and that I was sensitive to light. After blinking a few times, my vision finally came into focus, and I was staring directly at Sam Shoah.

CHAPTER SIXTEEN

Sam's Story

To say I was confused was an understatement. Could this be a dream? I tried to remember what happened the night before, but didn't really remember anything after saying goodbye to Anna.

"Sam?"

"He's alive," Sam replied with a wry smile. "Sorry about the drama, but it was the only way to get you here safely."

I had no idea where "here" even was and, given all the trouble they took to bring me here, I predicted they weren't about to divulge that information. I did know that I had to pee, so I attempted to get up and that's when the dizziness sent me plunging back down on the bed. My head was pounding and I felt nauseous, no doubt side effects to whatever drug I was injected with last night.

"Easy. You may feel some discomfort because of the Propofol."

So that's what they gave me. "Isn't that what killed Michael Jackson?"

"He would have done better with a Jewish doctor."

I heard some rumbling in the corner and looked over.

While I was still dizzy I was able to make out the identity of the third person in the room.

"Mustafa?" I said. Sam's puzzled expression reminded me that I had no idea what the man's name was, and that Mustafa was a nickname I gave him.

"Allow me to introduce you to Jacob Malakai. He's Mossad."

"As in the Israeli foreign intelligence service?" All those spy novels I'd read paid off. I suppose I should have nicknamed him Gabriel Allon, the Israeli spy invented by genre master Daniel Silva.

Jacob nodded.

My critical thinking functions started to come back online slowly, and I had some questions, starting with why a member of Israel's foreign intelligence service following me from the airport to Manhattan yesterday.

"That was for your safety," Sam said. "After I heard about Father Amar, I couldn't take any chances with you."

"What's going on?"

"I will tell you everything," Sam said. "But I'm going to need you to promise me something."

"What's that?"

"I need you to keep an open mind about what I am going to say. You are not going to like some of it, but I hope that by the end of my story you understand why I did what I did."

"Are you in trouble?"

Sam nodded. "And so are you. Your very way of life is in trouble."

The old man had my attention.

"I'm an illegal."

"Illegal? What do you mean?"

Jacob spoke up, "Illegals was a term used by your government to describe Russian sleeper agents who posed as ordinary American citizens. They built contacts with academics, industrialists, and policymakers to gain access to intelligence."

"Michael, I'm a spy."

Sam's words hit me like a punch to the gut. I didn't know what to say and Sam could sense that, so he told a story to give his admission more context.

"I was one of seven thousand prisoners left behind at Auschwitz after our captors led more than sixty thousand inmates on a death march westward. Most of us who were left behind were seriously ill due to the effects of our imprisonment. However, I was relatively healthy since I was part of a research study conducted on twins, and you already know that part of the story. Fortunate for me, children under fifteen were not selected for the march. Instead, we were left behind with no food, no water, and no medical care. We were left behind to die."

"This isn't new news, Sam."

"I never told you what happened next."

I piped down and prepared myself for what he was about to tell me.

"I still had some strength and was one of the first to spot the Soviet scouts who all bore bewildered expressions on their faces as they crept cautiously through the camp. They asked me questions and though I didn't speak Russian, I could tell by their tone that they were confused and had no idea what they had just stumbled upon. They ran off and soon after Soviet soldiers began to arrive and take over the camps. They set up field hospitals and the Polish Red Cross came to help with nurses, doctors, and paramedics in tow. They had their work cut out for them."

Jacob came closer to hear Sam talk. I assumed it wasn't the first time he heard this story, but when a Holocaust survivor talks of their time at the camps, one must listen reverently.

"Survivors suffered from malnutrition, bedsores, frostbite,

gangrene, typhus, tuberculosis, and a host of other ailments. Some who were healthy enough to leave trickled out in small groups and walked out of Poland on foot. I knew that I had nothing waiting for me back in Germany and stayed at the camp and befriended a Soviet officer named Serge Vaselenko who unofficially adopted me as his son. His father was some big shot in Moscow and Serge was called back to Russia where he took a post working in intelligence and took me along with him, though at the time I didn't understand why a Red Army soldier would want the responsibility of taking a Holocaust survivor who didn't speak the language back to his home country."

"Proof of concept for something?" I asked. Sam nodded.

"I spent the next five years in Moscow where I learned to speak Russian fluently. When I was ten, I was sent to a family we had placed in Canada and learned English and two years later we moved to a small farm town called Little Falls in upstate New York. When it came time to go to college, Serge selected Syracuse University for me for two reasons; its proximity to Canada and the fact that it had a strong psychology department."

"Why was it so important that you study psychology?" I asked.

By that point in time, our two countries were in a Cold War. Having been exposed to the horrors of war, Serge, who was by then the head the First Chief Directorate in the KGB, the sub-organization responsible for foreign intelligence activities, thought that we could use psychology to win the war."

"How?"

"Do you remember learning about Jane Elliot?"

"That teacher in Iowa who did that controversial discrimination experiment?"

Sam nodded. "That was done in 1968 as a way of teaching

the realities of discrimination after the murder of Dr. Martin Luther King. The Russians had been doing experiments like that for years. I was supposed to add to that body of knowledge and help identify ways of dividing the American people."

"Divide and conquer," I said disgustedly.

"A strange thing happened, though. I came to love America."

"You loved it so much you'd spy on it?" I did nothing to hide my anger at Sam. Here was a man I looked up to as a father and it turned out I knew absolutely nothing about him.

"I wasn't passing along intelligence, I was simply doing research, but I also played another role."

I looked at Sam with a raised eyebrow.

"You can imagine that sleeper agents living abroad live with a certain amount of fear and anxiety. I was a talented clinician, and Moscow Center, who I ultimately reported to, assigned me the role of therapist to my fellow illegals."

"How benevolent," I said sarcastically.

"Judge me all you want, but I found meaning in helping my adopted country. The Russians saved my life and the lives of countless others as they liberated camps across Europe. You grew up believing they were the bad guys, but I didn't."

There it was again, Sam proselytizing about meaning. But his story wasn't over and I needed to find out where it was going.

"None of this explains why we are here right now?"

"I'm getting to that. My research showed that it was possible to divide people if their beliefs could be exploited, but there wasn't really a way to do that on a large scale. Then the tech revolution happened, and everything changed."

I had the sense I knew where this was going but needed Sam to confirm it.

"Years ago, I learned that a sleeper agent we placed in the

US when he was just a kid had worked his way up into big tech and started using some technology you helped build to put the division of America into overdrive. Advertising so good people will think it's a service. Does that sound familiar?"

That was the phrase my old boss, BA, would drill into our heads every day as we created the future of marketing back in the mid 1990's.

"Are you telling me Bob Ahlers is one of you? The guy drove a pickup truck with American flags on the back and spends his weekends either hunting or fishing."

"Quite the cover, isn't it?" Sam replied. "He's been using your targeting technology to disseminate misinformation while exploiting confirmation bias. And he's at the heart of all this noise around the last presidential election and will almost certainly be involved in the next."

"So that's why you championed my application to the clinical program?"

"Partly," Sam admitted. "But you were so passionate in your personal statement about how you wanted to use research to drive change in technology adaption that I was touched. I knew you were right and pushed you forward as..."

I cut him off. "A penance?"

"No," he said sternly, "because I knew you'd find meaning in it."

There it was again. Meaning. The scapegoat for everything.

"Okay, so my old boss is a sleeper agent. I'll ask again, why are we here?"

Sam took a deep breath and let it out slowly. "We are here because I learned my people have gotten tired of waiting for your people to go into another civil war and are planning a catalyst that just might lead to another mass imprisonment, and I can't let that happen."

"What kind of catalyst?"

"What I am about to tell you is going to be very difficult to hear."

"More difficult than hearing you are a Russian national masquerading as an American?"

Sam nodded. "I'm afraid so. One of the things I learned about was how my people would conduct experiments using a combination of suggestion and a common class of drugs to treat anxiety disorders to determine their impact on the ability to manipulate behavior."

"What class of drugs?"

I knew from my training that there are a number of anxiety medications that psychiatrists could choose from depending the diagnosis. My son took selective serotonin reuptake inhibitors, commonly known as SSRIs, to treat his general anxiety disorders.

"SSRIs," Sam said without breaking eye contact.

The way he said it, I didn't like where it was going.

"And the suggestion component?"

"Disseminated through very targeted advertising."

"Like one found on a social media platform?"

Sam nodded again and gave me a minute to put it together.

"Are you saying that my son's death was a result of one of these Russian experiments?"

"They've figured out a way to encourage people to take their own life. They've also been experimenting with ways to encourage mass shootings. Have you noticed the rise in school shootings over the past twenty years or so? It's not random, Michael."

My blood was starting to boil. "Why my son?"

"They must have had someone who knew your son was on the right meds and then had a way of targeting him through his device."

"Very few people knew my son was seeking treatment for

anxiety and depression. In fact, I could count them on one hand: his mother, his psychiatrist, and the pharmacist."

Jacob felt the need to offer his two cents. "Unless there was a data breach. Do you remember hearing about one from your pharmacy or maybe insurance company?"

I remembered getting a standard letter in the mail about a possible data breach from the chain drugstore in New York that we'd get our prescriptions from, but since payment card data wasn't taken I didn't think anything of it.

"Yes."

"There it is. Someone knew your son was on an SSRI and did something with that information."

The question I had asked earlier had yet to be answered. "But out of everyone on SSRIs, why my son?"

"So they could track results," Sam replied and gave me time to put two and two together.

"My old boss, BA, would have the wherewithal to hack into a system. He also had the ability to send targeted messages. And because we were connected on social media, when I was still using it, he could see any elements of my life that I'd share publicly."

"Or see the condolences people would post on your page," Jacob offered.

"Let me get this straight, you get word that your country is doing some major social experiments here in the States and, in addition, are planning something big, but you don't know what it is. Were you planning on going to the FBI with any of this?"

Sam nodded. "Yes, I was going to turn my back on my country but didn't have any ins. One just doesn't walk into FBI headquarters and ask to speak with someone in charge of counterintelligence. That's where Jacob came into play."

"I met Sam at a talk he gave at the US Holocaust Museum. I lost my grandparents in the Shoah. We developed a relationship over the years and trusted each other. I knew who he worked for and he knew who I worked for. Say what you will about your current president, but relations between Israel and the US are very strong now and Sam came to me for an introduction to a counterintelligence officer in the FBI. It wasn't safe for him to go to them directly."

"Why's that?" I asked naïvely.

"My people have assets everywhere. I'd have been made immediately."

"Someone must have made you though, right? You must have known someone was on to you because you thought to put a coded message in the book you gave me."

"When we were coming home from the restaurant after your dissertation defense, do you remember seeing graffiti on the mailbox near my home?"

"Yes," I replied, "a butterfly or something. Why?"

It was Jacob's turn to talk. "The Russians have a group of highly skilled female intelligence agents who they nicknamed Butterflies. Like the insects they are named after, Russian Butterflies are masters of change. They are highly skilled at not only sexpionage but also eliminating targets. I knew that if the Russians found out that Sam was turning to the American authorities, they'd send a Butterfly after him. As it was unsafe for me to be seen with Sam, we devised a signal that if I heard anything about someone coming for Sam, I'd find a way to have a Mossad agent tag a butterfly on the mailbox near his home. We'd then extricate Sam from his home and make it look like he'd been the victim of a kidnapping. A reliable source told me that Sam had been made so we engaged the plan."

This was getting crazier by the second, but at least Sam was attempting to do the right thing by trying to go to the authorities.

"Any idea how you were made?" I asked.

Sam shook his head. "I was always very careful, and I didn't even get to meet anyone in counterintelligence at the FBI. Part of the reason I'd been stalling is that I didn't yet know what my people were planning on doing, only that it was big."

"Wait, so you still don't know?"

"No. The sleeper agent who I was treating missed an appointment. I presume that he's face down in an unmarked grave now."

"Did you treat him in person or remotely?"

"He worked out of state. We did tele-therapy."

"You must have known people in Moscow were listening."

"Of course. He didn't feed me information in our sessions."

"How did he get it to you?"

"In a similar way to how I've been communicating with you, through coded messages."

"If that's the case, then how did some intelligence officer from your side decode them?"

"He could be careless. I have to assume that they suspected something and tortured him and are now looking for me to find out what I know. But it's my turn to ask you a question."

"What's that?"

"Were you alone in Florida?"

"Huh?"

"Clearly you solved the puzzle to find the church in Pompano. Were you alone when you went there?"

Between the side effects of the drugs Jacob had me injected with the night before and being lost in Sam's story, I hadn't thought about my travel mate.

"No, actually." I then went on to tell Sam how Marie Charcot showed up at his house after the show, how she helped me figure out the codeword to solve the cipher that directed me to Fr. Amar, and how she took me down to

Florida on her private jet.

"I told you, she wanted to meet with me while she was on campus the other day."

"She wanted to invite you to speak to some mucky muck corporate types at some event she's planning. She thought your Holocaust story would be compelling for them to hear."

I couldn't help but think about the evening we had at the Ritz, and that's when I remembered her tattoo.

"There's something else."

"What?" Sam asked.

"She had a tattoo of a butterfly just above her hip bone."

CHAPTER SEVENTEEN

An Offer

The mood in the room changed instantly and I could see fear on the faces of both men.

"So, she's the one. And to think of it, I would have met with her if you weren't defending your dissertation the other day."

"Walk us through what happened in Florida," Jacob said with a sense of urgency I hadn't heard in him yet. Up until then he'd been as cool as a cucumber, now he was quite anxious.

"I took her with me to the church, and she walked around while I was in the confessional with Fr. Amar, but the thing is she never asked me anything about what we discussed."

"Maybe because she knew she was going to come back and put the screws to the priest," Jacob offered.

Sam offered an alternative hypothesis. "Or because she had another way of getting the information she needed."

"What do you mean?" I asked.

"She's a highly trained hypnotist. She could have put you in state and had you recount whatever Fr. Amar told you in minute detail."

"I don't remember her doing that at all," I protested.

"You said she came back to your house after you dropped Gianna to campus. What happened there?"

"We had some wine, and she used some exercise to help me figure out the codeword for the cipher."

"Did she tell you to relax and guide you through the experience visually?"

"Yeah, but…"

"Then you were hypnotized, Michael. Tell me, did she do anything odd or have any traits that you considered odd?"

I had to think about my time with her over the past few days and then remembered how she would sometimes touch my wrist. "She would sometimes graze my wrist with her hand and speak softly to me."

"That's an anchor. Done frequently enough that touch from her alone would be enough to start an induction into a hypnotic state without having to go through the guided visualization and relaxation exercise she went through on the couch. Did you ever find yourself just relaxing in her presence?"

I nodded. "Yeah, on the flight down to Florida I conked out for a while." I then remembered being woken up after leaving the church and arriving at the Ritz Carlton. "Come to think of it, I fell asleep after leaving the church and then again after making love to her that evening."

"You left that part out," Jacob said.

"That's how I knew about the butterfly on the hip."

Then I remembered what Jacob had said about Russian Butterflies being trained in sexpionage. Maybe that's why the sex was so good, she was a trained professional.

"So, if she was playing me to get to you, why did she hightail it out of Florida when Fr. Amar had no idea where you were?"

"I think it's reasonable to assume that she killed the

priest," Sam said. "Maybe she wanted to get away from the scene of the crime as soon as possible. You said she had a private jet. Fr. Amar wasn't found until the following morning, so Marie could easily claim she was hundreds, if not thousands, of miles away when he was found dead."

"The guy who took me to the airport said that she left the hotel around nine. Still, she's no closer to finding out where you are now that I'm here."

Jacob turned his attention towards Sam. "Did the priest know anything else? Anyone else in your network?"

"Network?" I asked.

"The word network is a stretch. I just had a few trusted friends, such as Fr. Amar, I could call on. I never told them who I worked for."

"Well did he know any of your other associates?" I asked.

"No."

"Then the only thing Fr. Amar could tell Marie is that he didn't know where you were. Why kill him?"

"Maybe she didn't believe him?" Jacob offered.

I had a sobering thought. "Wait a minute, Fr. Amar knew that I was going to see my ex-wife. She could be in danger?"

"Not likely," Jacob said. "Marie heard your entire conversation with your ex and since you didn't have any idea where Sam was, she'd have no reason to go after Anna."

"How could she do that?"

"She had a listening device on your phone. We found it last night after taking it from you. We had to make sure you weren't compromised before bringing you to this safe house."

I reached into my pocket for my phone and found that it wasn't there.

"Where's my phone now?"

"In the other room. We removed the battery just to be sure."

"How can you be so sure she didn't go after Anna?" I

asked. While she was my ex, I still had feelings for her in a small corner of my soul and didn't want her to get hurt over something I did.

"What exactly did you talk to Anna about last night, Michael?" Sam asked.

I recounted our conversation as best I could. Sam tried to comfort me again.

"Then I don't think she has anything to worry about. Hurting her only exposes her to greater risk and the ratio of risk to reward is too high."

"On that note, why did you need me to meet with her at all?"

"Because, Michael, for what I'm going to ask you to do I need you free of the guilt that holds you back and I knew the only way to start the process of shedding it was to have a healing conversation with your ex-wife."

While I certainly wasn't free of the guilt I carry as a result of my past life, it's true that I didn't feel it weighing me down as much. But now it was time for the million-dollar question.

"So, what are you asking me to do?"

"I need someone to find out what my people are up to and prevent it from happening."

"You want me to be a spy? I am a former tech guy turned psychologist, what do I know about spying?"

"Think about it, Michael, you are perfect for this. Modern espionage is more about electronic communication than it is about backroom meetings and the stuff of spy novels. Your background as a computer scientist is perfect. You also know human behavior and were the most promising student to come out of our graduate program in three decades. You can use those skills to gain the confidence of the people you need to infiltrate to find out just what the Russians are up to. What do you think?"

I think Sam's eighty-two years have caught up with him

and that he's completely off his rocker, that's what I think.

"Why not pick someone who knows what they are doing? Surely there's someone in the Mossad who can help," I said while looking at Jacob.

"This is between your two countries," he replied. "My country is enjoying a relatively peaceful time with Russia and we cannot interfere."

"What about the FBI? That's who you were going to go to in the first place."

"It was, but I'm afraid we are out of time. For us to convince them that there is a credible threat against the United States and for them to go through all the proper legal channels to mobilize an investigation would take too long. Michael, it has to be you."

So the fate of my country was now placed on my shoulders, no pressure there.

"Let's say I do this; your people know I'm connected to you. It's only a matter of time before they come after me."

"That's why we are going to engage what Jacob and I have dubbed the Lazarus Plan, which is ironic considering neither one of us is Christian."

While I've struggled with belief, there's a lot I do remember from my Catholic upbringing and recognized the name Lazarus. In the Gospel of John, he was a brother to two of Jesus's close followers, Martha and Mary. After being entombed for four days following his death, Jesus raised him from the dead and this miracle encouraged many to believe that Jesus was the Christ.

"I don't like where this is going."

"Michael, we are going to kill you and raise you up as a new man."

This isn't exactly what I had in mind when I entered graduate school to reinvent my life.

"And just how are you going to do that?"

"I mentioned that I had more friends than just Fr. Amar. I made another friend in Westchester years ago. His organization was known for making people disappear and creating new identities for them."

Now I really didn't like where this was going. "What kind of organization?"

"You could say it is a family business. Things being what they are these days, his organization has lost some pull, but it still operates in the shadows. And plus, Patsy owes me a favor."

Patsy? That's the name of Gianna's grandfather.

"That favor wouldn't happen to be getting one's granddaughter into the doctoral program in psychology at the University of Connecticut, would it?"

Sam flashed a smile. "It just might."

If I said yes to this, then the mob would arrange for my death, which I imagine would have to be somewhat public so that the news made it back to Marie and the Russians. Everyone I know would mourn my passing. Then again, my parents were both dead, I had no siblings, and my son was already gone. The only people who would really mourn me would be Anna, the people I met through the graduate program, and maybe some of my old co-workers, if they even remembered me.

"What would I do for money?" I asked.

Sam smiled because he knew that meant I was considering the proposition. He countered with, "Didn't you make millions in the tech industry?"

"Yes, but that's all in my name. If Michael Corrigan is dead, how will I get to use it?"

"Fortunately, Patsy knows a thing or two about moving money. He's a man of honor, and you will be fine financially."

With all this talk about me, I was curious to know what would happen to Sam. Would he also be part of this Lazarus

Plan?

"Do you get a new life as well?" I asked.

Sam closed his eyes, looked down, and shook his head.

"For this to work, Marie has to catch me. Then, when she does, she will come looking for you, but by then you will have already met your maker, so to speak."

All along I thought Sam's sudden departure from his house and the cryptic puzzles to find him was so that he could escape the fate his people had sentenced him to. Now I realized it was all a ruse to sell me on something he'd been planning for a while. He'd been grooming me.

"I'm an old man, Michael. My death will be my penance for the sins I've committed against this country and, importantly, it will have meaning. I represent just one life; if you don't succeed, millions will die, and your country will never be the same."

"No pressure," I said.

"You will find great meaning in helping your country, Michael. I promise. You will also find meaning in something else."

"And what's that?"

"Finding the people who killed your son and bringing them to justice."

He definitely had a point there. I carried my son's death on my shoulders for years and to learn it quite likely had been manipulated by my old boss lit a fire in me that was starting to burn into a rage. I knew that saying yes would seal Sam's fate, but I also knew that saying no just might lead to more pain and suffering than our country hadn't seen since the Civil War, over perhaps the last presidential election. I nodded my head.

Sam walked over and hugged me. "Thank you. Remember, in all of this, you must find courage in the face of danger."

It all goes back to Viktor Frankl, doesn't it?

"I will," I said. "But how will Marie find you?"

Jacob had a plan for that. "The minute you connect this listening device back to the circuit board on your phone and power it on, Marie will be able to hear whatever you say. All you have to do is say where Sam is, and she will find him."

That posed a problem for me, though. If she was close by, I may not have a lot of time to get away. On top of that, I still had no idea where we were.

"Where are we, anyway?"

"A Mossad safe house in the diamond district," Jacob replied and then added with a laugh, "the best place to hide a pebble is on the ground."

"We can't call just yet. I need to get some distance between us for my own safety. I'll head to Westchester and then have you call me, that way she'll think you are reaching out to me and you can tell me an exact address."

"That sounds good. In the meantime, I will call Patsy and put plans into motion. I'll hold off on calling you until I hear from him so we can time everything right. In a perfect world, you'd have an unfortunate accident on the way to see me."

"Where in Westchester does Patsy live?" I asked.

"Ninety Chatsworth Avenue in Larchmont. It's walking distance from the Metro North stop." Sam rattled off the address so quickly it betrayed just how well he knew Patsy.

"So what, should I just take the train up there?"

Jacob nodded. "I'd offer to give you a ride but there are a few more things Sam and I have to work out. You'll be fine on the train."

I'll be fine on the train? Apparently Jacob hadn't done the reverse commute during rush hour. Then again, it was Sunday so it shouldn't be that bad.

"Now listen, you can't say goodbye to Anna or Gianna, or anyone. Is that clear?"

I nodded. But there was one person I knew I had to say

goodbye to—Sam himself.

"But I can say goodbye to you."

Sam hugged me again. "You would have made a great psychologist, Michael."

"Thank you."

"Now go defend us in battle."

CHAPTER EIGHTEEN

Life is Contacts

After saying goodbye to my friend and mentor, I left the safe house, which upon exit, I learned was above a jewelry store on West Forty-seventh, just one block from Fifth Avenue. I remembered that there was a tunnel that I could take to Grand Central terminal at Forty-seventh and Madison and walked east. I passed two of my favorite Irish bars on the way, Connolly's Pub and Maggie's Place. Both were places Anna and I would visit frequently when times were good. It made me sad to think that I, as Michael Corrigan, would never go to either again.

I reached the north entrance to the terminal after passing Maggie's Place, but it was locked and had a sign saying it wasn't open on the weekends. I continued walking east and started to zig zag my way to Forty-second and Vanderbilt where I found an open entrance to Grand Central. As I entered, I thought of the nights I spent at The Campbell Apartment enjoying high-priced cocktails with my tech industry friends who commuted to NY from Connecticut. We liked that bar because it was convenient for commuters but still had a great New York feel to it.

The terminal was pretty empty. Most of the people there were clearly those who had a big night in the Big Apple and who missed the last train back. There were also a smattering of young couples who, no doubt, looked to get out of the concrete jungle where dreams are made of for the day and enjoy spring-like weather in the country.

I saw that there was a 7:45 semi-express to Connecticut which stopped at Larchmont leaving from track 39, so I bought a ticket from the Metro North app and made my way to the track. Thankfully, it was pretty empty, which meant I didn't have to share my seat with anyone, not that anyone would have wanted to share a seat with me. I looked like death warmed over considering the only sleep I had last night was drug induced and I hadn't showered at all that morning.

As the train pulled away from the station, my mind started to wander. I was still wearing another man's clothes, the ones I borrowed from my ex-wife's new husband, and that made me realize I'd already started to shed my old identity the night before. Then again, isn't that what I'd been doing for the past five years? At the time I considered it reinventing myself, but now I realized I was going through a rebirth. I wondered if this is what born again Christians feel like.

At first, I couldn't stop thinking about the hatred I had in my heart towards my old boss, Bob Ahlers, and knew that I had to confirm that suspicion and make him pay accordingly. While I was tempted to obsess on that for the entire ride, I knew that I couldn't as much more needed to be done before I could confront him.

I then started thinking about how I was on my way to meet a mobster who, up until recently, was, how did Gianna put it, in college. It felt surreal to think that the topic of conversation was going to be how we could fake my death, though I was more than just a bit curious to learn how that was going to go down as well as how I'd get a new identity.

As my train rolled along and clinked and clanged against the tracks, I started to doze as the motion and sound became quite soothing. Before I knew it, the conductor announced we had stopped at 125th Street and, in what seemed like no time, came back on the loudspeaker saying we had arrived at Larchmont station.

I exited the train and made my way to Chatsworth Avenue. Sam wasn't wrong, it was only a five-minute walk to number 90, a mid-modern-styled home that stood out amongst the center hall colonials that lined the street. It certainly looked more Studio City California than Larchmont New York, and I half expected to see the name Brady on the mailbox, not Mazzone.

I hadn't yet turned on my phone, as that would enable Marie to hear everything I'd say. I wondered if she'd be suspicious that I hadn't made a sound all morning, but hopefully any suspicions would be quelled after my untimely demise.

I stared at the house for a few minutes and wondered if one can just walk up to the front door of a mobster's home and ring the doorbell. I started walking up the front walkway and, just as my finger was going to push the button, the door swung open. Before me stood an older man who was easily six feet four inches tall wearing a track suit. His grey hair was perfectly positioned on his head and his chin jutted out in a way that made me think of Jay Leno.

"Never ring the doorbell, it makes the dogs go nuts and I don't like it when they go nuts," he said in a raspy voice which couldn't hide his thick New York accent. "Are you Sam's friend?"

I nodded and extended my hand and tried to introduce myself, "Mich…"

He interrupted me immediately. "Not here," he said and

pointed to his ear indicating that someone, likely the authorities, could be listening.

A moment later, I heard the sounds of two dogs barking. "That's what I was afraid of. They heard you and now they are going nuts."

Just then, two golden retrievers came into the doorway.

"This is Clemmy," he said as he petted the bigger of the two dogs, "and that over there is Tess, but don't get too close to her. She sometimes bites."

Clemmy allowed me to pet him, but Tess growled when I tried to do the same.

"Are you Irish?" he asked.

"Half Irish, half Italian," I replied.

"Tess doesn't like the Irish. Good thing you are only half because if you were full she'd have nipped ya."

Patsy bent down and pet both dogs. "Okay, calm down youse two. I'll be back in a bit." Then he walked out of the house, joined me on the porch, and closed the front door. I guess I wasn't going to get a tour of this mid-century modern masterpiece.

"I have an office on the side of the house. The original owner was a doctor and used to see patients here in the fifties, but for privacy there's no way to get to it from inside so we have to walk around."

"What kind of doctor was he?" I sometimes ask stupid questions when I'm nervous and this was no exception. What did it matter what kind of doctor he was?

"Pediatrician, but who gives a fuck?"

Patsy agreed with my self-criticism about asking stupid questions. He opened the door and that's when I noticed just how big his hands were. They were practically catcher's mitts. If Gary Carter had hands like that, I doubt he'd have found a glove to fit his catching hand.

Patsy pushed the door open and we entered the room,

which was tastefully decorated with a desk, a small couch, a coffee table, and two chairs. On the wall above his desk was a framed picture of a grey-haired man pressing a stethoscope to the chest of a young child. It was done in the style of Norman Rockwell's illustrations from *The Saturday Evening Post*.

"That's a picture of the first owner. He was a surgeon in World War II and was captured by the Nazis during the invasion of Normandy and forced to perform surgery on Kraut officers at gunpoint."

"Did you leave it on the wall as a sign of respect to him?"

Patsy looked at me as if I had three heads.

"It's an original by Norman Rockwell. Apparently he was buddies with the doc and it's worth a mint. I didn't want to risk damaging it by taking it down. Plus, I like it. It's a good conversation starter."

"Mr. Mazzone, did Sam tell you why I'm here?"

"Call me Patsy," he said, "and yes, he says you got a bit of a problem, but I don't want to know more than that. If Sam is asking for my help, it must be something bad."

"If you don't mind me asking, how do you know Sam?" This was something I'd been curious about since learning that Sam had some kind of relationship with Gianna's grandfather.

Patsy pointed back at the picture. "It all began with the doc on the wall. I bought this place back in the late sixties when my wife and I had our first child. Up until then we'd been living in The Bronx, but while I loved my old neighborhood, I wanted to give my kids something more than what I had. A lot of the guys had moved north to Westchester, so I followed them up here."

By "the guys" I assumed he meant mobsters, but I didn't want to ask another stupid question, so I held my tongue.

"Anyway, the realtor lady showed us this house and my wife fell in love with it. But here's the thing, the owners wanted to know who it was going to. They built the house and were the only owners and wanted to be sure it was going to a good family, so we had to meet with them. The doc and his wife were both Italian, which started us off on the right foot and I explained to them that I was in the restaurant business, which wasn't a lie, and that we had just started a family and wanted out of the city. The doc was quiet, as if he was used to his wife doing all the talking, and let me tell you something, Irish, she raked me over the coals like it was no one's business. That woman would have done well with the Feds or in one of my crews."

Irish. I guess I had a nickname now.

"Anyways, so they like us and sell us the house and move down to Florida. Pompano Beach to be exact, and a couple years later there's a knock on the door and it's your guy Sam Shoah who wanted to know if the doctor was still here. He told me he'd heard the story about the doc being forced to do surgery on the Krauts during the war and wanted to talk to him. I had the doctor's address down in Florida and offered it to this short little stranger and thought that'd be the end of it, but it wasn't."

It's no coincidence Sam wound up buying a vacation condo in Pompano Beach, I thought to myself, and wondered what he wanted with the doctor. I had to table that thought, though, and acknowledged what Patsy just said. "Sam has a way of making himself sticky," I replied.

"No shit, Irish. But here's the thing, I took an immediate liking to the guy. Now in my line of business being able to read people is the cost of entry and there was something about him that was sincere and trustworthy, and believe me, I don't come across that too often. So, we kept in touch. He never asked anything of me, ever, which is also unique. Most people come to me with certain needs, but not Sam. He was just a friend."

"He's a pretty amazing guy," I replied.

"When my granddaughter Gianna wanted to go to graduate school for psychology, I reached out to Sam because I knew that was his business. My father always told me that life is contacts so I figured it couldn't hurt, right? Next thing I know Sam offered to bring her application personally to the admissions committee. Then she got in and I knew I owed him a favor. And here you are."

"Sam helped me get into the program too," I said.

"What, twenty years ago?"

"No. Five," I replied and then told him the story about my previous career and how the loss of my son drove me to academia. Based on his body language, my story tugged at something inside the aged mobster.

"There's no harder thing to do in life than bury a child. Fucking Giuliani, thinks he cleaned up New York but he couldn't be more wrong. When the Italians were in charge, our neighborhoods were safe, but now you've got these crazy Albanians and all this MS-13 bullshit. One of those assholes got my son, Gianna's uncle. All because he looked at him funny in a nightclub."

"Did you find who killed your son?"

Patsy gave me one of the coldest stares I'd ever experienced in my life. "He's not a problem no more."

I wondered if that's the reason he'd been doing time recently, but assumed it was impolite to ask.

"I don't want to know why Sam's asking me to do what he's asked me to do, but need to let you know that there's no coming back from this. If you do it, you can never go back to being Mikey Corrigan again, capeesh?"

I'm not going to lie and say that I came to terms with this reality, because I hadn't; however, I knew what had been asked of me was incredibly important.

I nodded and looked at my watch. It was now 10:30 in the

morning and I was eager to know how this was all going to go down.

"So how does this work?" I asked. Patsy put a finger up to his lips indicating that I should be quiet.

"You hungry?" he asked.

As a matter of fact, I was starving, having not had anything to eat since the night before.

"Yeah," I said.

"Let's take a walk up the street. There's a great hot dog stand I go to on Sundays."

CHAPTER NINETEEN

Hello Peter Avellino

We left his house and took a left onto Chatsworth Avenue and then made a right onto Palmer. While walking past a seven-story building to the right of us, Patsy paused to tell me a quick story.

"See that park over there, Irish? I used to take my boys there when they were little. Did you spend a lot of time with your son?"

"Not as much as I should have," I admitted. "I was too wrapped up in my career when he was younger. I didn't just lose him, but his mother as well. My wife left me not long after he died."

"Some lessons you have to learn the hard way," he replied. For a mobster, he was very philosophical.

"So how does this work?"

"Well, we continue to walk this way and then we get in line at the hot dog stand. When it's your turn, you order."

All of a sudden, he was a comedian.

"I mean the business that Sam asked you about."

"There's a few moving pieces to it. First, we gotta arrange an accident where a poor unfortunate soul will be found.

Second we have to find a way to confirm that this unfortunate soul is Mikey Corrigan. Lastly, we need to establish a new identity for you."

Wait a minute, is he going to have to off somebody in order to produce a body? I can't let someone get killed because of me. Patsy must have noticed the change in my body language because he explained it right away.

"Do you know about City Cemetery on Hart Island?"

I shook my head.

"It's a big potter's field on an island off The Bronx. It's where unclaimed bodies from New York's morgues are buried three deep in unmarked trenches. Now many of these bodies are of homeless people without families, but others are of people whose families don't have the means to give them a proper burial. I have an associate, Anthony Bonasera, who owns a funeral home in The Bronx, and he's been known to intercede on a family's behalf to release an unclaimed body to his care where he will give it a respectful burial at no cost to the family. It's gotten to the point where they don't ask him too many questions about it now."

"That's very generous."

"Bodies come in handy every now and then. I've instructed Anthony to pick up a body with your measurements. When you say the word, that poor guy is going to be found behind the wheel of a burned-out car in New Rochelle."

"A car? But what would I be doing behind the wheel of a car? Plus, the registration wouldn't match, unless it's a rental, but then you'd need a rental agreement."

"Irish, anyone ever tell you that for a Ph.D. you can't see what's right in front of your face? Sam told me all about your fancy electric car. We are going to put the body behind the wheel of your Tesla. The batteries in those things have a way of catching fire."

Not my Tesla! It was my prized possession. Then again, it's

not like I'd ever be able to drive it again.

"But it's up in Connecticut. How are you going to get it down here?"

"This isn't my first rodeo, kid. It's on its way down now."

"Alright, so that's how they find the body, but can't they check dental records to prove it was me?"

"That's why we are doing it in New Rochelle. The medical examiner is my godson. No one will question his findings."

Now there's just the small matter of getting me a new identity, but no doubt Patsy had a guy for that too.

"In terms of a new identity, getting you a new birth certificate ain't a problem, so long as you have no objections being from New Rochelle. In addition to the ME, we've got someone in the office of vital statistics. It gets a bit tricky if you've ever been fingerprinted, as changing fingerprints is actually quite hard and ain't exactly pain free."

"Never been arrested," I replied. It struck me that the Russians must have done something very similar to the assets who were part of their illegals program, kind of like an illegal witness protection program.

"Good. Now as Columbo said, there's just one more thing."

"What's that?"

"We have to change your appearance. To start, you need to dress completely differently than you did before. But that's the easy part."

"What's the hard part?"

"Well, you are rather plain looking, except for those blue eyes, so that actually gives us a lot to play with."

Talk about a back-handed compliment.

"Look, I know I'm not Brad Pitt," I said, "but plain looking is a bit harsh, don't you think?" The truth is, I've always been self-conscious about my looks and it was a sore spot for me.

"Hey, don't get all sensitive on me, Irish. In this case, plain is a good thing. Your chin is normal, your cheekbones are normal, your ears are normal. All we have to do is tweak these things a little bit, change your hairstyle, and maybe have ya shave off a little around the mid-section and your own mudda won't recognize ya. Plus, if everyone thinks you've quit the oxygen habit, they won't even look twice at your ugly mug."

Speaking of putting on weight, I was starving and happy to see that we had approached a pagoda style structure across from what looked to be a huge high school. The sign read Walters Hot Dogs and, even though it was only 11 am, there was already a line out front.

"Ever been here?"

I shook my head and wondered what could possibly make a hot dog so special that people would wait in a long line for it outside.

"Get 'em with mustard. Trust me on that, Irish. These are the filet mignon of hot dogs."

Since we were now in mixed company, our conversation turned to more mundane matters.

"So, what do ya think of my granddaughter?"

"Gianna was one of my only friends in the doctoral program at UConn. She's very bright and will make a great therapist someday."

Patsy smiled. I could tell he had a soft spot in his heart for her.

"She's my first and only grandchild. When she came into my life, the world became a lot brighter for me. I'm going to offer her the office in my home, and she can use it for private practice when she's licensed."

My heart sank a bit when I heard him say that because it reminded me that I'd be taking my licensing exam in July. Oh well, just a dream I was giving up for the greater good.

"What's the matter?" Patsy asked.

"I'd be getting my license this summer," I admitted, but didn't expand given we were still in the middle of the line and no one else should be hearing the reasons why I wouldn't be taking the exam.

"I understand. Well, don't lose heart. These things have a way of working out."

We stood in silence until it was our turn to order. Patsy did the honors of ordering four with mustard, two sides of shoestring fries, and two black and white milkshakes.

"Your weight loss plan starts tomorrow, Irish."

Once the food was in hand, we sat down at an open picnic table to the left of the building and were relieved that the tables around us remained empty. According to Patsy, it was a tradition to eat the dogs in one's car, which was a non-issue for us since we walked here.

I took a bite and couldn't have predicted how much I would like this hot dog. "This is the best goddamn hot dog I've ever had."

"I wouldn't lie to you, Irish. Speaking of which, anyone ever tell you that you look more Guinea than Mick?"

Who was I to correct a mobster on using pejorative terms for people of Italian and Irish descent?

"My mother was one-hundred percent Italian, and my father was Irish."

"Where was your mother's family from?"

"My mother was born in Brooklyn…"

"Madonna Mia!" Patsy exclaimed. "I meant in Italy."

To say that my grandmother was proud of her Italian heritage was an understatement. She would constantly tell me stories about where she grew up in Italy and even took me there when I was a teenager.

"Lioni, in the province of Avellino," I replied, with proper pronunciation. There were two things that were never up for debate with my grandmother: making a tomato sauce from scratch and pronouncing Italian words appropriately.

"I'm impressed, Irish. Since we have to come up with a new name for you, how about we do what they did to immigrants when they came into this great country of ours?"

"What's that?"

"Name you after where your family is from. Tell me, what was your grandfather's name?"

"Pietro, but in America he was called Peter."

"How do you feel about Peter Avellino?"

"I think that has a nice ring to it."

"I'll make the necessary calls and make sure all the paper work is done."

Our conversation was interrupted by Patsy's buzzing phone.

"Yeah," he said while answering. "Okay, stand by." He then turned back to me.

"My guy Vincenzo says you got a real nice ride. Shame that we've gotta torch it. He's ready when you are. John Doe can be behind the wheel in twenty minutes."

These guys work fast.

"I wish the government could work at your speed."

"We tried with Kennedy. It didn't work out. You done?"

"Yeah."

"Good," he said, and then extended his hand to take my garbage. Patsy may be a mobster, but he was one of the most polite gentlemen I'd ever met.

I followed him away from the picnic table and over to the trash receptacles where he deposited our garbage and then walked with him the mile or so back to his place on Chatsworth Avenue. Another call to his phone informed him that everything was ready. All I had to do now was get a message to Sam to have him call me. Patsy dialed his number and they had a quick chat.

Then, in Patsy's office, I reconnected the listening device to my phone's circuit board the way Jacob showed me back at the safe house and then replaced the battery. I took a few deep breaths while the phone turned on and then waited for it to ring with Sam's call. Moments later, my phone was ringing with a call from a number I didn't recognize.

"This is Michael Corrigan," I said without betraying I knew it was Sam who was calling.

"Michael, it's Sam, look, I'm in trouble."

"Sam!" I said excitedly. "Everyone is looking for you. Where are you?"

"I've tried calling you all morning. All calls go to voicemail."

He just gave me the opening needed to explain why Marie hadn't heard anything from my phone today.

"I turned it off when I went to bed and forgot to turn it back on. It's not like I use the damn thing all that much."

"Forget about that. Look, some people are looking for me and you are the only person I trust. I tried to leave some clues as to where I am but I can't wait for you to unscramble them anymore."

"I'm sorry…"

The old man cut me off and said, "Where are you right now?"

"New Rochelle," I said. "I slept here last night after having dinner in the city. Where are you?"

"I'm in the diamond district. Forty-four West Forty-seventh Street, in an apartment just above Baron Jewelry."

"What the hell are you doing there?"

"I'll tell you everything when you get here. Do you have your car?"

I had to think quickly as there needed to be a good explanation for how I got my car given Marie knew I left it at my house.

"Yes, I thought I'd need it and had someone drop it off

early this morning."

"Good, because we can't take public transportation. How fast can you get here?"

"It's a Sunday and I'm only about 20 miles outside of Manhattan. Figure thirty minutes or less."

"The sooner the better. Call this number when you arrive," he said and then hung up.

Although I wouldn't hear the explosion, I knew that my car and poor old John Doe were about to be blown to bits somewhere in the neighboring town of New Rochelle.

RIP Michael Corrigan. Hello Peter Avellino.

CHAPTER TWENTY

Six Key Lessons

Later that Sunday afternoon, Jacob got word to me through Patsy that a woman matching Marie's description came into the safe house and marched Sam out, though she didn't kill him, not in the apartment anyway. There was no telling what she did with him after that.

Later that day, it was reported on the news that a doctoral student from the University of Connecticut had been killed in an automobile accident when his Tesla caught fire after it backed into a concrete barrier in the back parking lot of a pizzeria in New Rochelle. While it happened in broad daylight, surprisingly there were no witnesses.

I spent the evening at Patsy's place in Larchmont where I enjoyed Sunday dinner with him and his wife, Rina. After the meal, we retired to his den for an after-dinner drink.

"I have my people working on a birth certificate for you, but it will take a day or so which is fine because we can't take a picture for your license or passport until we do something about that face of yours."

Ah, that's right, my plain face.

"What do you have in mind?"

"We got a great plastic surgeon in the family. He can tweak that chin of yours, those cheekbones, and maybe give you more of a Roman nose to go with your new name."

Most people chisel their nose away when they have a nose job, I was going to get a bigger one. FML.

"I suppose I can't keep my blue eyes, can I?"

"No Sinatra, you can't. But those are easy enough to cover up with contact lenses. You wear glasses?"

I shook my head. I was proud to say at forty-six my vision was still twenty-twenty.

"Good, that makes it easier. I hope you get to see forty-seven."

Considering the journey I was about to undertake, I hoped so to.

"I've only known you for under a day, Irish, but I'm worried about you. I think you are getting in way over your head here."

I knew he was right, but did he have to be so blunt about it? Then again, maybe that was the Mafia way. Bosses aren't known for blowing smoke.

"Do you mind some advice?"

I knew nothing about infiltrating personal networks, computer networks, or building spy networks. I was also the least violent person I knew, so some advice from a mobster who lived into his seventies would certainly be welcome.

"Please," I replied.

"Let me see your hands, Irish."

I held them out for him to see. He grabbed me by the wrist and turned them so they were facing palms up.

"Your hands are soft. No callouses. You ever get them dirty?"

Now getting them dirty in my world and getting them dirty in Patsy's world were likely two different things.

"I spent part of my adult life with computers and the other

part trying to help people. My hands have always been clean."

"That's okay, Irish. A wise man once told me that the most powerful weapon we have is between our ears and whatever it is you have to do you are going to have to do it with your mind, not your hands. Capeesh?"

I nodded.

"When dealing with an adversary, and I assume you have them, the most important thing to do is never to let your emotions be the basis of your decisions. It's vital that you think critically and rationally at all times."

Easier said than done, I thought. I began to hate my old boss, BA, for the role he may have played in my son's death and wanted to act accordingly. Was he telling me to turn the other cheek?"

"So, let's say someone killed my son as they did yours. I shouldn't feel hate towards that person?"

"I'm not saying that at all. We are only human. What I'm suggesting is that you don't let your hate drive the decisions you make when retaliating. Think things through. Don't rush. If you put your emotions in the driver's seat all the time, they will inevitably steer you off the road. Which leads me to another lesson you need to hear."

"What's that?"

"Keep your friends close, but your enemies closer."

"Didn't Michael Corleone say that to Frank Pentangeli in *The Godfather II*?"

"There's a reason why I named my restaurant after the author of *The Godfather*. However, it doesn't make it any less true, though it's easier to do in a movie than practice it in real life. If you have someone who you've identified as an enemy, befriend them. Show them kindness. Build their trust and get them when they least expect it. You ever play chess?"

"I used to play with my grandfather. Why?"

"One of the most useful skills in that game is to be able to think the way your opponent thinks. That way, you can anticipate their moves and plan for them. You are going to have to do that as well. Put yourself in their shoes, try and build a little empathy with them, and you will be in a better position to strike against them."

"Get into their head. Got it." Shouldn't be too hard, I almost had a doctorate in clinical psychology after all.

"You got room in your head for a few more?"

"Yeah. I should be writing these down."

"Nah. The mind has an incredible ability to remember things that are important. Now look, you are going to sometimes face challenges that you couldn't anticipate and get yourself into a few jams. When faced with an imminent problem or threat, don't brush it off. Hunker down until you come up with a solution. Winners never quit and quitters never win."

Now he sounded like my old baseball coach. "Don't give up. Got it."

"Along with that, and this is very important, once you have a plan never share your personal plans with anyone you don't fully trust. In my experience, they will always use it against you."

"That shouldn't be a problem, I'm on a solo mission."

"A man needs friends, Irish. One last lesson for you; when dealing with anyone, always make sure that your decisions and wishes are always clear, precise, and deliberate. That way, they will never be misinterpreted. Relationships have died over misinterpretations and in my world that leads to violence. Always be clear about your decisions and intentions and leave no room for interpretation."

Six key life lessons from Patsy. I hoped I could keep them all in mind when I started down the road of learning what the Russians were up to, but feared it would be like trying remember the hundred things you have to consider when swinging a golf club—and my game wasn't that good these days.

We each took a sip of our drinks and Patsy looked over at me and said, "Before, when you asked about feeling hate towards someone who killed your son, you weren't talking about me, were you? You were talking about you. Correct?"

I nodded. "I recently learned that my son was killed by some of the people I'm going to be chasing down."

Patsy exhaled deeply. "I wanted nothing more than to torture the bastards who killed my boy, but I knew I couldn't do it directly. I had a sense that his death was a setup to expose me. Had I gone after them myself and pulled the trigger, I'd have been sent away for the rest of my life. You see, I anticipated what their endgame was and acted accordingly, not letting my emotions drive me. Capeesh?"

I nodded.

"Now anyone who you are going after won't recognize you because you won't be looking like you no more, so that can work to your advantage. Take your time. Think of it like a seduction."

A seduction was one way of putting it.

"Speaking of not recognizing me, what's the plan there?"

"A car will pick you up tonight and take you to a plastic surgery center we have an interest in up in Jersey where our doctors will work on you all night. After the swelling has gone down and you have recovered, you will come back to me and we will get you documents for your new identity. Then it's off to the races, Irish."

Forty-six years of being Michael Corrigan will be chiseled away tonight and I'll wake up in the morning as a new man. Well, the same man but with a different face anyway. Speaking of a new man, that new man was going to need some money and that was a subject we hadn't broached yet.

"I hate to bring this up, but I've got a lot of money from my former career sitting in investments and am going to need to be able to access it after this is all said and done."

Patsy fished out a packet of papers from his desk.

"Money is important, Irish. I've got all the paperwork ready for you to sign."

I looked over everything. It was amazing, Patsy had access to all my financial accounts and had Peter Avellino named as beneficiary to all of my assets, including my life insurance policies.

"Wait a minute. Aren't I technically already dead? Won't it look bad if these papers were filed after my death?"

"Check the dates, Irish. These are all predated a year and will be notarized by…"

"Let me guess, you've got a lawyer in the family."

"Something like that. He's good with wills and I know a judge or two in Connecticut where you live. Nothing will be in probate too long."

"Is there anything I can do for you?"

Patsy looked over at me as if I'd offended him.

"What I did today is a favor for an old man. Don't feel as if you owe me anything in return. However, if I ever need a favor from you, I'll ask."

"Sounds like a deal," I said and raised my glass towards him. "Salute."

Our glasses meant with a clink and he replied, "Cin cin."

We had one more drink and then I heard the sound of a horn honking outside.

"That's your ride, Irish."

I kept repeating Patsy's life lessons in my head on the drive to Jersey as I wanted to make sure I didn't forget them. Once I had them committed to memory, I closed my eyes and dozed off. Before I knew it, we were pulling up to an office park in eyeshot of where the New York Giants and Jets play their home games. I knew the rumors that there were bodies buried in the foundation of the old Meadowlands stadium that had been razed when the new Met Life stadium had been built a decade or so ago and wondered if Patsy had put any there.

I walked into the lobby of the building and was met by a nurse who confirmed my name and followed her to a pre-op room where I was asked to undress, shave, and shower prior to the procedure.

Once finished, I put on a robe and there was a knock on the door.

"Come in," I replied.

Two people in scrubs entered: one a man and the other a woman. They were two of the most attractive humans I'd ever seen in my life and, judging only by their looks, could have been Hollywood stars. I nicknamed them Brad and Angelina, even though that power couple had been consciously uncoupled for years.

They didn't speak to me at all and went right to their work, marking my face up with a sharpie and speaking to each other in a language that I couldn't understand; perhaps that was for the better because I didn't want to know what I was in for.

Angelina asked me to remove my robe.

"I don't have anything on underneath," I said.

"It's okay, we're doctors," she replied.

I've always been self-conscious about my physical appearance so I reluctantly untied the belt around my waist and dropped the robe to the floor. These two would be great poker players because they didn't let their expressions betray whatever thoughts were going through their heads.

Angelina marked my love handles and areas around my stomach while Brad made some marks on my back.

Apparently they were going to liposuction out all those stubborn areas of fat on my trunk that diet and exercise couldn't eliminate.

"Put your robe back on," she said.

"We'll be back for you in a few moments."

Those few moments felt like an eternity. There was a full-length mirror on the far side of the room and I gave Michael Corrigan one last look. Not a change was made to my appearance yet, but I had a hard time recognizing the reflection staring back at me. What was I about to do? Could I even do it?

I won't lie, I was scared about what the path forward looked like but remembered what Viktor Frankl said about having courage in the face of danger—it's another way to find meaning in life.

Yes, I was scared, but I was also resolved to do what had to be done not only to save my country but also strike back at the people who killed my son. And they would pay dearly for that.

CHAPTER TWENTY-ONE

Eyes of a Stranger

While it felt like an eternity, I only spent two weeks recovering from facial reconstructive surgery and body liposuction at the clinic in New Jersey. Every day, Brangelina would come in, remove the bandages that covered my face, evaluate the swelling, and put on new dressings. Once the swelling had gone down to what they thought was an appropriate level, they let me have a look at my new face in the mirror. Patsy was right, even my own mother wouldn't recognize me.

I still had a significant amount of swelling around my trunk and waist where liposuction was performed. As a result, I was told that I'd have to wear compression bandages for the next few months.

I was discharged on Sunday, April 21st which, it turned out, was Easter Sunday. That's appropriate, I thought to myself, as in a way I had been raised from the dead, though I had no delusions of being able to walk on water or turn it into wine. Brangelina came in to say goodbye and handed me a parting gift—a charcoal suit along with a new shirt, tie, belt, socks, and shoes.

"A gift from a friend of yours," Angelina said.

Brad then handed me a hat. "This friend believes a gentleman should always wear a hat when he's outdoors."

"And another," Angelina said and handed me a small plastic case with two octagonal flip tops on it. "Colored contact lenses. Those beautiful blue eyes of yours will now be hazel."

I'd never worn contacts and asked if she could help me put them in. After she showed me, I looked at myself in the mirror again and felt as if I were staring into the eyes of a stranger.

They left me alone to change and everything I put on felt as if it were custom made for me. I gave myself a once-over in the mirror and thought I looked just like a gangster out of central casting, or a venture capitalist. Which reminded me of a joke I heard once. What's the difference between a mobster and venture capitalist? It's a trick question, there isn't one.

Over the past few weeks, I'd had a lot of time to think about what my next move would be to find out what the Russians were up to, and part of that was dreaming up a back story for Peter Avellino. I needed to have a job where I could get access to people in high places and the best way to do that was to sell myself as a money man. Having grown up in the tech industry and having delt with my fair share of venture guys, I decided to make Peter a venture capitalist. If the suit fits…

It may sound a bit strange, but after putting on the suit, I felt a strange energy come over me. Wearing it gave me a confidence that I hadn't felt in a long time. No wonder why lawyers and bankers still wore these things. I put on the hat, a light grey fedora with a black ribbon, and walked out into the fresh April air. Spring was in full bloom and it was remarkably warmer out than it was when I arrived. I could feel a sense of new life blooming all around me.

A Cadillac SUV was waiting outside, presumably sent by Patsy. The presumption was confirmed when the passenger side window rolled down and an attractive female driver said, "Mr. Avellino?"

With the sexual escapade I'd had with Marie Charcot relatively fresh in my mind, I tried my best to let the head on my shoulders do the thinking and simply replied, "Yes."

"My name is Angela and I'm here to take you to Mr. Mazzone's house. Do you have any bags?"

I thought for a minute to go back and retrieve the clothes I came in with, those belonging to my ex-wife's new husband, but decided to leave them there. The guy who wore those was now dead.

"I got nothing," I replied and realized just how true that was. My car was gone and the house was likely jammed up in the Connecticut legal system or on the market to be sold. If Patsy's attorney lived up to the expectations the old man set, though, the proceeds of that eventual transaction would be hitting whatever bank account was set up for Peter Avellino. I was a man without a family and with only one friend in the world, Patsy, unless, of course, I could count Angela in that distinguished group. Time would tell.

Professional that she was, Angela came out and opened the rear passenger door for me. I glanced down at her left hand and saw that her ring finger was bare, a fact that I filed in the back of my head thinking it might come in useful in conversation. Hey, I had to start thinking like a single venture capitalist would and that guy would definitely hit on the girl. As much as it was outside of my comfort zone, I knew I had to go there at some point.

She got back behind the wheel and said, "If there's anything you want to listen to on the radio, let me know."

While I was recovering at the clinic, I hadn't watched TV or read a newspaper and was eager to hear what was going on in the world.

"Would you mind turning on talk radio?"

"Of course," she replied, and then used the touchscreen to turn on a conservative leaning talk station.

"Is FAB News okay?"

FAB stood for Fair and Balanced, which it certainly wasn't. In reality, it was more opinion than news, but their afternoon talk host, Chase Fielding, was wildly entertaining. He spoke at a rapid pace with his raspy voice, as if he drank energy drinks by the gallon and chased them with unfiltered cigarettes. At the moment he was spewing a conspiracy theory about how the influx of school shootings were false flag operations by the Socialist revolutionaries to force stricter gun control laws in the United States so that the average citizen would be left defenseless when they came to invade us. Actually, if what Sam said was true, those shootings were the result of mind control experiments by the Russians.

During a local news break, a broadcaster came on to talk about the latest news on the rise in protests and counter protests throughout the United States around the President's foreign policy with China. Protesters claimed that tariffs on imports from China were clear proof that the Republican president was a xenophobe while counter protesters provided the point of view that he trying to bring manufacturing jobs back to America. In the back of my mind I wondered what role, if any, my old boss BA played in motivating these uprisings. Sam mentioned he was behind a slew of targeted misinformation efforts to divide and conquer the US population.

"So, what do ya do?" Angela asked while Tom Selleck came on the radio to sell listeners reverse mortgages.

It was the perfect opportunity to get comfortable talking in the character of Peter Avellino.

"I'm a venture capitalist."

"Sounds fancy. What does that mean?"

"I invest in companies that show potential in exchange for a piece of the action."

"Oh, so you are kind of like a legit mobster."

Angela gets it.

"Except I don't have to break anyone's legs if they don't pay up."

"No. I'm sure you just take their business and then sell it off to some shmuck and still try to make a profit."

Yes, she definitely gets it. It was time for me to channel my inner alpha male—if I was going to sell myself as a venture guy, I was going to have to act the part.

"So, what do you do besides drive legitimate gangsters?"

Angela laughed out loud. "Look at you, Mr. Rico Suave, thinking you can pick me up. You gotta pair on you."

"Wait, I didn't mean…"

"I'm just busting your stones. I work as a waitress at Puzzo's on Arthur Ave. We are closed on account that it's Easter Sunday, so Patsy gave me some hours in his limo business. Time and a half plus tips isn't bad, especially when you have two in college."

Angela didn't look old enough to have two college-aged kids but whereas Michael Corrigan would just think it, Peter Avellino came out and said it.

"What, did you have them when you were ten?"

"That's a way to get on my good side. If my ex was as nice as you he wouldn't be my ex. Actually, if he was as rich as you he definitely wouldn't be my ex!"

I laughed. Angela seemed to have a great sense of humor. I could see where she'd be a fantastic waitress or bartender as she was both personable and engaging. I bet she made a mint off of tips.

"These supposed college-aged kids you have, what are their names?"

"Aaron and Jeremy. Aaron is going to school at Fairfield University in Connecticut and studying communications and Jeremy goes to Loyola in Maryland and is doing a semester abroad in France. He wants to get into the wine business someday."

"Two Jesuit schools both out of state. You know, there's a fine Jesuit college in the Bronx, right?"

"Ha! No, Ma, Fordham is too close to home!" Angela said, apparently imitating the deep voice of her boys. Luckily they are very smart and got good scholarships. And they are good kids, that's what's important. Do you have any kids?"

I had to get used to answering that question without hesitation. Michael Corrigan had a son, but Peter Avellino had no wife and no kids.

"No," I said, but Angela was a people reader and I knew she didn't buy it.

"Had to think about it for a minute, did ya? Word of advice, don't hesitate with a question like that. Women will think you are lying."

Note to self, pick up Lee Strasberg's book on acting.

"You look a bit tired there, Mr. Avellino, how about I stop yip yapping and let you have some quiet time. Okay?"

"Thank you, Angela."

While I enjoyed Angela's company, I had a more active day today than I did in the past two weeks. Brangelina warned me that, while it was only reconstructive surgery, my body would still take some time to heal and I used this quiet time to review Patsy's lessons in my mind.

Number one, don't let your emotions dictate your actions. To say I felt rage towards the man who, according to Sam, had something to do with the death of my son was an understatement, but I also knew that BA was an important link in the chain of Russian assets who were planning something against my country. Seeking revenge on him immediately would be counterproductive to my overall mission.

Number two, keep your friends close, but your enemies closer. I had to build confidence and trust amongst the operatives I uncovered in Sam's old world. What was it Patsy said? Befriend them and show them kindness. To do that, I was going to have to channel my inner Strasberg—maybe I should buy that book after all!

Number three, think the way your opponent thinks. I had to get into the heads of my targets and to do that I would channel everything I'd learned about personality theory over the past five years as well as tap into what I'd learned about people while working in the tech world. In order to do that I would have to observe their patterns and understand their personality traits. If they were active on social media, that would certainly help.

Number four, don't give up until you come up with a solution. I knew I would face resistance on this journey and would have to tap into my ability to be persistent. Fortunately, I learned a thing or two about persistence from my time in the tech world—investors just don't give you their money because you have asked for it. Even if you have a one-of-a-kind product that will change the world, persistence is a must when seducing the money men.

Number five, never share your plans with someone you don't fully trust. There should be a caveat to this one, "unless you are hypnotized." I unknowingly shared things with Marie Charcot because she was able to get into my head. Going forward, I had to be protective of the things I learned and the plans I made.

Lastly, make sure your decisions are clear, precise and deliberate. Communications wasn't always my strong suit, just ask my ex-wife. When dealing with my enemies, I'll have to make sure what I'm demanding is exact, especially when

I'm in the process of deceiving them.

As we drove over the George Washington Bridge, I found myself dozing off and didn't wake up until Angela parked the SUV in front of Patsy's place in Larchmont.

"Do I owe you anything for the trip, or was this taken care of?"

It was a stupid question on my part seeing as I had no way to pay her.

"Patsy said your money is no good here," Angela said and then got out of the truck, came around my side, and opened the door. "Happy Easter."

"Buona Pasqua," I said, using the Italian accent my grandmother taught me and tipped my hat to her.

I walked to the front door and was about to ring the doorbell when I remembered that Patsy didn't want me to use it before as it drove the dogs nuts, so I knocked gently. Immediately, I heard the sounds of dogs barking.

I heard a familiar woman's voice coming from inside telling the dogs to calm down. When the door opened, Gianna was standing in the doorway. Things were about to get more interesting.

CHAPTER TWENTY-TWO

Buona Pasqua

I stepped into the foyer of Patsy's home and my heart was racing as if I'd run here from Jersey. Out of all the people I met through UConn's doctoral program, Gianna was the one I was closest with. It was time to see just how good a job Brangelina did on my new appearance.

"You must be Peter. I'm Gianna," she said while offering her hand for me to shake. "Nonno has been expecting you."

I shook her hand and followed her from the foyer and into a small sitting room and then into the kitchen, which looked as if it hadn't been updated since it the house was built in the fifties. The dining room was off the kitchen and there were four people around the table and two empty chairs. I assumed one was for Gianna and the other was for me.

When I stepped into the room, I removed my hat and Patsy got up.

"Peter, so glad you could make it. I see you have already met my granddaughter Gianna, and this is my wife, Rina."

While I remembered her from the meal we had two weeks ago, the question was, did she remember me?

I walked over to where she was sitting and offered my

hand, "I see where your granddaughter gets her good looks."

"Welcome to our home," she replied in an accent reminiscent of my grandmother's.

Patsy then motioned to a man who looked to be around my age. "And this is my son, Joseph."

He had dark hair that was slicked back, a squared jaw, and hands as big as his father's When I shook his hand, he held eye contact longer than usual and squeezed mine with a firm grip. I got the sense he was testing me. No words were exchanged between us, which was just fine by me.

"And this is my daughter-in-law Sabrina. She owns a bakery just over the line in Connecticut and brought her famous cannoli nachos for dessert."

"Very nice to meet you, Sabrina," I said while extending my hand.

"Likewise," she replied.

"Now that your friend is here we can eat, right, Pop?" Joseph said.

Patsy looked over at his wife and nodded at her. She then got up from the table and went into the kitchen. Gianna and Sabrina followed. This was, after all, a very traditional Italian home. Knowing Gianna, I'm sure this must have chewed away at her.

"Would you care for a glass of wine, Peter?" Sabrina asked.

I normally didn't drink wine in the afternoon but didn't want to offend my hosts so accepted the offer. She filled the small, 6oz glass in front of me with wine from a jug. The glass was just like those seen in traditional Italian trattorias; no long stem, just a basic short and skinny glass one might use for orange juice.

"Joseph and I made this wine last year. Let me know how you like it."

I took a sip and discovered that it was stronger than any wine I'd ever tasted.

"It's good," I said, suppressing a cough.

Patsy and his son laughed. "Homemade wine is an acquired taste. Joseph used to cut his with 7-Up when he was a kid."

"I'd cut it now if you had any soda in the house, Pop."

"Too much sugar in that crap. It's no good for us no more."

The women came back with a big bowl of ravioli with tomato sauce.

"We got these from Borgatti's this morning," Sabrina said. "I hope you like ravioli, Peter."

When it comes to ravioli, Borgatti's is, by far, the best. It's a small shop on East 187th street in the Bronx known for homemade pastas and one that my grandmother would swear by.

"Is the pope Catholic?" I asked, earning a chuckle from Rina.

As the guest, the bowl was passed to me first and I took a scoop and then passed it over to Gianna, who was sitting to my right. I held it for her as she put some onto her plate. The bowl went around the table counterclockwise until it ended with Patsy who was sitting to my left.

I grabbed a fork and was about to dig in when Patsy said, "Before we eat, would anyone like to offer thanks?"

Everyone's eyes shot downward as if they were trying to avoid being called on in class. Gianna bravely volunteered.

She crossed herself saying, "In the name of the Father, Son, and Holy Spirit, Amen. Dear Lord, thank you for the food we are about to eat, thank you for the health of everyone around this table, and thank you for offering your only Son for our salvation. Amen."

"Amen," everyone around the table replied.

"And God bless the cooks," Patsy added and then raised his glass. "Cin cin."

We all raised ours, said the same, and took a sip.

The pasta course was followed by lamb with some vegetables and bread and the salad course came out after that. When that was finished, Patsy declared we should wait until after we clear the table before bringing out dessert.

All the women got up to clear the table, but I felt bad for making them do all the work. On top of that, I felt the need to walk around so offered to help.

"Rina and Sabrina, you rest," Patsy said. "Peter and Gianna can take care of the table."

I knew that Brangelina did a good job on my appearance because Gianna gave no hint of knowing who I was. However, that was based on looks. I had to concentrate hard to not bring out any of my old mannerisms or give any indication that I knew anything about her as we went to work in the kitchen.

"You scrub and I'll dry?" she asked.

"Fine by me," I said, but had a problem. I was still wearing my suit jacket and didn't want to get it dirty. Gianna sensed I was concerned about this and offered to take my jacket and then handed me an apron.

"You may want to roll up the sleeves on that fancy shirt of yours. What do you do, anyway?"

It was now or never. Strasberg don't fail me now!

"I'm a venture capitalist."

"In the legit sense or are you a loan shark?"

"Legit, but some would say there's a very grey area between us."

I cleaned a serving dish and handed it to Gianna to dry.

"How do you know my grandfather?"

I couldn't just say that my old dissertation advisor, who she had known, introduced us so had to come up with another explanation quickly.

"He helped me out with something not too long ago. Since I didn't have any family in the area, he invited me for Easter dinner, which felt more like lunch."

"Yeah, they like to eat early on holidays. Where are you from?"

I was relieved she that she didn't probe into what my business with her grandfather was; of course, she was smart enough not to pry.

"Northern California," I replied. It wasn't too hard to believe that a venture capitalist would be from the land of Silicon Valley. "What do you do?"

"I'm a graduate student studying for my doctorate in psychology."

"That sounds exciting. What field in particular?"

"Clinical," she replied. "I want to be a therapist."

"How long does that take?"

"I'm on track to complete it in five years, but it can take up to seven or eight depending on how many classes you take and how long it takes to do your dissertation."

"What's a dissertation?" It was a silly question coming from Michael Corrigan, but not from Peter Avellino.

"It's basically a way for the university to see that you can handle running your own research project independently."

"What are you focusing your research on?" I asked while handing her a pot.

"I'm exploring if a history of child abuse and trauma has any impact on acceptance of aggression later in life."

"So, if someone is abused as a kid, how might that impact how forgiving they are on witnessing that behavior in someone else?"

"You are the first person I've ever said that to outside of my field who actually understood that."

Shit! I thought to myself. I should dumb myself down a bit.

"Have you drawn any conclusions yet?"

"Yeah, but I'm trying to repeat my experiment with a more clinical sample. Most of my subjects have been undergraduate students at the university and it's a pretty homogenous population."

"Hey Gigi and Peter, why don't you come back to the table," Patsy said as a statement, though it technically was a question. "We can finish the dishes later. I want some of Sabrina's nachos."

I removed my apron and hung it where I found it and followed Gianna, back to the table. I had known her for four years and never heard her called Gigi by anyone else but me when I was trying to get under her skin. How I wished I could rib her about that, but I had to stay in character.

Sabrina brought out her famous cannoli nachos which were basically fried triangle-shaped cannoli shells that could be dipped into homemade filling. If Borgatti's was the king of raviolis then Sabrina was the queen of cannoli!

Rina poured coffee for anyone who wanted it and Patsy offered Sambuca to anyone who was interested. I hadn't eaten much in the past two weeks and was bursting at the seams when the meal was over.

"Any word on that missing professor?" Sabrina asked.

Gianna shook her head. "It's like he disappeared into thin air."

"What's this about a missing professor?"

"There was a semi-retired professor on campus who just went missing one night about three or so weeks ago. I was actually at his house the night he disappeared."

"Why were you there again anyway?" her concerned father asked.

"I was with my friend Michael and we went back to the professor's house to drop off his car."

"What, did the old guy have a bit too many?" Joseph asked and tipped back his wine glass for effect.

"Michael had just defended his dissertation and the two of them went out to dinner to celebrate. Michael drove and

Professor Shoah left his car on campus. Michael was just bringing it back to him and I followed in his car."

I knew that I needed to show some interest in this conversation, so I stepped in. "And when you went back, what did you find?"

"All the lights were on, the door was open, and the house was ransacked. There was no sign of Professor Shoah anywhere."

"And then your friend was in that terrible accident," Sabrina said. "That was so sad."

"What's this?" I asked.

Gianna looked down at her plate, she was clearly still upset about it.

"Michael, who I was with that night, died in a car accident a few weeks ago. He basically dropped off the face of the earth for a few days before that. I can't be sure, but I'm guessing he was looking for Dr. Shoah. The two were very close and Michael was very concerned about him."

"That's horrible."

"It smells funny if you ask me," Joseph offered.

"Stop it, Joey," Sabrina said while slapping him on the shoulder.

He stared at her if to say, 'Don't call me Joey in front of guests.'

"Tell them about that lady," Sabrina said.

"Michael and I had gone to see this famous hypnotist Madame Charcot that night and when we were at Dr. Shoah's, she shows up and claimed that she wanted to talk to him about appearing at one of her events. Apparently, she's also some big-time motivational speaker. Anyway, a few weeks ago she calls me and asks if I'd heard from Michael because he was supposed to call her, or something. I think she may have had the hots for him." Gianna laughed as she said this.

"What's so funny?"

"Michael was a lot of things, but he was no ladies' man, I can tell you that. He wouldn't know what to do with a woman like Madame Charcot."

I wanted to take offense to the accusation, but it was absolutely right on the money.

"When was this?" I asked.

"It was a Sunday, so two weeks ago today. It was early in the morning too, which I thought was odd. Anyway, I told her I hadn't heard from him and then later that day I found out he'd been killed in a car accident down this way in New Rochelle."

"Did he have family down here?"

"His ex-wife lived in the city, but his son is buried there so maybe he was going to visit the grave site."

"It's just so tragic. You said he just finished school, right?" Sabrina asked.

Gianna nodded. "He was going to graduate with his doctorate in May."

"I'm sorry about your friend," I said to offer my condolences.

"The funeral was sweet. It was so crowded they couldn't do it in the small church on campus so his ex arranged to have it at St. Paul's in New York. The whole department went, as did a lot of his former colleagues. His wife gave a beautiful eulogy."

I was touched. I had guessed that my funeral would have been a small affair. Now I was curious as to what Anna had said.

"And then that woman called you again?" Sabrina asked.

"Yeah. Out of the blue Madame Charcot calls and says that she heard about my research and wanted to see if I would be interested in speaking at one of her executive events. She said she'd been looking for someone to give a talk on bullying and aggression in the workplace and who better than a graduate student in psychology to talk about that?"

"She paying you?" her father asked.

"That's the thing. Normally you do this just for the exposure, but she offered me the same speaking fee as the big-time corporate people on the bill."

This was definitely out of the ordinary and something wasn't right about it. Marie Charcot was a Russian operative posing as a motivational speaker and it couldn't be coincidence that she put Gianna on her speaker's list.

"When and where is this event? If I can, I'd love to come see you."

"May fifteenth at Radio City Music Hall here in New York."

"We are all very proud of you, Gigi," Patsy said to his granddaughter. "Peter, you've had a long day and must be tired, but I'm wondering if you might want to take a walk around the block with me."

This was a welcome offer. Not only did I need to warn Patsy that his granddaughter was potentially in danger, but I really needed to stretch my legs.

"I'd love to," I replied and then got up from the table.

CHAPTER TWENTY-THREE

My Consiglieri

On Easter, when it was me, Anna, and Tyler, we'd always go for a walk after dinner and my son always called it the bunny hop. What I wouldn't give to have one more bunny hop with them.

"The team did a good job," he said as we walked up Chatsworth Ave towards Palmer.

"I was praying that Gianna wouldn't recognize me."

"That's why I brought you here. She's very observant, my granddaughter. If she didn't catch on, I doubt anyone else will."

We made a right onto Palmer and walked a block or so until we got to number 1880, a seven-story building that had seen better days. We walked into the main lobby and the rust-colored cement floor and plaster walls suggested that this was a pre-war building. By the smell of it, maybe even pre-World War I.

"The doctor who owned my house had a brother who lived in this building. When he passed, the doc asked if I wanted to take over the lease because it was rent controlled. I only pay five hundred a month and now they get about two grand, easy. One of my guys lives here now."

"Are we stopping by for an after-dinner drink?" I asked as we stepped into the elevator, which had a manual door that had to be shut before the security door would come down. It was so old and slow that I imagined it was powered by hamsters running in a wheel.

"No. You need a new license and passport, and my guy is about to make that happen."

We got off at the top floor and made a right down the narrow hallway until we reached number 7D. Patsy knocked twice, paused a beat, and then added a third tap with his knuckles.

A man of approximately sixty years of age opened the door. He was tall enough to play professional basketball and had his grey hair styled long, as if the seventies never ended. He had a perfectly trimmed mustache above his lip and was dressed in a sleeveless tee-shirt and sweatpants.

"Pasquale," he said. "Buona Pasqua."

"Buona Pasqua, Bobby. How's your mother."

"Good days and bad days," he said. She's resting now, thanks for asking.

"Bobby, this is Peter Avellino, who's a friend of mine. Peter, Bobby and I have known each other a long time."

"Forty years now," Bobby said.

"Bobby here is going to take your picture and do a little magic."

"I've got everything set up in the guest bedroom. Follow me."

We headed down a short hallway and walked into a makeshift photography studio. In the corner was a computer and what I recognized to be an ID card printer. We had a few at MyLife.

"I borrowed that from the DMV," Bobby said. "Peter, stand in front of that backdrop. I'll give you a minute for your eyes to adjust to the light."

While I did so, he walked over to the computer and hit a few keys.

"Okay, say formaggio."

I gave my best tough guy look into the camera, heard it snap a picture, and then my face came up on screen. Bobby showed it to me, and I nodded my approval. A moment later, my new driver's license spat out of the printer.

"This is a legit NY State driver's license," he said as he handed it to me. "It's even a real ID so you won't have any trouble in airports."

"Thank you," I said and looked it over.

I noticed that my new birthday was April 16th, 1972 which made me two years older than my real age. I also committed my new address, 55 Interlaken Avenue in New Rochelle, to memory.

"The passport is going to take a few days," he said and then handed me a manilla envelope with a return address from the New Rochelle office of vital statistics. That's three certified copies of your birth certificate and a new social security card."

If our government could work this efficiently the United States would be unstoppable.

Bobby handed me something else. "This is a passport application. I've already filled it out and all you have to do is sign it and attach a picture to it. I'll take another one so that it doesn't match the one on your license as that would be suspicious."

We repeated the picture ritual again and a moment later a different printer came to life and my image came out of it on photo paper.

"We have a guy at the passport office who will expedite it. It will be mailed to your house."

I gave Patsy a look.

"I forgot to tell you, you are now the owner of a lovely home in New Rochelle."

"Did I get a good interest rate on the loan?"

"Loan? You paid cash. Which reminds me, I've got something for you," he said while he reached into his pocket and fished out a key ring as well as an ATM card.

"You now have a checking account at the Bank of New Rochelle. PIN number is the last four digits of your new social security number and I suggest you change it. Also, my godson works in the financial planning side of that bank and he's going to work up an investment plan for your portfolio. The tech business was good to you."

Even after giving my wife half of everything in our divorce, I still had a comfortable amount of money left over.

"Oh, and one more thing," Patsy said. "Now that you have a license, you can use this."

He tossed me a small rectangular object which. I looked into my hand and noticed it was a key fob for an Audi.

"I know you miss your Tesla, but it would not have been smart getting the same car you had before. I figured a venture capitalist would drive an import and we have a friend who runs an Audi dealership. We got you an A5. I hope you don't mind midnight blue."

"Cash price?"

Patsy nodded.

"I have it parked in the lot out back," Bobby said.

"How long until the passport will be ready?"

I had no idea where my travels were going to take me, but given that Sam was working for the Russians, I had to assume I'd be leaving the States at some point.

"Like I said, we will expedite it, but it still takes at least a week. Unfortunately, it ain't like the old days and you can't get by with a forgery."

"It is what it is," I said. "Thank you both for all your help."

Our attention was diverted from a voice coming from the other room. "Bobby, I need some help."

"Alright, Ma!" he said.

"Go take care of your mother," Patsy said. "I won't forget this favor you did for me."

"Anything for you, Patsy."

We exited the bedroom and made a left down the hall while Bobby made a right to head to the master bedroom.

"Thanks for all of this," I said to Patsy.

"It's the least I could do for Sam," he said.

I'd been so wrapped up in what just happened, I forgot all about what Gianna said about her participating in an event with Marie Charcot.

"Listen, remember that event that Gianna got invited to?"

"Yeah, by that speaker woman?"

"She's no good, Patsy. She's the one who was after Sam and the key reason he and I are in this mess. Look, I know you didn't want to know anything, but her life may be in danger."

Patsy closed his eyes and sighed.

"Since this now involves my family, you gotta tell me something I really don't want to know."

I told him everything that happened after Gianna and I left Sam's house up until my meeting up with him two weeks ago. I even mentioned what Sam said about my old boss, BA, having something to do with my son's suicide.

"The Russians, huh? And you were going to go at this alone?" he asked. "Why are the smartest people so damn stupid?"

"What choice did I have?"

"I know some guys who are connected to the Russian mob in New York. One of them owes me a favor. Let me poke around for you."

"Thanks. What about Gianna?"

"We've got some time before that event. Any sudden moves now might tip this Charcot woman off. We've got to play it carefully." Patsy looked down and shook his head.

"What?" I asked.

"So much for a quiet retirement. Just when I thought I was out, they pull me back in!" he said in his best Al Pacino impersonation. "Consider me your consiglieri, Irish."

The elevator stopped in the lobby and we opened the door to exit. We walked over to the building's parking lot and I tapped the unlock button on the key fob and I saw two flashing red lights in my peripheral vision.

"Want a ride home?"

"Thank you, but I'll walk. I need to clear my head before going back inside. Call me tomorrow."

"But I don't have a phone."

"Check the glove compartment."

I got into the car and opened the glove box. In it was the latest model iPhone.

"I assume a former tech guy like you can work that thing."

"It's been a while since I've had one, but I'm sure I can figure it out."

"There should be a business card in there with some info on it regarding your phone number and Apple ID. In the back seat, there's a briefcase with a laptop in it."

I looked over my shoulder and saw a leather laptop bag.

"Coach, huh?"

I was never a fancy briefcase guy, preferring my old L.L. Bean canvas bag to the thousand-dollar model sitting behind my passenger seat.

"You gotta look the part."

I knew Patsy was right. Just as Marie had to look the part of a motivational speaker, my portrayal as a venture capitalist had to be as authentic as possible.

"I'll call you in the morning. Tell your family that I'm sorry

I had to leave so abruptly."

"Of course. They will understand."

"Thank you, Patsy."

He just moved his right hand to the side of his face and gave a small wave, like old Italian men are apt to do.

I pushed the start button on my new car and heard the engine roar to life. It had been a while since I'd driven a gas-powered automobile and I forgot the thrill I used to feel after ignition. I pulled out of the driveway onto Palmer Ave and headed to my new home in New Rochelle.

CHAPTER TWENTY-FOUR

A Promise

I pulled onto Interlaken Avenue and found it to be a beautiful tree lined street straight out of Mayberry. I half wondered if sheriff Andy Taylor was going pop out of one of these houses and wave at me while I drove by.

I pulled into the driveway of number fifty-five and it led directly to a one-car garage. I didn't see a clicker in the car, so I parked it just short of the garage door and had a look at the house. The front of it was a combination of fieldstone and stucco and an American flag was placed to the right the front door. As a whole, the home looked sturdy.

There was still plenty of daylight out and, given it was a beautiful spring day, there were kids playing in the backyard of the home to my left. By the looks of it, they were enjoying a spirited game of Wiffle ball.

I found the key for the front door on the ring of keys that Patsy gave me and made my way inside. I expected to find an empty house and was surprised to see that the parlor I walked into from the hallway was furnished, albeit with the furniture of the previous owners who, I assumed given their decorating style, were quite old.

Along the back wall there was a couch with a flower print pattern covered with plastic and I imagined it hadn't been removed since the Kennedy administration. In front of the couch there were two old-fashioned chairs facing each other and a coffee table sat between them. I immediately nicknamed the chairs Edith and Archie as they were similar to those featured on the classic sitcom *All in the Family*.

In front of the coffee table sat a vintage RCA console TV and to round out the mid-1950s look was an old-fashioned hi-fi system in the corner, complete with turntable, radio tuner, and built-in cabinet speakers. I wondered how many cocktails were consumed in this room while the family made room for daddy.

A small eat-in kitchen was accessed through the parlor. The stove and sink looked to be originals while the refrigerator was updated—in the 1980s, judging by the choice of a yellow-colored model. I opened a door in the kitchen which led to a narrow staircase, clearly leading down to the basement. I walked down a hallway and found a formal dining room that led back to the main foyer.

A carpeted staircase was positioned directly in front of the front door and I walked up it to check out the upstairs rooms. As I ascended, the smell of mothballs came over me and I was praying that the previous owners hadn't left closets full of clothes. Which reminded me, I had to go shopping since I literally had no clothes other than the ones I was wearing.

To the left and right of the top of the stairs there were two modest bedrooms. There was a full bath halfway down a narrow hallway and I peeked in and immediately noticed the previous owner's affinity for the color pink. A vintage cast iron sink, toilet, and tub—all pink!

The master bedroom was located at the end of the hall and, while not big by today's standards, it was twice the size of the bedrooms at the other end of the hallway. It housed a queen-sized bed and old-fashioned dresser which I opened and found some new clothes—Patsy had thought of everything. The small walk-in closet also had some new threads as well as a new suitcase.

Fortunately, the previous resident's love of pink didn't extend to the master bath, though the mint green sink, tub, and toilet weren't much of an improvement. It didn't really matter, however, since I wasn't planning on making this my forever home. It would be where I spent the night tonight. After that, who knows?

I made my way back downstairs and turned on the TV to see if it actually worked. Sure enough, it did, but the picture was fuzzy so I turned it off and walked over to the hi-fi. I slid the top open and saw that there was a record on the turntable —Perry Como's *Pure Gold*. I turned the power on and after a few crackles "Catch a Falling Star" was coming out over the speakers. I had to admit, the sound quality was amazing.

My attention was stolen away from the crooner's voice by the sound of a telephone ringing in the kitchen. It was an old-fashioned rotary dial wall-mounted model and I questioned whether I'd crossed through some space-time continuum upon entering my new home.

"Hello?" I said, more as a question than as a statement when putting the receiver to my ear.

"It's Patsy. How do you like the place?"

"It could use a decorator."

"Yeah, well beggars can't be choosers, Irish."

"I didn't expect to hear from you tonight," I said.

"Yeah, well, your story about the Russians got me thinking and since it now involves my granddaughter, I made a call to a friend in Brighton Beach."

I remember Patsy saying something about having a connection in the Russian mob. I'd never been there personally but was aware of its reputation of being the epicenter of Russian organized crime.

"I know a guy, Dimitri Popov, who's high up the food chain in Bratva, the Russian Mafia. He had an issue with credit card fraud and asked for my help as he heard I knew the judge on his case. Anyway, I made his problem go away. I called him earlier and asked if he had a moment to talk to a friend of mine."

"And?"

"You are expected in Brighton Beach tonight. This isn't something that can be done by phone. Too many people listening these days."

"You aren't coming?"

"Listen, Irish, I'm on parole. If I'm seen on Easter Sunday talking to a guy with known ties to the Russian mob, I'll be toast. Relax, he's a reasonable man. Just remember, if he helps you, you will owe him a favor."

"What could I possibly do for him?" I asked.

"Believe me, he'll think of something. Dimitri will be waiting for you at the Ocean View Cafe right on Brighton Beach Ave. Good luck."

I hastily packed a bag as I didn't know if I'd be coming back here or not, and headed out.

Thankfully, Patsy stocked the master bath with some toiletries and I took a quick shower before heading out to Brooklyn; one never gets a second chance to make a first impression.

On the way to the highway, I had to pass the cemetery where Tyler was buried and decided to make a quick stop to pay my respects as I hadn't been in a while and it was something I always did on major holidays.

After passing through the main entrance of Holy Sepulchre Cemetery, I made an immediate left and drove about twenty yards before parking in front of a maintenance shed. Daylight was fading and I knew the cemetery would be closing soon.

Tyler was buried next to my mother and stepfather, who both passed away in a car accident back in 2004. I missed them every day but was grateful for the fact that they got to know Tyler and that they weren't alive to hear the devastating news that he killed himself.

I stood in front of his headstone and noticed that someone had planted some Easter flowers. Typically, whenever I came, I brought something to pretty up his headstone, whether it be a plant or, at Christmastime, a wreath. I didn't have anything today because I hadn't planned on coming but made a mental note to bring something extra special when I came back.

When visiting my parents, I used to pray in front of their headstone, but I'd all but lost the faith I was raised with. Instead, after Tyler died, I just talked to him. I looked around to make sure I was alone as I didn't want anyone to think I was crazy. Satisfied that I was in the clear, I started to talk to my son.

"Hey buddy. You have no idea how much I miss you. I think about you every day. What do you think about my new look? Long story there, I'll be sure to tell you if we meet again someday."

Years ago, I was convinced there was an afterlife with an all-knowing and all-loving God overseeing it all. What bullshit. If there's a God who loves us like his children, why is there so much suffering in the world? Why would He let an innocent child like Tyler die, the victim of some human experiment? Hell, why would He let something as evil as the Holocaust happen? The Jews were His chosen people, right?

"I promise you this, son, I'm going to find the people who did this to you and take them down."

I saw some movement out of the corner of my eye and noticed a butterfly fluttering in the wind just to the right of me. Up until recently I believed that butterflies were symbols of rebirth, transformation, and hope, but Jacob and Sam taught me that they were also beautiful angels of death. There was something about this one, though, that captivated me and I followed it until it landed on the headstone directly in back of Tyler's in the next row.

I could only see the back of the stone from my vantage point so had no idea who was buried there, but thought they must have died recently as the ground was still disturbed and there looked to be a number of flower arrangements around the stone. My curiosity got the better of me and I walked around. What I saw made a chill run straight down my spine.

I was looking at my own headstone. Michael Corrigan January 1973-April 2019. I immediately knew the horror Scrooge must have felt when looking at his own grave in Dickens' *A Christmas Carol*.

But it wasn't Michael Corrigan buried six feet below where I was standing. It was a poor, unfortunate John Doe who was slated to be buried in a mass grave on Hart Island until Patsy worked his magic. I made him a promise too, that I'd work like hell to make his death mean something too.

I walked back to Tyler's grave to say one last goodbye. I kissed two of my fingers and tapped them on Tyler's headstone and said, "Dad's got to go to Brighton Beach to meet some Russian gangster. What the hell have I gotten myself into?"

While backing away from the stone, I accidentally tripped and stepped on the flowers in front of it. I bent down to pick them up and reposition them and realized that they were artificial, which I thought was odd because it's customary to bring living plants when paying respects to the dead—the whole circle of life thing. When putting them back, I felt something fall out and make a small thud on the ground. I picked it up and saw that it was a small camera.

I started to panic. Why was there a camera hidden in a fake

plant in front of my son's grave? I knew cameras like this were used in modern-day security systems and could send a live feed to a mobile device or computer, but who would be interested in spying on people coming to see my son? I was afraid that this could mean the Russians didn't buy the fact that I died in a car accident and that going through the trouble of altering my appearance had been for nothing. I started taking deep breaths to prevent myself from going into an all-out panic attack.

If someone was interested in Tyler's visitors, I wondered if they were also interested in mine. I walked back to the headstone for Michael Corrigan and fished through the dying flowers in front of it, but there was no camera. Why Tyler's but not mine? I decided to stash the camera in my pocket—in addition to sending a stream to a device, it had a microSD card in it, and I was curious as to what could be on it.

A moment later, a maintenance man in a golf cart came by to tell me that the cemetery was about to close. The name tag on his overalls read Jimmy.

"I was just about to leave," I said and then started to walk back to my car but then turned around. "Hey, I got a question for you, Jimmy."

"I gotta answer for ya," he said, with a thick New York accent. New Yorkers always have answers.

"This is going to sound crazy, but I found a small camera in a flower in front of that headstone. Do you think that's weird?"

"Not at all," he replied confidently. "We've had a lot of vandalism here as of late and the diocese has been planting those little cameras all over the place to catch the bastards. Pain in the ass for me since I have to charge them all the time."

After hearing that, my pulse returned back to normal and I could breathe a sign of relief. One of the first things I learned in psychology was the law of parsimony which dictates that, given multiple explanations of an event or observation, the one that is simplest is the most preferred. It was certainly simpler to believe Jimmy's explanation than the one my mind went to—that it was left there to spy on Tyler's visitors hoping to catch me. I guess everything I'd been through over the past few weeks had been getting to me.

I walked back to the Tyler's grave and replaced the camera and then went back to the Audi and headed off to Brooklyn.

CHAPTER TWENTY-FIVE

Brighton Beach Memoirs

Traffic was lighter than usual given that it was Easter Sunday, and it took me just under an hour to get from New Rochelle to Brighton Beach in Brooklyn. It was dark out and my mind was preoccupied with what I was about to do, so I didn't exactly take in the neighborhoods I had passed through. I was too worried about my pending meeting with a Russian gangster named Dimitri.

I was able to find parking on a side street adjacent to the Ocean View Cafe and walked in just after 8pm. The place was empty, and I questioned whether I heard Patsy correctly when he told me where to go.

Just then, a beautiful young woman with long, straight dark hair entered in from what I assumed was the back room of the restaurant. "Can I heylp you?" she asked in a thick Russian accent.

"My name is Peter Avellino. I'm here to see Dimitri."

"He's beyn expecting you. Follow me please."

We walked through the empty dining room and into a back room that was also empty. Off the backroom was a kitchen which was humming with activity; the smells of grilled meats wafted towards me. I assumed they did a brisk takeout business as an evening rush seemed unlikely.

We went down a flight of stairs which led to a storeroom for holiday decorations and old furniture. In back there was a door that looked to be a heavier duty than ones typically seen in basement offices. This one looked as if it could withstand gale force winds, and perhaps a battering ram.

There was a camera above the door and my guide looked into it.

"Please stand here," she said.

I did as told but didn't smile for the camera as I assumed the man on the other side would assume that smiling was a sign of weakness.

I heard a number of locks disengage on the other side of the door. When it opened, I was staring at two identical twins who looked as if they could have been professional wrestlers. In my head I referred to them as The Bolsheviks after the '80's tag team billed from Russia. Members Boris Zhukov and Nikolai Volkoff, neither of whom were actually from the USSR, would come to the ring waving the flag of the Soviet Union and sing the Russian national anthem—I half expected them to do the same. In back of them was a bearded man sitting in a chair behind a large wooden desk.

I walked into the room with my heart in my throat and was immediately frisked by both men. If the professional wrestling careers don't pan out, they could easily get a job with the TSA. One of them took my phone, powered it off, and placed it on the desk.

They didn't say a word to the seated man, but just nodded to communicate that I was clean of any weapons or listening devices.

"Leave us alone," he commanded. A thick beard covered his face and a mountain of hair sat on top of his head, making him look more like Yanni than a Russian Patsy Mazzone.

"I understand we have a mutual friend."

"Yes, I was sent by…"

Dimitri put his index finger to his lips to suggest I should stop talking. "There's no need to tell me who you were sent by. Can I offer you a drink?"

I shook my head. In spite of that, he opened a desk drawer, removed a bottle of vodka, and poured two glasses.

He raised his glass and said, "Zdorov'ye." I did the same and we emptied the contents of our glasses at the same time.

I wasn't much of a vodka drinker but had to admit the warmth from the alcohol helped calm my nerves a bit.

"Why are you here on your Easter Sunday instead of spending it with your family?"

As a Russian Orthodox, his Easter would be celebrated next week.

"I don't have a family," I replied.

Dimitri countered with, "Everyone has a family, maybe you haven't found yours yet."

I wasn't in the mood to get into a philosophical discussion so decided to cut to the chase.

"Are you familiar with what a Russian Butterfly is?"

The mobster's face turned to stone, suggesting that he knew all too well what one was.

"Why do you ask?"

On the car ride down, I carefully considered how much information I was going to tell Dimitri. If I told him too much, I ran the risk of tipping my hat should he still feel a sense of duty to his home country and tell any political connections that people in the States got wind of a secret plan. If I didn't tell him enough, it was likely he'd choose not to help me as I'd be giving a sign that I didn't trust him. I opted to start at a high level.

"It turns out a friend of mine is a Russian spy who was living in deep cover here in the States. He was looking to defect and somehow his handlers got word and sent a Butterfly after him."

I was surprised when Dimitri's stone-cold expression gave way to a heavy dose of laughter.

"You've been watching too much TV, my friend. The illegals program has been done in this country for quite some time. Who needs deep cover spies when computers do all the work?"

It's possible that Dimitri wasn't aware of the full extent of the program, or that he was pushing me to give up more information, so I clarified more about what had happened to Sam.

"I met one of these Butterflies. She came down to Florida with me as we were following a clue to track down my friend…"

"Your friend the illegal, I presume?"

I nodded. "It led us to a priest who my friend knew and he sent us somewhere else. The priest was murdered that night."

"Why do you think she was a Butterfly?"

I told him how I'd noticed a butterfly tattoo on her body while having sex with her that night.

"Lots of American women get tattoos like that. It doesn't make her a killer. Plus, Butterflies seduce men who can offer them something. What could you offer her?"

"Maybe she thought I would lead her to my friend?"

"Is it possible that she was into you? You are not a bad looking guy, my friend."

I couldn't exactly tell Dimitri that I didn't look like this when I met her. What would she have found interesting in me anyway? No, she was definitely after something. That was the most likely explanation.

"But don't you think it's too much of a coincidence?"

Dimitri poured two more vodkas for us and sat back.

"My friend, I don't know you, but I think you have to be

open to the possibility that you are being played."

"Why do you say that?"

"Let's say, hypothetically, that as a Russian man of means I may have been known to fund some, let's call it, research, for some friends of mine back in Moscow. Through grants from some foundations I started as a way of, let's say, reducing my tax liabilities and washing some money."

As someone who has conducted research at a major university, I knew just how valuable grants were. That many illegals, like Sam, wound up in academia was on purpose because, as academics, they could get low-level contacts on the fringe of power. For example, their research might be sponsored by the department of defense and findings from that research would be considered valuable to their handlers back home. While legitimate grants would be used to fund the research, it's possible that grants from people like Dimitri could be used to fund their lifestyle.

"Okay. So, theoretically, you could have funded some illegals through grants. So what?"

Dimitri smiled. "Since 2011 the number of grants that I and some of my colleagues have been asked to fund has decreased significantly. Either my country has found a better way of funding illegals, or the purge of ten years ago led to the end of the program."

"What purge?"

"My friend, in 2010 the US government arrested ten deep cover Russian agents who were deported in a prisoner exchange program. My country had to play it conservative and assume that they had rolled over on their fellow illegals and that our network was busted. If anyone stayed in the States after this time, it was of their own volition."

"They were burned?"

"To a crisp!" he said and poured a third round.

"It just doesn't make any sense. Why would Sam lie to me

about everything?"

Dimitri put his arms up. "I can't tell you why people do what they do, but I do know a bullshit story when I hear one and you, my friend, have stepped into some bullshit."

Now my mind was swirling. Sam admitted to being an illegal and having information that the Russians were up to something that could jeopardize the American way of life and went so far as to suggest it might lead to a potential holocaust. If he was lying about all of that, it meant that my death was faked for no reason and that I didn't need to go through a surgery to change my appearance or adopt a new identity. If that were all true, why involve me at all? No, Dimitri was wrong, I wasn't being played.

"I'm sorry I cannot help you too much, my friend," he said.

"Me too," I replied, but then had a thought—if the illegals program was over, it meant that Dimitri had lost a way to clean some money and reduce his tax liabilities. Assuming he was right and that some of these burned illegals had remained in the States and were in hiding, might they have reached out to him for support?

"These grants you funded, do you know where they went?"

"Of course!" he said defiantly, as if I questioned his business sense. "We kept close track of them for tax reasons. Everything had to be on the up and up."

"Would you mind sharing any of that information with me?"

"You are persistent, my friend, I will give you that."

He then picked up the phone on his desk and said something in Russian to whoever picked up the phone. A few minutes later the woman who led me down to Dimitri's office came back with a stack of folders.

"Thank you, Iggy."

Funny, I didn't peg her as an Iggy. A Helen, maybe, but not

an Iggy.

Once she left, Dimitri went through the folders.

"Now I have no way of knowing which of these is from the illegals program and which were legit as I needed to have plausible deniability if the government caught on, but here goes; Stanford University, National Institute for Health, University of Connecticut…"

I interrupted him. "Hold up, was the research grant for UConn from the psychology department by any chance?" My research was self-funded, but I figured Sam may have put in a grant for something.

He looked through the file quickly. "No. This was for the biology department."

Biology? That meant there could have been someone else at the university who may have been part of the illegals program.

"Does it say who requested the funds?"

"Yes," he replied. "Dr. Anton Levy."

Sonofabitch! I thought to myself. He was the pompous ass who gave me a hard time in my dissertation. I thought it was random that he showed up, now I had to challenge that assumption.

The stack of folders in front of Dimitri was still pretty big. I was curious to know when the most recent request was.

"What's the last request for money you got?"

Dimitri laughed. "My friend, I get requests for money all the time. These are only the grants."

Given that his grant requests had died off after 2010, it's possible that some illegals came to him for money outside of the grant channel. It was worth exploring.

"Has anyone come to you recently with any out of the ordinary requests?"

"You really like to pry in my personal affairs."

"I really don't mean to. I'm just trying to put this puzzle

together. Assuming that the program has dissolved, like you said, maybe one of them came to you for funds."

"To be clear, I wouldn't know who is an illegal and who isn't, but that said, I did have someone come to me and ask for a rather large sum recently. Told me he'd double my money within a year. Now I get pitches like this all the time, but I vetted the guy and he's done quite well for himself in tech."

"Bob Ahlers," I blurted.

"How did you know?"

I explained how my friend, the self-confessed illegal, told me how Ahlers was also in the program and involved in using targeted advertising to manipulate behavior.

"Ahh, Russian collusion," Dimitri joked.

I was tempted to tell him how Ahlers' work cost my son his life, but it would betray my new identity.

Now my Spidey senses were tingling. With the revelations that Dimitri had funded Anton Levy's work and that my old boss reached out to him for money, I knew that there was something bigger at play, but what? Was my country really in danger or was it all a con? And if a con, what was my role in it?

"Tell me, what did Ahlers say?"

"He came to me and five of my other friends in this business with the supposed opportunity of a lifetime. He asked us each for two million dollars and guaranteed us a hundred percent return or he'd pay us back in full, with interest. After we vetted him and saw that he was worth ten times that, we agreed to the investment."

"Do you have an address for Ahlers?"

"Let me see," Dimitri said while investigating a piece of paper. "He lives on a farm in Vermont. He listed that as part of his collateral."

So, he still has the farm up north, I thought to myself. In

years past, I had many pleasant experiences at that place.

"And you don't know how he's going to double your money?"

"I've learned not to ask too many questions about that. Besides, if he fucks me, I can get him."

"Listen, thanks so much for your time, Mr. Popov. I appreciate it."

"Good luck, my friend. I trust you are a man of honor like the man who sent you?" He said it more as a question than a statement.

"Meaning?"

"I believe the Italians call it omertà, my friend."

Ah, he wants to make sure I don't divulge this to anybody.

"This conversation never happened."

"Excellent. The boys will see you out."

We shook hands and I left the room and found The Bolsheviks waiting for me. They walked me up the stairs where I said goodbye to Iggy and walked out into the cool April air, though I didn't drive back to New Rochelle. Instead, I fueled up at a gas station, purchased a large cup of coffee that tasted like salty motor oil, and headed north to the green mountain state.

CHAPTER TWENTY-SIX

Matlock Returns

After graduating Stanford, I moved back east and took a job working in development at a start-up advertising agency called Modulation Media, which was the brainchild of Bob Ahlers, a software engineer, and Gerard Allen, an advertising executive. The two met at their previous employer, Prodigy, one of the first dial-up Internet service providers.

BA had first gotten into the tech business in what could best be described as a software scheme.

As a teenager in the 1980s, he was already an adept programmer and, as a hobby, he and some buddies started creating computer viruses. At first, it was just an act of high-tech teenage rebellion, but BA had an idea—create the virus and then sell the vaccine. He and his friends formed a company called Antidote Software and made a mint doing this until someone caught on to their scheme and threatened legal action unless they stopped. Being still only teens at the time, the kids got spooked and the person threatening them stole their idea and formed a company that was later sold to Microsoft for hundreds of millions of dollars. The tech world is not just full of piracy, it's full of pirates too.

As a computer engineer myself, I worked for BA and learned the value of energy drinks, sugary snacks, and sarcasm. Eighty-hour weeks were the norm, but none of us cared. We were in the trenches creating the future of advertising and loved every second of it.

One day, I overheard a conversation between a fellow developer and a guy who ran our media business. They were dreaming up a solution for sequential advertising, meaning if someone saw an advertisement offering twenty percent off of a product's price and didn't respond, they'd next see a follow-up ad for twenty five percent off, etcetera. The thing is, they didn't know how to check for an exposure, so they couldn't place the offers in sequence. A few months earlier, someone came to me with a similar need, to customize a website based on something the site "knew" about a visitor. I wrote a piece of tracking code to handle this and told my colleagues how it could be a solution to their problem. A promotion soon followed, and I started to lead all efforts around targeted advertising. As an introvert, I didn't seek to capitalize on this fame and my technology was later replicated by a pirate at a company called Netscape who nicknamed the tracking code a cookie. The rest is Internet advertising history.

I remember being mesmerized by BA as a visionary. Make no mistake, the guy was completely bonkers—he once gave a talk in 1997 about something he imagined called Digital Current—an invisible force that would run through every house in the world and power common household devices beyond computers. He gave the example of a refrigerator being connected to the Internet that could automatically place an order for groceries once it determined the household was low on key items. We all laughed at the time, but today we have Internet-enabled fridges with voice-activated intelligent agents built in. I guess he wasn't so nutty after all.

He cashed out of Modulation Media after it went public. While he had an earn out, the new board didn't mind his lack of presence since he had a tendency to ruffle feathers. Besides, his partner Gerard had a great head for business and oversaw exponential growth for the company. BA took some of his proceeds and bought a farm in Vermont and was generous enough to have the entire company camp up on his property every August. The parties there were legendary. Invitees were made up primarily of tech nerds and type A salespeople who, after alcohol was introduced, all lost their minds. Many relationships began and ended at BA's summer parties.

I was on my way up to the farm now not for recreation, but fact finding. I needed to figure out a few things; first, did he have anything at all to do with my son's death? Second, why was he asking for ten million dollars from a bunch of Russian mobsters? While I believed what Sam had told me a few days ago about BA being involved with some experiments that could have impacted Tyler, after meeting with Dimitri I wasn't certain whether that was true. I didn't know exactly how I was going to uncover any link BA might have had to Tyler's death, but I did have a sense for how I could better understand his need for capital.

With my new persona as a venture guy, I'd meet him and let it slip that I was actively seeking investment opportunities. If he was hungry for cash, he'd pitch me the opportunity.

One of Patsy's rules was to think like your opponent thinks and I knew just how BA thinks. He likes to get into philosophical discussions late in the evening over cocktails and I could certainly hold my own in that regard.

It was approaching 11:30 pm and I was fifteen minutes away from what I knew was a favorite watering hole of his called the Silo, an American restaurant near Mt. Snow that was built around an old grain silo. I pulled in to the parking lot right around a quarter to twelve and, sure enough, a pickup truck with two American flags hanging out the back and a personalized license plate that said VT PATRIOT was parked out front. I knew right away it was his. It was Easter Sunday, after all, and he was escaping his family. A brilliant tech guy, yes, but not what you'd call a family man.

"Kitchen is closed, but the bar is open," the bartender said as I walked inside.

"When's last call?"

The bartender laughed. "Whenever BA over there decides to go home."

BA looked at me and slurred, "I've got room for one more."

"What's your poison?"

"You have Angel's Envy?"

The bartender nodded.

"Two fingers, neat," I replied.

"Bourbon man I see. Tell you what, Bobby, give me one of those."

"Sure thing, BA."

The bartender went to work, and I settled into a seat.

"Escaping the family?"

"Pardon me?"

"Has to be. I mean, what brings you to a bar on Easter Sunday dressed like Matlock?"

I looked over my suit and second-guessed my choice of going with a lighter colored one. Come to think of it, that was the second time I thought of Andy Griffith that day.

"I was in Springfield for Easter with my parents and have a team offsite at the resort near Mt. Snow tomorrow. They had availability tonight, so I decided to come early."

"The Grand Summit?"

I nodded.

"Nice place. What do you do?"

"I run a venture capital firm and am taking the team out to show my appreciation for a strong first quarter and to brainstorm some new ideas. We are hungry for growth."

"You don't say." He leaned in and I could tell I had earned his attention.

I'd been in his shoes before, though, and knew that the number one rule is not to look too eager. This had to be a slow dance, a seduction. He wouldn't try to take me to bed without a little foreplay.

"My name is Bob Ahlers, but everyone calls me BA."

"Peter Avellino," I said and shook his hand.

"Eyetalian, huh?"

"100%."

He raised his glass and said, "Salud."

I did the same to him.

"What kind of work are you in?"

"Well, I spent a lot of time in the tech industry and then retired early. Keep one foot in the game, though, as an investor mostly. Just something to keep my mind going. Can't hunt and fish all day, right?"

"I suppose not. Got any tips for me? I did well in tech in the nineties but lost my shirt on a few bad calls."

"Like what?" he asked.

"Pointcast," I replied quickly. It was the first dog that came to mind. It was a news service that pushed headlines to a user's computer as a screen saver, but IT departments loathed it as the service ate too much bandwidth and slowed internal networks to a crawl.

"Got in when it was valued at four-hundred-and-fifty-million and got out when it went under a hundred."

"Ouch!" he said and laughed. "We all have tales like that. My biggest flop was caskets-dot-com. Turns out people really wanted to see those in person before purchasing one for a loved one."

"It's amazing how some crazy ideas got funded. The launch parties were fun though, right?"

"It was a crazy time. But man, if we could have predicted the bubble bursting, we could have made a fortune."

One way to make a fortune when you can predict a down market is through short selling. I wondered if that's what he was referring to.

"A big short?"

BA smiled and nodded.

"Think of it. If you knew when AOL was going to tank, you could have sold a ton of shares on margin and then bought them at a rock bottom price and kept the difference, after paying Uncle Sam of course. We could have made billions."

BA easily made hundreds of millions when Modulation Media went public. How much more did he need? That's the thing, though, in the '80's MTV coined the phrase "Too much is never enough" and that's the way guys like BA looked at money.

"If only there was a way to predict the future," I said and emptied my glass. I noticed BA's was empty too and asked the bartender for another round.

"Maybe there is," he said wryly.

"What are you talking about?" I asked.

"What causes market volatility?"

"Uncertainty," I replied quickly.

"Bingo. What if we could predict uncertainty and capitalize on it?"

"And how would we do that? Political unrest? Civil war?"

"Hey, buddy, I don't have any answers for you on that, but if there were a way to know, would you be interested?"

"Sure," I said. "And can you tell me what Wednesday's Powerball numbers will be?"

"You got a card on you? If you are serious, we can continue

this conversation another time. My head is a little funny."

Unfortunately, I hadn't planned on actually conducting any real business so didn't think to make up any business cards, but a real venture guy would always have a card on him. I had to think fast.

"Actually, we got some of those millennials on our staff who feel as if printed business cards aren't green so it's company policy not to have them. I'd be happy to give you my mobile number though."

"Sure," he said and reached for his phone.

I gave him my new number and watched as he plugged it into his address book. I thought it would be important for me to have his, too.

"Hey, BA, do me a favor and text me to make sure you got the number right."

"Good idea. I've had a few."

He shot me a note and my phone buzzed to life with his text.

"Great."

I could sense that he was antsy to leave, but still didn't have a sense of whether or not he had anything to do with Tyler's death. Then I remembered what Jacob suggested about him possibly hacking into my pharmacy.

"Hey, you don't know any hackers, do you?" I asked.

"I used to dabble for shits and giggles," he said. "Why?"

"Know anyone who could get into a pharmacy database?"

BA had an ego and, were he able to do it, I knew he'd flaunt it.

"About six years ago, an old friend of mine who had started a cybersecurity business had been pitching a drugstore chain in the northeast, but they held off on acquiring his services claiming to have an unbeatable security system in place. He wanted to prove to them that they needed his services but couldn't get into the damn system."

I really didn't like where this was going.

"So, he went to you for help?"

"You know how they said the Titanic was unsinkable?"

"Yeah."

"Well, it's sitting on the bottom of the North Atlantic. There's no system that I can't get into, so I did him a favor. It took me two weeks, but I got into their system and was able to pull a file of all customers and prescriptions filled over a two-year period. He brought that to his next meeting, and they signed with him on the spot, even after he tripled his fees."

Pirates!

"And what did you do with that information?"

BA just laughed. "That's a story for another time, Kemosabe."

At that moment, I knew he had to die but I had to remember what Patsy told me, to keep my friends close and enemies closer as well as not to act too emotionally. St. Michael the archangel had to sheath his sword for now and uncover what Anton Levy's role in this whole scheme was.

"Why you asking about hacking, anyway?"

"Let's just say I might need your services in the future, but that's a story for another time."

The moment between us was interrupted by Bobby the bartender. "Uber is waiting for you out front, BA."

"Yeah, yeah. Watch my truck, will ya?"

"Will do."

Once BA left, I settled up my tab with Bobby and made my way south. I was tempted to drive straight back to New Rochelle, but could barely keep my eyes open so I stopped off at a Hampton Inn right off of I-91. Besides, tomorrow I needed to head back down to UConn to see if I could learn anything about Anton Levy's research and it didn't make much sense to go all the way home only to go north again. I was out before my head hit the pillow.

CHAPTER TWENTY-SEVEN

Puzzle Pieces

I'd always had the most vivid dreams when my sleep pattern changed. Last night I dreamt that Tyler was still alive and that I was trying to make my way home from a business trip in order to see him in a play. My plane kept circling an airfield and then suddenly started losing altitude. I had the sense that we were going to crash and braced myself in my seat but woke up right before we hit the ground, sparing myself the pain of going through a plane crash, albeit one dreamt up by my subconscious.

After opening my eyes, I was a bit confused as to where I was and then remembered stopping off at a roadside motel after leaving The Silo. I looked at my face in the mirror and was still getting used to the new me. Thankfully, the swelling was all but gone, though I did need a shave. I went to the small overnight bag I packed before leaving New Rochelle, took out a toiletry case and then lathered up my face with shaving cream, though didn't shave my entire face. I figured that I'd try the five o'clock shadow look and just cleaned up the neck.

I then removed my contacts stared at my blue eyes in the

mirror. I didn't think I'd ever get used to the brown ones, but not wearing the contacts wasn't an option. From what I was told by my friend David, Michael Corrigan's blue eyes were unmistakable and, although I had a new face, I couldn't risk my eyes giving me away, so I put a fresh pair of contacts in.

I took a quick shower and then got dressed in some business casual clothes. Although I was going to a college campus, a middle-aged man trying to dress like a college kid would stand out, as would a guy wearing a custom fitted suit. As such, it was khakis and a button-down for me.

I went down to the lobby and took advantage of the free continental breakfast, grabbed a cup of coffee, and hit the road.

It took me just over two hours to drive the one-hundred-and-twenty miles from West Dover, Vermont to the UConn campus. When I pulled through the main entrance just after noon, Spring fever was definitely in the air. I saw students playing ultimate frisbee and sunning themselves on the grand lawn, taking advantage of an unseasonably warm day, a gift after a long, cold winter at the rural campus.

The biology building was located directly across from a small cemetery on campus, which led many of us to joke about where the department really got its cadavers for its Gross Anatomy class. I parked my car in the garage adjacent to the campus's basketball arena and walked down the road to the bio building.

On the way, I had to pass the theatre where Gianna and I had seen Marie Charcot's show and there were throngs of students out front protesting a right-leaning comedian who was coming to campus later in the week. I wasn't too familiar with Nick Di Paolo's comedy, but he must have said something in support of the current Republican president as protesters carried signs depicting the two of them embracing as if they were on their honeymoon. Of course, some signs compared the comedian to Hitler, showing just how unoriginal these protestors were. They'd find a way to compare Mother Teresa to Hitler if she had said anything that went against leftist doctrine.

The Torrey Life Sciences building was named after a botanist who taught at the school for over forty years. It had recently been remodeled to bring it into the twenty-first century and part of the renovations included an interactive digital display for finding the room numbers of faculty and staff. I walked up to the kiosk and typed Levy into a search field and found that his office was in room 194. It also said what his class schedule was and when his office hours were. At the moment, he was currently giving a lecture in room 154. I decided to take a walk to that lecture hall and eavesdrop outside the door.

I peeked in and saw that just about every one of the hundred and fifty seats were taken. Given the size of the glass, Dr. Levy used a microphone and that allowed me to hear what remained of his lecture.

He was talking about viruses and how they evolve through natural selection, albeit at a quicker rate than more complex forms of life.

"A virus's job is to reproduce in a host and then spread to another host where the process continues. Now, a virus doesn't want to be stupid. It doesn't want to kill the host because, if it does, then the virus dies too. So that's why it has to evolve quickly. So what you tend to see when a new virus is discovered is how the first groups of people to get it might get very sick and die. Over time, though, the virus mutates so that people get sick, but not so sick that they die from it."

While peeking into the lecture hall I saw a student in the front row with her hand up.

"Oh good, we have a question. Someone is paying attention," Levy said in a condescending tone.

"Could a virus be used in warfare?"

"Well, it seems we have a diabolical thinker among us. In fact, the British attempted to use smallpox as a weapon in 1763 during the Siege of Fort Pitt. In World War II, the Japanese planned to use plague as a biological weapon against US citizens but didn't pull the trigger on it as the Empire wound up surrendering before it was to go into action. The big problem with germ warfare, aside from the immorality of it all, is the collateral damage that is done because of it. You could actually wind up infecting your own soldiers, thereby hurting your cause while attempting to advance it."

"What about as part as economic warfare?" blurted out another student.

"You must be in the business school," joked Levy.

"Finance major," the student admitted.

"I know of a computer scientist who made a lot of money creating viruses and then selling a program to combat them. He was a real scoundrel! Like real viruses, his computer born ones would mutate and that would encourage his customers to purchase subscriptions for his service. It was a great business model, until he got found out."

He had to have been talking about BA, it would have been too much of a coincidence otherwise. So, Levy knew my old boss, but I needed to figure out how exactly they were working together and what they wanted with Sam. He must be a threat to their plans, but how?

"Right now, my research team is researching a novel virus that causes mild, flu-like symptoms in some lab animals and no symptoms in others. In some animals, though, the virus is unpredictable, and we are still trying to figure out why it's such an anomaly. If this virus got out now, there'd be no telling who would get sick and, human nature being what it is, hysteria would ensue, under the right conditions."

As a doctoral student in psychology, I knew a thing or two about hysteria and, though I'd hate to give Levy any credit, he's right. A virus like the one he was describing would lead to panic on a scale we haven't seen in a hundred years. Given the ease at which information—and misinformation—flows these days, mass hysteria would certainly be an outcome.

"Now imagine that my team also had developed a vaccine for this virus. If we weren't as ethical as we are, we could force an outbreak of that virus and then sell access to that vaccine for high profits since we'd have a monopoly on it."

"Wouldn't that require FDA approval?" asked the business student.

"Of course," Levy replied. "But we could file for emergency use authorization. If we had the right contacts in government, that wouldn't be a problem."

The buzzer announcing the end of class sounded before he could take another question. I stepped aside as students filed out of the lecture hall and then waited for Levy and followed him.

After about ten steps he turned around quickly and challenged me.

"Can I help you?"

I could have sworn I saw fangs in his mouth.

"I'm sorry, I'm a bit turned around. I'm looking for the department chair's office."

"I'm the department chair, but I don't have any meetings on my calendar," he said and then started walking again. "Who are you and what do you want?"

I didn't think I would get anywhere playing the venture capitalist card with him. Besides, given the connection between him and BA, if word got out that the two of them randomly met the same venture capitalist, it would suggest that someone might be on to them. I had to think of something quick—something that might be able to take advantage of Levy's massive ego. I noticed he was carrying a textbook and had a flash of inspiration.

"I'm with McGraw Hill and looking for an author to write a textbook on virology. All my research suggests that you've forgotten more about viruses than most will ever learn."

We had stopped walking once we got to door number 194. He entered in a six-digit passcode which I glanced at and committed to memory.

"You people never give up," he said while pushing is door open. "I get hundreds of calls and emails each term from publishers looking to slap my name on a book. I tell them all the same thing; I barely have enough time to teach, let alone write."

"I'm sorry to trouble you, Dr. Levy. I should let you know that we are prepared to offer you ten times the standard advance of ten-thousand dollars."

Sam had recently written a textbook on psychological tests and measurements and griped that the standard advance for doing so was only ten grand. I was curious to see if an offer of one hundred thousand would appeal to Levy, as it would more than match his yearly salary. If he turned that down, it would suggest that he was in on the mysterious money-making scheme BA referenced last night.

"Buddy, I wouldn't do that for a million dollars, now please leave me alone, I'm due in my lab."

Levy dropped his bag in his office and then quickly exited, leaving me in the doorway.

"I assume you can see yourself out," he said while walking down the hall.

I pretended to walk away but doubled back once I was sure he was out of sight. I entered the code I observed him punch in and was relieved when I heard a click suggesting the lock disengaged. I pushed the door open and entered his office.

Was it possible he was going to take a page out of BA's playbook and release a real virus into the world with the hopes of capitalizing on it? If so, how was he going to pull that off without getting caught? Surely, they could link an outbreak of a virus he and his team were studying back to him. Also, wouldn't his having a vaccine ready to go be too convenient? Most governments would be able to see right through that scheme. Also, if this was the case, how did it link to BA's plans on making big bucks short selling stocks? I had the sense that I had pieces of the puzzle in front of me, but didn't know how to put them together.

Like that of most academics, Levy's desk was a mess. It was littered with invoices, journal articles, and a stack of while you were out memos, but nothing that I'd call incriminating. I decided to leave his office but heard the sound of approaching footsteps outside the door. Seconds later, I heard the lock to the door disengage. Levy, the vampiric virologist, was back.

I looked around and saw that the only place to hide was in a small coat closet. I quietly stepped inside and prayed he wouldn't need anything in there. By the sound of it, he had walked over to his desk and then made a call.

"I just got the latest numbers back. The virus has mutated again and this time it's much less lethal. We only lost five out of one hundred lab mice over the past fourteen days, and only the older ones at that. We should be ready soon."

That confirmed that he was planning on releasing a virus. If I knew where, maybe I could stop it.

"I've thought of that," he said in reply to something the person on the other end of the phone said. "We'll release it in Russia where we have a sister research team working on the same virus and can blame the outbreak on them. I have a friendly asset at a medical clinic in Wales, Alaska who can store the virus for us until we are ready to infect the mule and send him over from there, it's just across the Bering Strait from Russia. After it spreads, it will only be a matter of time before it finds its way to the States, and then we move onto the second phase of the operation."

Damn you, Sarah Palin, for claiming you can see Russia from your house. Now some egomaniac virologist from Connecticut was going to take advantage of that

"Mark my words, Bob, this will shut down the economy. Between the short selling you will lead and my selling the vaccine, we'll make billions."

So, it was a multi-pronged scheme; spread a virus, take advantage of the ruined economy, and sell the vaccine.

After a long pause Levy continued. "Yes, I know we still need someone to ferry it over, that's what the old man is for."

Another pause while Levy took another question.

"All he has to do is wind up on shore. Again, we'll infect him before he goes over and he'll spread it to whoever he comes in contact with. To maximize exposure, I'll let it leak to some of the old man's former friends that a credible threat is crossing the Bering Strait. The Russian coast guard will pick him up, fly him to Moscow, and that will become ground zero."

I could tell the virologist was getting impatient with the questions coming from the other end of the phone because his tone turned harsh.

"Christ almighty, enough with the inquisition. It will be ready for transport tomorrow morning and I'll send it to the medical clinic in Wales by FedEx."

Another pause.

"I'm a goddamn scientist, Bob, I've shipped biological specimens before and they cannot go on commercial flights. It's not my first rodeo."

Another pause.

"Well why didn't you tell me you'd front the money to fly

me private? That makes everything simpler. I'll just take the sample on the plane with me."

Another pause.

"It's literally going to be half a dozen Q-tips sealed in airtight transport tubes each no bigger than a test tube."

Another question from the other end of the phone.

"I'll put the tubes in a cryobox. Happy?"

Another pause.

"No, it's just a term, we don't need to transport the samples cold but I can't risk exposing the tubes to UV light because it will kill the virus. The cryobox's job is to protect it. Now where will I meet this plane?"

I heard the sound of Levy writing something down.

"Let me read this back to you, Deerfield Valley Airport in Dover, Vermont. I knew I should have studied tech instead of viruses. But hey, in another six months I'll be able to buy a fleet of planes."

Another pause.

"Don't worry about that. When I finally get to Wales I'll stick one of the swabs up his nose myself. Satisfied?"

Another pause.

"I'll be decked out in PPE"

Another pause.

"Personal protective equipment! This conversation is over."

Levy hung up the phone and exhaled loudly. I heard him walk over to the closet where I was hiding and hoped he couldn't hear my heart pounding through my chest. I heard him pick something up, presumably his computer bag, and then exited his office. I waited for ten minutes to give me a buffer before doing the same.

I considered my next course of action. Going to the authorities wasn't practical as I had absolutely no credibility as Peter Avellino, a man who literally appeared out of thin air just a few weeks ago. On top of that, I had faked my own death by working in collusion with a known mobster and, while I knew the identities of at least two illegals plotting against the United States, all my evidence about their true identities was circumstantial. I knew that Marie Charcot was possibly a highly trained Russian spy, but couldn't exactly prove it by pointing to a tattoo on her hip that I, as Peter Avellino, shouldn't know anything about.

I did know, however, that my friend and mentor, Sam Shoah, was still alive and was going to be used to mule a virus between Alaska and Russia. I had to get to Alaska in time to try and help him.

CHAPTER TWENTY-EIGHT

Know When to Hold Em

Aside from getting stuck in traffic between Manchester and Hartford, the drive back to New Rochelle was uneventful. After arriving at 55 Interlaken, I called Patsy to ask for a meeting as I needed his advice on how I could go about rescuing Sam from his current predicament. He and Sam went way back, and I figured I could use all the help I could get. Patsy told me he'd be at his restaurant, Puzzo's, all day and to meet him there for an early dinner.

I took a quick shower and then put on one of the new suits that Patsy gave me. I needed to ask him for a big favor and wanted to look my best while doing so.

It would only take me an hour to get to Arthur Avenue, which meant I still had a little time to kill before I was expected at the restaurant, so I investigated flight options to Alaska and learned that there was no real easy way to get to Wales, where Anton was going to infect Sam and have him mule the virus across the Bering Strait into Russia.

The most efficient route took me direct from JFK Airport in New York to Seattle where I'd connect to Anchorage. From there I'd go to Nome where I'd take a puddle jumper to

Wales. When I arrived, there wouldn't be any five-star lodging; the best I could do was rent one of two trailers located next to the airfield, presumably for flight crews who needed overnight accommodation. Levy was right to take BA up on his offer to fly private and, while I had financial means, finding someone who could ferry me to a remote part of Alaska on short notice seemed unlikely.

I checked the weather in Wales and it looked like the daily high would only reach fifteen degrees, which meant I needed to get some warmer clothes. I headed out to the Pedigree ski shop in White Plains and bought a new coat, hat, gloves and thermal undergarments, all on clearance. The salesperson was so happy for a late April windfall that he threw in a duffle bag for half price. I put everything in it and stored it in the trunk of my car.

Patsy told me to park in the small lot behind Puzzo's and, sure enough, there was a prime spot waiting for me when I arrived. I entered through a back door, walked down a narrow hallway where the restrooms were, and then entered the main dining room, which only had a few guests in it. All looked to be middle-aged women enjoying an early dinner after shopping on the avenue.

I didn't see Patsy anywhere and walked to the front of the restaurant where the bartender asked, "Can I help you?"

"My name is Peter Avellino. I'm here to see Patsy."

The bartender, who had short hair and puffy face that made him look like an overweight Ray Liotta, extended his hand and said, "I'm Alfred. He's expecting you. Follow me."

I followed Alfred back through the dining room and into the hallway I walked through when coming in from the backdoor. There was a doorway in-between the men's and ladies rooms which led down to the basement. It felt like déjà vu from my experience with Dimitri Popov.

"Peter Avellino to see you, Patsy. Want me to send some

food down?"

"You hungry?" Patsy asked.

If I wasn't hungry before walking into the restaurant, the smells that hit my nose while walking through it primed by appetite. "I could eat."

"Have Mario send down some things," Patsy instructed and then Alfred left us alone. Unlike Popov's office, which was basically a desk in a small storeroom, Patsy's was more like a private dining room. *If these walls could talk*, I thought to myself.

"So, what have you learned?"

I gave Patsy an overview of what Dimitri Popov told me regarding the illegals program and how I learned my old boss was up to some financial scheme involving short selling. I concluded with how a scientist, and former colleague of Sam's, was going to use him to mule a virus over to Russia.

"And our government wanted to take the Mafia down. They probably funded research on this virus to begin with. So, what do you want to do?"

"First, I need to save Sam. If we can pluck him from the equation, their plan goes to shit."

"Maybe," Patsy said. "Though they could just find someone else to act as the mule."

"I thought of that too, but Sam, given his former role as a deep cover Russian agent, is key to getting the powers that be in Moscow to take action. Since he was part of their illegals program, they will take it seriously and grab him the moment he reaches the Russian shoreline."

"I get it, but there's another angle to play."

I raised an eyebrow.

"Their entire plan doesn't hinge on Sam; it really hinges on him being infected with a virus and then being ferried over to Mother Russia." He paused to see if I was tracking what he was saying.

"So if they don't infect him with the virus, their plan falls apart."

"Exactly. But the key will be to convince them that they did infect him, or whoever they wind up sending over there if your rescue attempt succeeds. If they believe they are still in control of this hand, it will be all the sweeter when we lay our cards on the table."

Patsy was channeling his inner Kenny Rogers—gotta know when to hold 'em, know when to fold 'em.

"Which means that we somehow have to switch the virus samples with a placebo."

"Any idea how this Dr. Levy is going to transport them?"

"He's flying private," I replied.

"Out of where?"

"A regional airport in Dover, Vermont. The virus samples will be on cotton swabs and he's putting them in some kind of transport tube and then in another box for protection."

"Protection from what?"

"Ultraviolet light. Apparently it kills viruses."

Patsy paused and thought for a moment. "We have associates in the Aircraft Mechanics Fraternal Association, maybe they could help."

There was a knock at the door.

"It's Alfred," the bartender said from the other side of the door.

"Come on in," Patsy replied.

The bartender wheeled in a cart with enough food for the Russian army. There was a meat and cheese spread, salad, pasta, and chicken topped with prosciutto, eggplant, and mozzarella.

"I hope you like Sorrentino," Patsy said. After placing all the food on the table, Alfred left.

"So, the million-dollar question is, how do you switch the samples?"

I didn't answer right away as I needed to consider a few courses of action.

"Remember what I said, Irish, when you have a tough problem don't rest until you come up with a solution. It sometimes helps to think out loud."

"There are a few courses of action we could take. First would be to get inside his lab before he collects the samples and kill the virus so that he takes something inactive to Alaska."

"I got guys who can do bacon and eggs, but I imagine there's some high-tech security in these university labs."

"Bacon and eggs?"

"I sometimes forget you are an academic. Another word for breaking and entering."

Silly me.

"Plus, I don't exactly know my way around a lab and could wind up infecting myself with whatever Levy is planning on transporting."

"What else you got?"

"We could do a switch-a-roo with the samples he collects. I can put some cotton swabs in a collection tube and switch them for the ones with the virus on them, but that means I have to get close enough to him to make switch."

"That's some Mission Impossible shit right there, Irish. Even if you could get in a position to make the switch, too much can go wrong."

"Such as?"

"Well, do you have any idea what these tubes look like? If the tubes you bring are different in any way, shape, or form, he'll know that something was up. Plus, then you are walking around with some unknown live virus on your person. I don't like it."

"Well, plan C would involve killing the virus once he's collected it, but I'm not sure how to do that."

"There's a solution to every problem, Irish."

I knew I couldn't just brush this off. Too much was at stake including Sam's life, the health of my fellow Americans, and the US economy.

"Don't give up, think it through."

Unfortunately, at that moment, I was stuffed from the feast we'd been eating and felt as if all the blood left my head and went right to my stomach. I needed to move. "Can we take a walk?"

"Good idea."

We went back upstairs and then through the dining room and Patsy stopped at just about every table to thank people for coming to his place.

"The restaurant business is very personal," he said. "Treat people like family and show your appreciation for their patronage and your restaurant will always be full, provided the food is good."

"This your only place?" I asked.

"Nah. I have another in Ft. Lauderdale, but I haven't spent much time there recently. If you ever make it down, it's called Cafe Martorano and there will always be a table ready for you."

We walked outside onto Arthur Ave and headed down the street.

"Belmont has changed so much," he said. "Look at this," he said while pointing to a homeless man harassing someone at a neighboring restaurant. "All these people want to do is eat in peace and you've got riff-raff like this bothering people. That's what got me sent to college a couple years back."

"What's that?"

"There was a bum who used to harass people for money right in front of Puzzo's and no matter what I did, he wouldn't go. I'd give him money to leave, but he just came back. So, I had someone encourage him to leave."

I could only imagine what that entailed.

"Anyways, some hanger-on who was in my restaurant was wearing a wire and it caught me giving the order to take care of the bum and I did two years for it. Two years for a broken finger."

It's ironic that a guy like Patsy, whose criminal enterprise was about as wide as it could be, got pinched for taking care of a bum who was harassing his patrons. You can't make this stuff up.

We continued to 187th Street and saw a crowd of people in front of someone running a shell game.

"These tourists will never learn. The pea isn't under any of those shells," he whispered to me.

We stood by and watched five people lose their money and then left.

"I was sure I could follow the cup the ball was under."

"I'm sure you did. It's a classic sleight of hand trick," Patsy said.

I wondered if I could play a sleight of hand trick with the cotton swabs Levy was going to pack in the shipping container.

"Let's keep walking, Irish."

We continued down 187th and then Patsy started lamenting about a tanning salon that had opened in the neighborhood.

"Madonna Mia," he said. "The health department made us buy a bunch of UV lamps for Puzzo's to kill bacteria in our kitchen and dining room. We can't even be in the room when those things are on because of the damage they could do and you've got these sciocchi bathing in them just so they can get a tan before summer. They may as well smoke in them things and get two cancers for the price of one."

Patsy's rant made me think about something I overheard Levy say back in his office, that he had to protect the virus samples from UV light because that could kill it.

"Where did you get those UV lamps?"

"Home Depot. What are you thinking, Irish?"

I told him the idea he inspired, and a big smile came over his face.

"You know, that just might work. I'll call one of our union contacts today and you make your way up to Vermont. Have you thought about how you are going to get to Alaska yet?"

I ran through all the hoops I'd have to jump through if I flew commercial.

"You can't do that. Too much can go wrong. One delay and Levy would be too far ahead of you."

"You have any better ideas?"

"The brass in the Aircraft Mechanics Fraternal Association has a plane they use when visiting local chapters. I can make sure it will be waiting for you in Vermont."

We walked back to Puzzo's and Patsy accompanied me to my car in the back lot.

"How does she run?"

I had to admit, while I missed my Tesla, the Audi was a thrill to drive.

"She doesn't drive, she flies."

"Well, you better fly on up to Vermont, Irish. Good luck to you."

"Thanks, Patsy."

I got in the car and left the Bronx. I stopped at a Home Depot in Connecticut on the way up, purchased what I needed, and went straight back to the Hampton Inn I stayed at the night before in Vermont. I walked through the plan in my mind a few times and then called it a night.

CHAPTER TWENTY-NINE

One Step Up

Tuesday morning's alarm felt as if it came at me out of nowhere and I was tempted to hit the snooze button, which would break one of my cardinal rules, which is to never use the snooze.

My ex-wife was a snooze button aficionado. Anna would hit the damn thing no fewer than six times every morning, which served two functions; it got her another hour of sleep and it royally pissed me off. I once questioned her as to why she didn't just set her alarm for an hour later, and she growled at me. There were some things I did miss about that women, but her reaction whenever I questioned her judgment wasn't one of them.

I was waiting for a call from Patsy's union contact as he was key to what I needed to accomplish that day. I was on the clock as Dr. Anton Levy was almost certainly on his way up to Vermont from his lab and we'd have to move fast.

Time passed slowly while I waited for the call and that reminded me of a psychological fact; time always feels slower when you are waiting for something to happen. If you ever want to test this out, sit on a chair with nothing in front of you and set a timer for 10 minutes. Don't think about anything else except waiting for it to ring and that ten minutes will feel like an eternity. Conversely, repeat the exercise and actively daydream without thinking about the timer; time will feel as if it went by quicker.

I made another cup of coffee from the instant machine in my room and started thinking about Sam and how his life might come full circle, albeit not in a good way. When he was a child in Auschwitz, Sam and his twin brother were involved in medical experiments. Sam was the control subject while his brother was the test. Now his fellow illegals were setting him up in another experiment of sorts, but this time as the test subject. At a minimum, I knew that I had to kill the virus and that's what today would be about. Ultimately, though, I wanted to free Sam so they couldn't try to use him as a mule in the first place. Not exactly your typical Tuesday.

Speaking of which, I walked over to the wall where my newly acquired hand-held ultraviolet light disinfector lamp was charging. According to my research, I would need to expose Levy's cotton swabs to this light for at least three minutes in order to kill the virus and my only hope of doing that was if this union guy could find a way to get me on the plane.

I hit the floor to do a few push-ups to help pass the time when the phone finally rang to life.

"This is Peter," I said, and was surprised to hear a woman's voice on the other end.

"Peter, my name is Tamika Bradley, I'm with the Aircraft Mechanics Fraternal Association where safety in the air begins with quality maintenance on the ground, how are you today?"

I didn't know if she was setting me up for making a donation to their organization or if she actually was going to help me.

"I'm a little anxious," I replied.

"I understand from a mutual friend that you need our help with something, is that right?"

"You could say that."

"Well, I'm on my way to the airport now and can pick you up. Where are you staying?"

"The Hampton Inn off of 91."

"That's about fifteen minutes away. I'm going to bring you something to change into and when I see you I'll tell you the plan, m'kay?"

"That sounds fine."

"See you soon."

Now that contact had been made, I could take a quick shower and get ready. I was still sporting the five o'clock shadow but knew that I had to take on the look of an aircraft maintenance man, so I was inspired to shave most of my face, but kept a mustache. Hopefully, Tamika would have a spare hat and safety goggles as I needed to reduce the chance that Levy would recognize me from our brief conversation yesterday. I evaluated myself in the mirror and was tempted to start singing "YMCA" as I looked like the damn cowboy from The Village People.

Tamika called to tell me she was in the parking lot and I gave her my room number. A few moments later, a knock at my door told me she had arrived and when I opened it I saw a short African American woman who looked as if she could play linebacker for the Miami Dolphins. Her posture suggested a no-nonsense attitude and she handed me a blue windbreaker and a hat; both said DEA on them.

"I was expecting coveralls."

"Yeah, well, you can't always get what you want. From what I understand, you have to get onto that plane and search for something with none of the passengers looking, right?"

I nodded.

"While there are a few maintenance problems that require passengers to get off a plane, nothing would really require that they leave all of their belongings on board while a search of the aircraft is made. I checked the flight records for the plane and it recently came back from Mexico, so you can use that as a reason to check for drugs. I've got a couple of local officers who will meet us at the airport, West Dover isn't a big town and the local PD handles the airport, which is a pretty plum assignment because the only flights that come in and out of it these days are private."

"Don't I need a gun and badge?"

"They'll have that for you. I looked at the flight plan the pilot filed and it's scheduled to leave Vermont in an hour and then fly to Billings, Montana where it will stop to refuel before heading to Anchorage for more gas and then off to Wales, which frankly I didn't know existed before today. Our mutual friend tells me you need a similar trip and we've got a bird that is a bit more fuel efficient and can take you all the way to Seattle and then direct to Wales, so you'll be ahead of them even though you are leaving a bit later."

"What do DEA agents wear in addition to a windbreaker like this?"

"I'd go with a dark suit. Do you have other bags besides that overnighter? It's pretty damn cold in Alaska."

"It's in the trunk of my car."

"Fine, but let's take mine. Guessing a fine-looking man like you has a fancy car that no DEA agent could afford. I've got a black Suburban and it fits the part better."

I changed into a suit, slipped on the DEA pullover, and added the hat. I was feeling good, as if I were finally a step ahead of the bastards I was after. I looked at myself in the mirror and tried my best Clint Eastwood meats Jimmy Caan tough guy impression and liked what I saw. It was game on.

CHAPTER THIRTY

Two Steps Back

Deerfield Valley Regional Airport had been permanently closed by the FAA until 2015 when it was reopened by a group of investors who wanted an easier way to get from White Plains airport in Westchester, NY to their ski homes in Vermont. Given the fact that this airport was resurrected by the hedge fund crowd, I'm sure there's been more than a little Colombian snow on the planes that fly in and out of this place. But of course I'd think that; I was DEA now.

When we arrived at the airport, we drove to the hangar where the union's plane was undergoing pre-flight maintenance and Tamika took my bag and stowed it in an overhead compartment. She then deposited me in the small office for the airport police where I had a good view of everyone who'd be coming in and out of the small terminal. Anton Levy hadn't arrived yet, but a middle-aged man dressed as a pilot was seated in the waiting area sipping on a cup of coffee.

A small jet was visible just outside the doors leading to the tarmac and I saw Tamika go outside to begin her inspection.

The two airport officers she introduced me to were named

Greg and Jim and both looked the part with matching crew cuts and bulging muscles under their form-fitting DVRA PD shirts. Each had radios on their chest and guns on their hips. Greg, the shorter of the two, handed me a badge and a sidearm.

"The badge is official DEA, courtesy of an off-duty agent who had a bit too much to drink at après ski one night and the gun is one of ours, but don't get any ideas because it's not loaded."

I looked at the badge and identification card that came with it. "Joe Elliot? Isn't he the lead singer of Def Leppard?"

"It's better to burn out than fade away," Greg replied.

Jim, who was a good four inches taller than Greg and sported a dark tan, reviewed the plan with me.

"We are going to wait until they are on the plane and then, while Tamika is finishing her pre-flight check, we'll approach. You explain that because this plane was recently in Mexico you have to do a routine check to make sure there are no drugs on board. We will keep the passengers occupied. According to the manifest there are three passengers who are coming on board plus the pilot, so we'll have to play zone defense."

I wondered who the additional two passengers were, as Anton didn't indicate anyone else would be coming with him when I overheard his phone call yesterday.

"It sounds so simple," I replied.

"The best plans are the simplest," Greg replied, paraphrasing the law of parsimony.

I was becoming worried that Levy might recognize me and wanted to see if there was any way I could alter my appearance even more.

"Hey, you guys don't have a pair of sunglasses laying around do you?"

Greg and Jim looked at each other and laughed.

"We have a lost and found full of them," Greg said and then reached into a closet and grabbed a cardboard box. "Take your pick."

I fished out a pair of Ray-Ban Aviators, appropriate given the setting, and put them on. Satisfied that the shades and DEA hat would do the trick, we waited for the virologist to arrive, which he did ten minutes later, though I didn't see anyone else with him.

He didn't look like a chair of a biology department when he walked past on his way to greet the pilot. Gone was the poor-fitting suit of an academic and in its place was what I could best describe as a walking J. Crew catalog. Form-fitting pullover with button-down shirt underneath, khaki pants, and high-end boots. His long hair was pulled back in a ponytail and his face was freshly shaved, though his pale pallor still suggested he could be a creature of the night. He was carrying a duffle bag in one hand and a laptop case in the other.

I watched him as he exchanged some words with the pilot and stepped out of the office in an attempt to hear better.

"Captain Parker, this is my business. I'm telling you, there are three layers of protection here and there's no chance the virus can escape unless someone literally opens the transport tube. It's perfectly safe."

I assumed the samples were in the laptop bag since that was the bag he kept patting when talking about the samples.

"I still don't like it, but BA is paying me double for this trip, so I'll deal. Are you ready to go?"

Levy nodded and the two got up from where they were sitting and walked out through the doors leading out to the tarmac. I waited a few minutes for them to get settled and motioned over to Greg and Jim to let them know it was go time.

Tamika was standing on a ladder doing a fuel level check

on the wing of the plane and nodded to indicate it was time to play DEA agent. The two cops and I walked up the stairs leading up to the plane and I saw that the cockpit door was still open and that the pilot was running through a pre-flight checklist.

"Excuse me, Captain," I said in a stern voice while flashing the badge I was given. "My name is Joe Elliot with the Drug Enforcement Agency. We understand this plane recently came back from Mexico."

"That's right," he replied. "The owner and I were there last week as he was in a fishing tournament, but I can assure you there was nothing to declare on the way home."

"We aren't with customs," I replied. "It's just standard operating procedure to do a quick sweep for drugs. Would you and your passenger please follow these officers off the plane?"

"What's going on here?" Levy said indignantly, clutching his laptop bag.

"Just a formality sir," I said while holding my arm out. "Now what I'm going to need you to do is go with the captain and these gentlemen while I conduct a thorough search of this aircraft."

"The hell you are," Levy declared.

Greg and Jim were still on the ladder and I heard what sounded like three M80s going off outside.

"What the…?" I asked.

Levy gave me a wide smile. I looked outside and saw the two officers laying in a pool of blood on the tarmac, just to the left of the plane's short staircase. I prayed the third shot didn't get Tamika but assumed the worst.

"We are going to have two more people on this flight, Captain," Levy said.

I was tempted to make a run for it, but knew the gunman was still outside and, unfortunately, the gun by my side was useless. I was trapped.

I heard the sound of footsteps coming up the staircase and the next person I saw enter the plane stopped me dead in my tracks. It was Sam Shoah, and he seemed okay.

"Sam!" I said. "Look, you are in trouble. We have to get out of here."

Sam looked over at Levy.

"I told you it would work."

"Sam, what are you talking about. I was about to go to fly to the damn Arctic Circle to save you. Anton is going to have you mule a virus over to Russia and…"

"Save your breath, I know all about the plan."

"You do?"

"Of course. I devised it."

"But I heard Levy say to BA, 'That's what the old man is for.'"

Anton laughed. "Yeah. Baiting you to Alaska. I knew you were in my closet the entire time. Originally we thought we'd get you in Wales, but now that you are here, our job is much easier. What was your plan anyway?"

"Fuck off," I replied.

Another person entered the plane. It was Jacob, the Mossad agent who brought me to the safe house in the diamond district.

"We've got to stop meeting like this," he said, this time with a Russian rather than an Israeli accent. He took my gun and frisked the rest of my body. He removed the UV wand I had in my pocket and showed it to Levy.

"So, you were going to try and kill the virus. I'll give you credit for that."

Sam, my friend and mentor, betrayed me, but why? I had to know—it was the least he could do for me. I turned to him and asked, "Why?"

"I served my country dutifully and the powers that be

burned me. I lived a secret life that put my own in danger day after day, and for what? To be told that the Information Age has rendered my services obsolete! I couldn't marry, have a family, or even earn a decent living in this country. In a place where all people care about is climbing the ladder, I was stuck on the first rung."

"And when the program was over, they burned you."

"They burned all of us!" Sam shouted. "And then Russia changed. Oligarchs emerged, the things we all believed in were flushed away."

"And Anton, is he an illegal like you?" I asked.

"No. A few years ago he came to the clinic on campus and I pulled him as a client and learned how he lamented how the women's basketball coach made millions and he didn't even break the six figures. So it got me to thinking, could I exploit his skills to get back at my country for burning me?"

"So, he wasn't an illegal?"

"No, but BA was. I didn't lie about that. In fact, his teenage hobby of profiting off of viruses inspired the entire plan. But he also was necessary for two additional aspects: money and misinformation. Your technology is going to help us with the latter."

"My technology?"

"You see, Michael, we are going to create mass hysteria once the virus you ferry over to Russia makes its way back to the States. That hysteria will be fueled by a misinformation campaign about the virus that will cause such a panic that people will be afraid to leave their homes. They won't go to work, school, or seek refuge in whatever religion they practice. The economy will crumble, America will be in shambles, and we'll be richer than we ever could have dreamed.

The plan was diabolical, but I was still unsure why he needed to involve me. He owed me an answer.

"Why me? Why not just release the virus and cut the theatrics?"

"We needed to release it outside of the United States. There are only two other labs in the world working on this particular virus: one in Moscow and another in China. If we released it here, Anton's plan to capitalize on the vaccine would have looked suspicious. We chose Russia over China as we have ties to the Russian intelligence community and could get them credible information that an American intelligence asset going under the alias of Peter Avellino was planning an act of aggression against Russia. We knew they'd whisk you away to Moscow for interrogation and the virus would begin to spread from there."

"So, you infect me with the virus and I mule it over. What happens when I tell them everything I know?"

"They will never believe you. After all, you faked your death and had surgery to change your appearance. The story is so preposterous that they will beat the crap out of you until you tell them something that sounds reasonable, and by then it will be too late."

"What about Marie Charcot? Was she in on this too?"

Sam laughed. "All we know is that she isn't one of us. She was probably just someone who was trying to help you. There's no reason to believe that she had anything to do with any this."

"And that whole thing about Russian Butterflies?"

"They are very much real, but it was all part of our story. The fact that she had a tattoo was purely coincidental."

"So, she didn't kill the priest?"

"No. That was Jacob. The good father was collateral damage. Another chess piece to push you into action."

So why did Marie leave after our marathon love-making session if not to kill the priest? I guess she really did have a pressing business matter. There's that law of parsimony again.

I was also curious about why Sam had the priest send me back to New York to meet with Anna and wanted to be assured that she was out of danger.

"So why have Fr. Amar send me to New York to meet with Anna?"

"That's easy. We always knew we were going to get you in New York. That was simply our way of getting you right where we wanted you."

"And all that project Lazarus stuff, that was just to set me up to make me appear as unreliable as possible to the Russians?"

Sam nodded. "Now if you don't have any more questions, we have a long day of flying ahead of us."

Sam nodded towards the man I knew as Jacob who withdrew a small hypodermic needle from his jacket and I felt Sam and Anton grab both of my arms. They were both remarkably strong for an old man and vampiric biology professor respectively.

"Sleepy time," Jacob said.

I felt a pinch on my neck and almost immediately my vision went blurry and the voices of those around me dropped in pitch and became muffled.

CHAPTER THIRTY-ONE

A Lost Soul

When I came to, I was shivering on a boat in an icy sea floating towards a mass of land I assumed to be Russia. As consciousness came back, I realized that I had a slight cough, my nose was running, and my head hurt beyond belief.

I was alone on the vessel and noticed that it was on cruise control and traveling at a low speed. I wondered how long I'd been on board and then heard the engine start to sputter and then go quiet. They must have given the boat only enough fuel to get so far in case I came to earlier and decided to make a run for it. While the coastline was in sight, I still had a ways to go to get to shore and I was now just bobbing up and down with the current, helpless.

From seemingly out of nowhere, a blue and white vessel came barreling towards me and slowed until it was parallel with my boat. Next thing I knew, I was being shouted at in Russian by someone I assumed was from their version of the coast guard.

"I don't speak Russian," I shouted back in English.

Upon hearing my native tongue, soldiers drew their weapons and pointed them at me. Instinctively, I raised my arms above my head and a sailor lassoed one of the cleats on my boat with the expertise of a cowboy and pulled my vessel next to his. As our ships touched, a rope ladder was sent down and I had no problem understanding that they expected me to climb it.

Once I reached the deck of their ship, I was welcomed by five soldiers pointing guns at me. I noticed that, in addition to their head coverings, all were wearing face masks. One of the soldiers handed me one and motioned that I should put it on.

I did as I was told and two soldiers gave me a wide berth as they escorted me to a small cabin in what appeared to be a sick bay as evidenced by the big red cross on the entryway to that part of the ship. A towel and change of clothes were resting on a cot and my escorts motioned from a distance that I should grab the towel and clothes. Once I did, they escorted me to a shower facility and mimed that I should clean myself, which I was more than happy to do given I hadn't showered since the morning I left Vermont. I undressed in their presence and, while they kept their distance, I wasn't exactly happy about giving them a free show.

I was freezing and couldn't tell if the chill running through my body was from being exposed to the elements for as long as I'd been out at sea, or for some other reason, so I was extra thankful for the hot shower that followed. Once I was done washing, I toweled off, put on my new clothes, and then the soldiers escorted me back to my cabin in sick bay where I spent the time laying on the cot. While the chills I'd been experiencing left temporarily while I was in the shower, they were back, and with a vengeance. My teeth started chattering and my body began to shiver.

After a while I heard a knock at the door and I opened it to find someone in a nurse's outfit wearing full protective gear including a gown, face covering, and respirator. She was holding a tray with what looked to be a bowl of soup on it and mimed that I should not approach her. Apparently, no one wanted me near them. I went back to the corner of my room and watched her place the tray on the table. She exited without saying a word.

I dipped a stale roll into the broth, which tasted like a hot but watered-down chicken broth and it worked a bit to warm me up. When I was done, I started to feel dizzy so I lay back down on the cot and covered myself with the blanket they provided me. This ritual repeated three times a day for almost two weeks.

During that time, I felt as if I had the flu and felt feverish and as if someone were constantly sitting on my chest. I developed a terrible cough and felt as if I wasn't getting enough oxygen into my cells. Every day, someone dressed from head to toe in what looked like a biosafety suit came in to take my vital signs including temperature, pulse, blood pressure, and oxygen level, but not once did anyone ask me any questions. On day five, they started to draw blood twice a day and on day seven they started sticking long cotton swabs up my nose, as if they were giving me a standard flu test.

Some nights, I shivered so badly that I thought I started to hallucinate. On day ten, I could have sworn my dead son came to visit me and encouraged me to stay strong.

I was a relatively healthy forty-six-year-old man and couldn't tell you the last time I'd had the flu, but this did something to me that I never wanted to experience again. However, as quickly as these symptoms set in, they disappeared as quickly. By day twelve I started to feel human again and by day fourteen I felt completely fine.

That morning's nasal swab and blood draw would be my last. Later that afternoon I was transferred from sick bay to the brig. And that's where the interrogation began.

Every few hours two men, who, at best, could be described

as thugs would frog-march me down the hall to an interrogation room where I would be strapped into a chair and asked the same series of questions numerous times: what's your name? Who do you work for? What is your mission?

While Michael Corrigan was technically dead, I decided against identifying myself as Peter Avellino as it would eventually come out that wasn't who I really was. So, I decided to answer as Michael Corrigan.

Repeatedly, I'd say, "My name is Michael Corrigan, I am a doctoral student at the University of Connecticut, and there is a plan against my government by ex-deep-cover Soviet operatives." I told them all about Sam Shoah and his master plan involving a world-famous virologist and ex-tech titan. I even mentioned Marie Charcot's name, which I didn't think would do me any good as, apparently, she wasn't with the Russians after all, but I kept her as part of my story as she could be a witness in whatever farce of a trial I might have. At least it would be on the record.

Each time I went through the story, the person not asking questions would inflict some form of pain on me telling me that I couldn't be Michael Corrigan because Michael Corrigan was dead. It started mild and got more severe as the interrogation continued and my torturers were almost clinical about how they went about it, as if they have done this countless times before. First they started plucking my fingernails, then they'd break a finger. Eventually they started punching me in the stomach, then ribs.

It took all my remaining strength to not show any emotion during this process as I felt doing so would give them satisfaction. To diminish the sensation of pain, I used advanced breathing and visualization techniques I learned as a therapist to focus my mind elsewhere. When the pain was mild, thinking about my own childhood would do the trick but when it became more severe, I needed to focus on something greater. That's when Tyler came into play. I thought about how his life ended too early and how the Russians may have had something to do with it. I knew I had to fight for my own survival in order to bring those who had anything to do with his death to justice, and that alone gave me enough meaning to bear all the pain I'd been experiencing.

By day five I was asked to provide my testimony with something covering my eyes, which greatly disoriented me because I couldn't tell where and when the blows would come. Unfortunately for me, they moved up from my torso to my face. By day seven, I'd been punched so many times, it didn't even hurt anymore.

I knew that had to remain consistent in my replies even though not telling them what they wanted to hear only led to more pain. I took a class on criminal psychology which taught me that the human mind can be deceptive for only so long. Eventually, a guilty person will change his or her story ever so slightly, thereby opening up an opportunity for further scrutiny.

Even a strong-willed person who was telling the truth, though, might to start telling their captors a different story if they knew it would lead to a reprieve from beatings. While I was tempted to start making things up just to get them to stop, I thought of my son and how badly I wanted to get back at my old boss for his role in Tyler's death. I thought of Sam Shoah and how his betrayal needed to be dealt with. Lastly, I thought of the evil Dr. Anton Levy who infected me with a virus with the hopes I'd spread it throughout Russia, and have it come to the United States just so he could get rich taking advantage of a down economy and, of course, selling a cure. My desire to get back at each of these monsters fueled my will to stay consistent in my replies. What could would stopping the pain be if I had to lose my soul in the process?

On day eight, before the questioning began, the interrogator instructed the thug who had turned me into his own personal punching bag to grab me by the back of the head and push my face into the drain that was in the center of the floor.

"Do you know why there is a drain in this room?" he asked.

I knew that it was a rhetorical question, so I didn't bother answering. I prepared myself for another beating, but it didn't come. Instead, the interrogator said, "We are going to try something different today," he replied and then took out a syringe.

"Let's see how your story holds up with Sodium Pentothal running through your veins."

I held out my arm and didn't resist. The injection made me dizzy and I have no recollection of what I said before completely giving into the tiredness that came over me.

When I woke up, I was disoriented and started choking on what felt like a tube running down my throat. I tried to open my eyes, but they were covered by something. I started to panic and began flailing my limbs until I heard a door open and someone approach my bed.

"He's awake," an accented voice said in English.

"Okay, sir, What I need you to do is breathe out on the count of three. One, two, three." I exhaled and felt the tube exit my trachea.

"Your throat is going to be a little sore, but I will give you something for that in your IV."

While I couldn't see anything, I could tell that my vital signs were being taken as a blood pressure cuff tightened around my arm and I was asked to open my mouth for a thermometer to be inserted.

"Somebody will be in to check on your shortly."

While I felt weak, the pain I assumed would be running throughout my body wasn't there, as if I'd been given a dose of some kind of painkiller. I was hesitant to try and reach over my head to try and remove the bandages that were covering it because the last time I remembered being awake, I'd lost a full range of motion in my shoulders. With some hesitancy, I reached over my head and started to unwrap my dressing and was surprised that I did so without trouble. Where were the stiffness and pain?

Once the covering was off, I opened my eyes and realized I wasn't in the small cell in the ship's brig nor was I in the interrogation room or the cabin in sick bay. As my eyes continued to adjust, I saw that I was in a large, private hospital room apparently on a high floor given the view I had of a city. But what city?

I heard the door to my room open up and a woman's voice say, "Welcome back to the world of the living, Michael." I didn't need to wait for my eyes to adjust to know who said those words. I'd recognize her voice, and smell of her perfume for that matter, anywhere. It was Marie Charcot.

CHAPTER THIRTY-TWO

Behind Blue Eyes

She walked across the room and sat at the edge of my bed and said, "I bet you have some questions."

I had a million, and certainly wanted to know where I was, Moscow? New York? Purgatory? However, what I really wanted to know in that moment was why she called me Michael when she must have known Michael Corrigan was dead.

"How did you know…"

My throat was incredibly sore, and it hurt to speak. Thankfully, Marie had cut me off before I could even finish asking the question. I watched as she pulled out her phone, tapped its screen a few times, and played an audio file. I heard my voice say, "Dad's got to go to Brighton beach to meet some Russian gangster. What the hell have I gotten myself into?"

I remembered speaking these words at my son's grave just before going to Brighton Beach to meet with Dimitri Popov and then remembered that was just before finding the camera hidden in the plant in front of Tyler's headstone.

I started to say, "The camera…" but Marie cut me off.

"We placed it there as we didn't believe the news that you died in a car accident and figured that at some point you'd stop by to pay respects to your son."

"You said we. Who are you with? The Russians?"

This earned a laugh from Marie. "No, not the Russians. I work in counterintelligence for the United States."

"FBI?"

"No, our organization isn't as high profile. It was put into place after the 9/11 attacks and, while it has a formal name, we just call it The Company. Biowarfare has been on our radar ever since the post-9/11 Anthrax scare and we've been paying attention to virologists working with novel viruses. Since state universities get both state and federal funding, we can keep a close eye on their scientists. During a random check we picked up a conversation between Anton Levy and a presumed former Soviet deep cover agent that led us to believe they may pose a threat to the United States."

"So that's how you knew about Sam?"

Marie nodded.

Anton was the only one of the three who wasn't a former highly trained Soviet cover agent. That he would be the one to screw up made sense. In fact, he practically told his class what his plans were. Loose lips sink ships, and, in this case, master plans.

"They had me believe that you were a highly trained seductress looking to take Sam Shoah back to Russia."

"I wasn't looking to kill Sam, but I was looking to find him to question him. Regarding the seduction, as crazy as it sounds, I was into you."

"How did you come up with your cover persona?"

"What I told you was true. I was a former Wall Street trader who took a year off and became fascinated by hypnosis. When I parlayed that into a motivational speaking career, it caught the attention of someone at The Company and I was approached to join. In fact, all of us have unique covers. We even have a major hip-hop artist in The Company."

She had to be talking about Kanye West, I thought to myself. I was curious as to why someone who earned such a high income would spend any amount of time working for the government.

"So what do you get out of it?"

"I find it meaningful to be able to give back to the country that has given me so much."

There it was—meaning. It all goes back to Frankl.

"Now, I bet you want to know where you are and how you got here."

I nodded.

"Well, you are at a hospital in Stockholm, Sweden where you arrived after being airlifted off of a Russian coast guard vessel in the Barents Sea."

I remember being picked up in the Bering Sea after being set adrift there from Alaska, but the Barents Sea was on the other side of Europe. "How the hell did I get there?"

"The ship that picked you up took the Northeast Passage. Sam Shoah reached out to a connection he still had to let the Russians know that an American intelligence asset was going to attempt to enter Russia from the Bering Strait and that's how they knew to pick you up. However, because you had visited your son's grave, The Company was able to monitor your movements and we learned exactly what your old mentor and his two conspirators were up to."

"How did you…"

"I knew this guy who invented a technology that turned smartphones into sneaky eavesdropping devices in order to serve more relevant advertising to people. Sound familiar?"

I nodded. The smartphone that Patsy gave me actually wound up saving my life.

"Well, hate to break it to you, but the intelligence community has been using your technology under the Patriot Act ever since it was passed. We heard everything that you said and did over that time period."

"But how did you get the Russians to send me to Sweden?"

"Once we realized what Sam, Anton, and BA were up to, we reached out to clue the Russians in and they took interest as part of the plan was to release a novel virus in their country and be set up to take the blame. That's why you were quarantined in a sick bay for two weeks; they knew you were contagious with a novel virus and didn't want to take any chances. Fortunately, since Dr. Levy let it slip that there was a lab in Moscow working on the same virus, they were able to work with scientists in that lab and put together a treatment protocol for you. They also developed some tests to make sure you were no longer contagious. Once you were in the clear, they transferred you to the brig."

After that sank in, I realized that meant the pain I'd endured was all for nothing if the Russians knew I was telling the truth.

"What about the beatings I took after telling my story a hundred times?"

"I'm sorry about that, but we had to assume that was a mole feeding back information to Sam. They had to make your treatment look legit."

"Mission accomplished. And Tamika and the cops at the airfield in Vermont?"

"Collateral damage, I'm afraid."

"So I was a pawn in your game as well as theirs?"

"Yes, and their plan has been ruined, but they don't know it yet and I was hoping you would help us do one more thing."

One more thing? I'd already lost my identity in this whole

process, not to mention the new career I'd worked five years to launch. What else could she want?

"I'm not sure what else I can offer at this point."

Marie closed her eyes and took a deep breath in order to prepare herself for what she was about to say. "A man you trusted betrayed you, another wanted to ruin an economy by releasing a novel virus, and a third, who was responsible for the death of your son, masterminded a plan to make them all rich beyond belief. What I'm offering you is a chance to get back at them.

The thought of these three men meeting justice gave me some solace.

"What are you thinking?"

"We've been working with the Russians for the past six weeks on a misinformation campaign about a mystery virus running through Moscow. Now this news is only being targeted to certain people in the United States so as not to alarm anyone in Russia, or all of Europe for that matter."

I smiled because she was using BA's targeting tactic against him, but did she just say six weeks? It made me wonder how long I'd been in Sweden.

"Wait, how long have I been here?"

"Almost two months. Since you arrived you've had numerous surgeries to fix the bones that were broken during your interrogations, as well as some other things. You've been in a medically induced coma since then."

While I was curious about what other things she was referring to, I was interested in hearing more about how she thought I could help.

"Right now we have them nervous, particularly BA who we know already started to try and short sell certain industry stocks including hospitality and financial services as he anticipates an economic collapse."

"Why did he start selling before knowing that the virus

was Stateside?"

"The US economy is at an all-time high and he wants to maximize profits. If he sells on margin at the peak and then buys back once he thinks the stocks hit rock bottom, he'll make a killing, pardon the pun."

Right then I knew my old boss had a big problem on his hands. If he sells high and then has to buy back those shares at the same price, or higher, he'll lose his shirt, and the shirts of anyone who invested with him, including at least six Russian mobsters from Brighton Beach.

"But the virus won't cause the pandemic he's hoping because it won't reach the States. He's going to lose everything."

"On top of that," Marie added, "we have the SEC on him."

"If you have him covered, what do you need me to do?"

"Actually, we don't need you to do anything. But we are offering you the opportunity to tell him how you really feel about the death of your son."

I knew exactly what I wanted to do to BA, but was curious to know how she wanted to handle Anton and Sam.

"What about the others?"

"While the Russians are willing to give us Ahlers, they want Sam back. We are going to arrange for a prisoner swap and once he's back in Russian custody, it won't be long before he's in an unmarked grave."

"And Anton Levy?"

"He's not one of theirs, so the Russians don't want him. We will deal with him as a threat to national security."

"So what are you going to do about him?"

"Are you sure you want to know?"

I shook my head. As her words were still ringing in my ears, I considered how much I wanted to get them into the same room so that I could see the expressions on each and every one of their faces when I walked in.

"We've been monitoring all three and they are all keeping their distance from each other. BA remains on his farm in Vermont, Levy is back at the University of Connecticut, and Sam is buying his time at his condo in Pompano. From what we can tell, they don't communicate electronically with each other, not even in code."

"We'll have to lure them into a trap," I said.

"What did you have in mind?"

"What if there was a way to get them all in the same place at the same time?" I asked.

"And how do you suppose we do that? From what we can tell, they aren't talking to each other."

After a few moments of reflection, I had a thought, inspired by something Patsy taught me—to think like your opponent.

"What do all three of these men want?" I asked.

"Money," Marie said.

"Yes, but each is driven my something more. Levy is slated to make a killing from selling the vaccine, but what really drives him is to be admired as a savior."

"What about BA?"

"He's already got enough money for multiple lifetimes. He's driven by his ego—he wants to prove that he can pull levers and move markets."

"And Sam?"

"Sam Shoah wants to reap the rewards for the sacrifices he made while at the same time dolling out a penance for his former masters for their turning their backs on him."

I paused for dramatic effect. "In a way, they all want to be God—creator, savior, and ultimate judge."

"You know who else wanted to be God?" I asked, inspired by a memory from the days when I was a good Catholic.

"Who?" Marie asked.

"Lucifer."

"Didn't St. Michael the archangel send him to hell?"

I nodded. "And all the other evil spirits who prowled about the world seeking the ruin of souls. It's too bad that Michael Corrigan is dead," I said. "It would have been poetic if I could have completed this as him."

A wide smile came over Marie's face.

"What?" I asked.

"Remember how I said you had multiple surgeries to repair broken bones and some other things?"

I nodded. I'd been waiting to ask her what those other things were.

"Fair warning, you are about to see something that's going to shock you."

"What?" I asked, and then she got up from the bed, extended her hand for me to grab, which I did, and she led me into the bathroom.

"See for yourself."

I looked into the mirror and saw that Peter Avellino was gone and my old face was back. It was refreshing to see my blue eyes again.

"How did..."

"You were beaten so badly that all the work you did to alter your appearance was ruined. I had a picture of you that I pulled down from MyLife that I gave to your surgeons and they were able to work some magic. Welcome back to the land of the living, Michael Corrigan."

"What about me new identity as Peter Avellino?"

"Jesus wasn't the only one who could bring someone back from the dead. The Company has many talents in that regard."

"And my money?"

"It will take some time, but it will all be taken care of."

"Does anyone know yet? Anna? Patsy? Gianna?'

"No, and they won't until all of this business with Sam,

Anton, and BA is taken care of. To that end, we still need a plan."

How could I thrust them all into hell? Patsy would know what to do, but I couldn't reach out and had to figure this one out on my own. I closed my eyes and thought hard until I had another flash of inspiration.

"What is it?" Marie asked.

"I don't know exactly what we are going to do, but I know where I want to start."

"And where's that?"

"Our stomping grounds."

CHAPTER THIRTY-THREE

Love is all We Have Left

For all intents and purposes, Sam Shoah set me up to be the fall guy for his plan; admittedly, I walked right into it. I gave him everything he needed to manipulate me and, like a master chess player, he knew exactly what levers to pull to thrust me into action. Ironically though, the man he introduced me to, Patsy Mazzone, taught me what I needed to know to strike back.

I remembered that Sam met Patsy when he was looking for the former owner of Patsy's home, the World War II doctor who was forced to perform surgery on Nazi officers at gunpoint. Patsy knew the doc had left New York for the warmer climate of Pompano Beach and it's no coincidence that Sam bought a place there. I wanted to know what the relationship between Sam and the doc was, as I had a hunch that there might be a clue there.

With some help from Marie's organization, I learned that the former owners of Patsy's house on Chatsworth Avenue were Dr. Santino Lionetti and his wife Carol, who moved to a condo on the beach in Pompano in the late sixties. Both had been dead for well over three decades but their daughter,

Arlene, was still alive and living in nearby Ft. Lauderdale. I thought she could tell me something I could use to set a trap for Sam.

Through some research, I learned that she and her husband were members of a country club in neighboring Plantation and that she was on the membership committee. I set up a tour of the Ft. Lauderdale Country Club and asked Marie to join me so we could pose as a couple.

We arrived at the club dressed as if we were about to play a round and were greeted by a woman with salt and pepper hair who sported a wide smile. "You must be the Mazzone's."

The decision to use Patsy's surname was a calculated one. If she remembered that a Mazzone purchased her childhood home, it would help to build rapport.

"When I saw that name on my sheet for today I made a note to ask if you are any relation to Patsy Mazzone of Larchmont."

"What a small world," I said. "Patsy is my father."

"The world is about to get smaller," Arlene said. "My parents sold Patsy the house on Chatsworth Avenue."

"I love that mid-century colonial!" I said with excitement.

"My mother designed it," Arlene said proudly.

For the next hour, Arlene showed us around the grounds including both eighteen-hole courses, the pro shop, the driving range, and locker rooms. We ended our tour in the exquisite dining room.

"So, what do you think?"

Marie whispered something in my ear.

"Well, Arlene, we love the facilities but were hoping for a place with a pool and some tennis, for the kids."

When I said that, Marie coughed a bit.

"Well, we hear that a lot from our younger members. I can tell you that we have some of the most reasonable initiation fees and yearly dues in town."

I needed to get Arlene off of golf and talking about the old days before I asked about Sam.

"So how old were you when you moved here from Larchmont?"

"Oh, my husband and I were already married when my parents moved down here. My dad sold his practice in Larchmont and got a job working for a cruise line as a ship's doctor. Mom ran the ship's gift shop after selling her business. They saw the world and got paid for it."

A tall man came into the room and sat down at our table. He was slim and what remained of his hair was grey at the temples and dark on top. He kissed Arlene on the cheek.

"This is my husband, Don. Donnie, these are the Mazzone's from Larchmont."

"Any relation to…?"

"Yes, we covered that already."

"Nice to meet you both," Don said. "Don't let me interrupt."

"What kind of business was your mother in?" Marie asked, focusing the conversation back to Arlene's mother.

"She was a clothing designer," Arlene said nonchalantly.

"Arlene is being humble about her mother. She was one of the most influential designers of her day. In fact, Greg Cassini was her apprentice."

"Oleg," Arlene corrected her husband. Well, back in those days, women didn't get the credit they deserved," she lamented.

"So you stayed in New York when your parents moved down here?" Marie asked.

"Well, funny story. Donnie and I had two kids up in New Rochelle and then his job took us down to Plantation."

"I never should have sold that house on Interlaken Avenue."

Did he just say Interlaken Avenue?

"What number?" I asked.

"Seventy-five," Don replied.

That was just two doors down from mine.

"Anyway, we moved down here and were only about fifteen minutes away from Mom and Dad."

"And that was a blessing," Don said. "After the twins came, your mother was a lifesaver."

"Twins?" Marie asked.

"I was supposed to have a large baby girl and I came home with two boys. Our daughter always said, 'Mom, if you were going to have two, couldn't one of them have been a girl?'"

Don jumped in. I got the sense he liked to hear himself talk. "I traveled a lot for business, and it was great to have her mother around so much."

Now that we had established a good rapport, I thought it was a good time to ask about Sam.

"Hey, do you remember your mom or dad ever talking about a man named Sam Shoah? My father told me how one day he answered the door and a man was there looking for your father because he heard about a former Army officer who was captured and forced to operate on German soldiers."

"That asshole," Don said.

"I sense there's a story there," Marie offered.

Arlene scolded her husband lightly, "Donnie, be nice."

"I never trusted that man. He was a real club member."

"Club member?" Marie asked.

"A member of the asshole club. In fact, he could have been the president," Don clarified.

"Why not, if you don't mind me asking? My father thought there was something funny about him too."

"For one, he hit on her mother at your father's funeral."

All this time, I thought Sam was interested in the doctor due to his wartime experience. I had to consider he may have been after the doc's wife.

"Is there any reason to believe Sam knew your mother at all?"

"Well, it's possible, but I'd need to know where Sam was from. My mother was from a very small farm town in upstate New York."

"What town?" I asked.

"Little Falls."

That's the same town Sam moved to after leaving Canada when he was young. So that's it, he knew the doc's wife and tried to make a play at her. If true, I believed I had something I could use to lure the old man into a trap.

"It's getting late and we have to get the kids from school," I said.

"Oh, what school are they in?"

On the way to the course, I remembered passing by a Catholic elementary school called St. Gregory's and gave them that name.

"Oh Donnie, that's where we sent our kids," she said while rubbing her husband's arms. "Is Sister Peter Marie still there?"

Judging by Don and Arlene's age, I had to imagine that if this manly sounding nun taught their kids, she was long in the ground by now.

"I'm afraid not."

"Good. For a woman of God, that nun was a witch," Don replied.

"Another club member?" Marie asked.

"Could have been VP," Don said and laughed.

This earned a punch in the arm from Arlene. "Don't speak ill of the religious."

"Club member," Don mouthed behind her back.

"It was nice meeting you both," Marie said. "My hubby and I have a busy afternoon so we have to get going. Thank you for your time."

I suppressed a laugh and the two of us got up, walked back to the car, and drove back to Ft. Lauderdale.

The Ritz Carlton in Ft. Lauderdale wasn't as busy as it had been the last time we were there. Given what we had to discuss was sensitive, we didn't dare talk out in the open so ordered room service from Marie's room. Unlike last time, we had separate accommodations this time around.

Marie took a sip of wine and said, "So the old man had the hots for another man's wife. How do we use that to lure him, and his accomplices, into a trap?"

I was so lost in thought that I didn't hear a word of what Marie just said.

"I wonder if he loved her."

"You know, if you ever want someone to keep a secret, tell it to a man because they never listen anyway."

"I'm sorry, I was just thinking that if Sam loved the doctor's wife, it would explain why he came looking for her back in the sixties and also explain why he followed them down to Pompano."

I could see Marie's wheels turning. "He's eighty-two and judging by Arlene's age I'm guessing her mother would have been much older than that right now. So he could have been cougar hunting, but what difference does that make?"

"Sam had it drilled into me that there are three ways of living your life with meaning: through fulfilling work, by having courage in the face of danger, and through love. Sam told me that he found great meaning in his work and, given the nature of that work, he must have had courage in the face of danger. The only thing missing for him was love. Maybe that's what the doc's wife represented for him."

"I'll give you all of that, but how can we use it to get these guys into the same place at the same time?"

I got up and walked towards the window which had a view overlooking the Atlantic Ocean. The sea was a little rough and I noticed how the wind was whipping the palm trees back and forth. Just off-shore, I saw a very close call between three people who were kite surfing.

"A collision course," I muttered.

"How do you suppose we do that?"

"The old man is practically in hiding and isn't going to want to travel, so we will have to find a way to get the other two down here."

"What would draw each of them to Florida?" Marie asked.

I smiled and thought of a line from *The Godfather*. "We'll make them an offer they can't refuse."

"Want to expand on that, Don Corleone?"

"Levy's plan is to start selling a vaccine for the virus, but he's not exactly a renowned virologist. When you think about it, he's just another university scientist. It would help him tremendously if he could get featured in a high-profile piece on viruses."

"We'd need to bring a big-named journalist in on what we've been doing and that's not a risk I feel we can take."

I thought of my ex-wife Anna and how her new husband was a hot shot investigative journalist with *The Times*. "What if there was someone we could trust?"

"Such as?"

"Philip Jenkins."

"Your ex-wife's husband?"

"Someone has done their homework."

"It's my job. But why would he offer to help?"

"Phillip needs a big story in order to get promoted to the editor role for *The Times'* science section. If you promise him the scoop on this story after these three demons are dealt with, he'll do anything you want."

"Let's say he agrees, why do the interview in Florida? Why

not at Levy's lab in Connecticut?"

"Maybe a cluster of cases of a novel virus is discovered in Ft. Lauderdale and that becomes part of the profile piece on Levy."

Marie was quiet for a moment as she thought it through. "Okay, so we get him down here, what about BA?"

"Ahlers is easy," I said. "He's looking to short the market on a scale that hasn't been seen since the housing bubble burst in 2008. He's secured investments from six Russian gangsters, maybe the Italians want in."

"Italians?"

"Patsy told me a about a place he owns down here Cafe Martorano that will always have a table waiting for me. I'm sure some friends of his down there might be interested in a face-to-face sit-down to hear how they can get in on the action."

"And maybe Phillip might want to have his first meeting with Dr. Levy there as well. Which begs the question, how do we get the old man there?"

Love is all we have left, I thought to myself. For some reason these lyrics from a U2 song popped into my head.

"If Sam did love the doc's wife, would he attend a philanthropic event in her honor?"

"What kind of event?"

"The doc's wife was a very influential clothing designer. What if her alma mater decided to offer a scholarship in her name and host an awards dinner at..."

"Cafe Martorano," Marie finished my sentence.

I smiled and nodded.

"You know, we could use someone like you at The Company," Marie said. "I can put in a good word with the bosses."

"How do they feel about interoffice romances?" I asked brazenly. I'd never been one to be so impulsive and am not sure what came over me, but couldn't help myself."

"The policy is simple," Marie replied while walking towards me and unbuttoning her blouse. "Don't ask, don't tell."

CHAPTER THIRTY-FOUR

Fall from Grace

I'm a big fan of movies and, to me, *The Godfather* is the best movie ever made. At the end, when Michael takes out the heads of the rival families, plus Mo Greene, I can't help but feel happy that he struck back at the men who attempted to kill his father, those who succeeded in killing his brother, and the one who was planning on betraying him, Tessio. Michael Corleone, though, is a tragic character. He never wanted to take part in his family's business, nor did his father want that kind of life for him. In taking over the reins of the family, he too became a sinner and, while his intentions were good, wound up selling more than just a bit of his soul to the devil.

My stepfather always said that the road to hell is paved with good intentions and I had to question how much asphalt I'd be laying down on that road today. If everything went according to the plans Marie and I had been laying for the past few weeks, three men were about to lose their lives and one of those was one I considered a father figure. I suppose Sam Shoah is my Tessio.

Since my ex-wife's husband could not know that I was still alive, Marie made the approach to Philip and promised him the story of a lifetime. Knowing that it would clinch his new job if it came to fruition, he grabbed at the chance to profile Dr. Anton Levy, chair of the University of Connecticut's biology department, in exchange for the full story which would follow.

Before Philip was allowed to approach Levy with the opportunity, I worked with Marie's technology staff at The Company to plant some misinformation about a cluster of people of Russian descent in South Florida who were suffering from a mystery illness. During my dissertation defense, Levy accused me of falling victim to confirmation bias when analyzing my data. Ironically, he would fall victim to the same thing as there wouldn't be anything in the mainstream media about a mystery illness in Ft. Lauderdale. In effect, he believed what we sent him because he expected it to be true and disregarded anything that suggested otherwise. Karma is a bitch.

After ensuring Levy read our communications, Marie instructed Philip to approach the virologist about an interview and invited him to have their first meeting at a private room at a fancy Italian restaurant in Ft. Lauderdale. Philip, however, was over fifteen hundred miles away in New York when Anton Levy showed up for their seven o'clock reservation. He was seated in one of three private dining rooms and told that his dinner date was stuck in traffic. He was offered a complimentary beverage while he waited.

Unbeknownst to Levy, a wall separated him and my old boss, BA, who had come down to Florida to meet with who he thought were some Italian wise guys looking to invest in the opportunity he offered to the Russians in Brighton Beach. To make that approach seem all the more legitimate, Dimitri Popov offered to broker the meeting and flew down with BA and met him at the restaurant. This addition was Marie's idea, who thought Popov's support would ensure BA would meet with the Italians. The two of them sat in a room waiting for some made men who would never show.

Marie and I waited in a small office just off the kitchen and watched a video feed of all three rooms on closed-circuit TV. Levy seemed agitated as his ego was grappling with the fact that he was being kept waiting. BA, on the other hand, was placated with cocktails and seemingly enjoying Popov's company.

Meatloaf may have believed that two out of three ain't bad, but we needed to bat three for three and Sam Shoah had yet to show. Weeks ago, we sent him an invite to an event supposedly hosted by the Southeast Alumni chapter of the Parsons School of Design where the inaugural Carol Lionetti scholarship would be bestowed on a worthy student from nearby Cardinal Gibbons High School. If he truly loved Carol, we thought he'd show as it would have meaning for him. We started losing hope at twenty minutes past seven but breathed a sigh of relief when he approached the host a few minutes past seven thirty. He was brought to the third private party room where he was surprised to find that he was all alone.

The room he was brought to had three tables set up in a horseshoe format; in the open space between the tables there were three chairs. Sam was asked to sit in the center chair. While I was watching on a poor-quality video feed, I could tell by his body language that he knew he was done for. Marie gave a signal and one of Marie's colleagues, dressed as a waiter, secured Sam's arms behind his back and placed a cover over his head.

I turned my attention to the room BA was in and watched as another of Marie's colleagues approached my old boss with a drink and then surprised him with a jab which landed on his nose. Dimitri Popov helped to secure BA's hands and Marie's guy put a bag over his head. Together they frog marched him to the room where Sam was and sat him to Sam's left.

Levy went down easy. Clearly he'd never been in a fight before because when Marie's guy came in to subdue him, the virologist cowered in the corner and just slithered down the wall like the snake that he was. With a bag over his head, he was led to the room where Sam and BA were.

"It's now or never," Marie said to me.

I gave myself a quick glance in the mirror and was amazed at how much I looked like my old self. Never was I so glad to have what Patsy called a plain face. When we walked into the room, Dimitri Popov and his five associates from Brighton Beach were already seated at one of the tables in the room while Marie's colleagues from The Company were seated at another. At the head table was a man I didn't recognize who had a face that looked like it was shaped with the precision of a laser and a high top haircut that suggested that the Cold War was still alive and well.

"FSB," Marie whispered.

She and I took seats next to him at the head table; I made sure to be front and center. Marie gave a signal to the three men standing behind Anton, BA, and Sam and their hoods were removed in unison.

Once their eyes adjusted to the light and they realized who they were looking at, I saw each man's face go as white as a ghost. I heard the sound of water trickling and saw that Anton Levy had started to wet himself.

I looked at my old boss directly in the eyes. "Hi Robert, remember me?"

"Michael, I…I."

I raised my hand to indicate that he should stop talking.

"You were a brilliant programmer, and I learned a lot from you, but you ultimately decided to use your talent for evil. You used the technology we created to divide people when it could have brought them together. And, of course, you used it to encourage acts of violence and even suicide. Let's not forget your plan to profit off of a down economy. For these sins, you will be punished.

I then turned my attention to Anton Levy.

"And you, Doctor Levy, who had the audacity to challenge my research when you were planning what amounts to an act of terrorism against the United States and, quite possibly, the world. What do we do with you? Oh wait, I've got some unfortunate news, the virus never left Russia. As a matter of fact, I didn't spread it to anyone because the Russians were tipped off about your plan before you put me on that boat. Word of advice, when you have a master plan centering on ecoterrorism, don't go and tell a bunch of undergraduates."

I looked over at BA.

"Of course, this means that your plan to short the US stock market is going to fail miserably and the millions of dollars you've taken from the generous Russian men seated at this table will have to be repaid, assuming, of course, you can come up with that kind of cash. I saw the Dow today. Record growth."

I then turned my attention to the man whose eyes I'd been avoiding since the cover was ripped off of his head. My old friend and mentor, Sam Shoah. The man had the gall to teach me the importance of living life with meaning.

"You know, Sam, when I was being beaten to within an inch of my life, I have you to thank for the will to live. I kept thinking how I needed to survive so that I could convince the Russians what you were up to. And, of course, I had to survive so I could get back at the man responsible for my son's death. At any number of times during my inquisition I could have rolled over and given up, but there had to be meaning in my suffering, so I chose to fight on. And here we are. Do you have anything to say for yourself?

"I underestimated you," was all he could say.

I nodded at each of Marie's men standing behind the three demons in front of me and each removed a sheet of paper with seven lines of text printed on it. These pieces of paper were then placed in the laps of each seated man.

"On the count of three, I want each of you to read what is on this paper in unison. One, two, three."

All three men started to say, "St. Michael the Archangel, defend us in battle. Be our defense against the wickedness and snares of the Devil. May God rebuke him, we humbly pray, and do thou, O Prince of the heavenly hosts, by the power of God, thrust into hell Satan, and all the evil spirits, who prowl about the world seeking the ruin of souls."

"Can I get an Amen?" I asked.

I stared at the three men and waited for one of them to say something, but all I heard was the sound of a woman counting. I looked over to my right and saw Marie's lips moving. "Three, four, five…"

As the numbers increased, I felt myself pull away from the scene in front of me. Once she got to ten, I opened my eyes and found that I'd been transported fifteen hundred miles away, to the Jorgensen at the University of Connecticut.

CHAPTER THIRTY-FIVE

Ordinary Time

To say I was confused would have been the understatement of the year. I was wide awake and staring at Marie Charcot and realized I was on stage. I heard someone in the audience shout, "Hey, we want to know how it ends."

"I'm sure you do," Marie said. "But the union says the show has to end at eleven and I have to cut it short. How about a round of applause for Michael Corrigan for being such a good sport.

I was still confused as to what had just happened and Marie could tell.

"Don't worry, you were in a deep hypnotic state and what you just went through was very realistic. Follow me to the green room after the show, and I will debrief you."

She then turned her attention to the audience. "I always love coming to the University of Connecticut. you all for coming and go Huskies!"

The auditorium erupted with applause, the curtain was closed, and the houselights went up. Marie removed her headset microphone and its wireless pack that was attached to the waist of her jeans and then asked me to follow her off the stage.

A young man, who I assumed was her assistant, handed her a towel and bottle of water.

"Do you have another one of those for Mr. Corrigan, Dan?" Marie asked.

"Of course," he said and handed me a cold bottle of water.

"Follow me, the green room isn't far."

While I was eager to get Marie's take on all I had just divulged to twenty-five-hundred people, I needed a breather.

"Actually, can I just have a few moments to collect my thoughts? I could use some fresh air."

"Of course," Marie said and then walked me to a side door that opened up to a small balcony littered with cigarette butts. I've never been a smoker but felt as if I could use something to calm my nerves. Fresh air would have to do the trick.

"I'll give you a few minutes. When you are ready, I'll be in the green room, which is just down the hall and to the left."

The door closed behind me. Now alone on the balcony, I took a few deep breaths to center myself. I took a long pull on the bottle of water Marie's assistant gave me and eventually the disorientation I had felt after coming out of state dissipated. After a few more deep breaths and some more H20, I felt ready for Marie's analysis.

I went back into Jorgensen and found Marie in the green room, which was a glorified lounge with surprisingly modern furniture given the age of the theatre. Marie had taken a seat on an oversized chair and motioned for me to take a seat on the couch adjacent to it. I laughed.

"What's so funny?"

"Usually I'm in a chair like that and my patients lie on the couch."

"Well no one said you had to lie down, just get comfortable."

I sat up and stared at her. "So doc, give it to me straight."

"I have to say, that was one of the most vivid FLPs I've ever done."

"FLP?" I asked.

"Sorry, shorthand for future-life progression. You wanted to be an intelligence officer, huh?"

"Yeah. It was my dream when I was in college."

"I can tell you hold some resentment against your ex-wife because of that. It would have saved you both a whole lot of heartache if you could have just leveled with her when you were younger."

"Hindsight is 20/20," I replied.

"And my goal with the FLP exercise is to make foresight 20/20."

"There are a few themes that emerged from your FLP, but before we get into the real heavy stuff I have to know, what's your pre-occupation with *The Godfather* and *Columbo*? You made multiple references to both throughout your FLP."

"*The Godfather* is my favorite movie of all time. In many ways, I identify with the tragic nature of the Michael Corleone character as he was thrust into a world he never really wanted to be in. As far as *Columbo* goes, I'm obsessed with the show. It broke all the rules of what a police drama should be. The audience knows within the first few minutes who did it and the fun of the show is watching Detective Columbo put it together. I like things that break the rules."

"Well, now that we have that out of the way, let's begin. It's clear that someone in your life betrayed you. I get how your wife did so you by having an extramarital affair, but I'm curious why your subconscious also picked Sam as a betrayer."

"Me too," I said. "He's always been a father figure to me and has never hurt me."

"Tell me more about your real father."

"Birth father, or stepfather?" I asked.

"Ahh," Marie said as if a lightbulb had gone off in her head. "Birth father."

"He ran out on me and my mother when I was a teenager. I haven't seen him since."

"There you go. As a father figure, you projected some of that resentment onto Sam and your subconscious dreamed up a scenario where he took on the role of betrayer. Patsy was the other father figure in your FLP. Could he represent your stepfather?"

I laughed. My stepfather was certainly no mobster, but he was a real people person and creative problem solver. "My mother's second husband was everything I wanted in a father and more."

It never ceases to amaze me how much parental relationships impact behavior. When we are little, we put so much faith and trust in our primary caretakers because we have to. When that trust is broken, it causes wounds in us to show up slowly over our lifetime. As a clinical student, most of the people I've treated in therapy for relationship issues had some form of childhood trauma that impacted them negatively as adults.

"Another thing that is clear is how much you blame yourself for your son's death. Why?"

"Because I wasn't there for him when he needed me. I was always working and when I learned he was being bulled on social media, something that I helped to create, I internalized his suicide as being my fault."

"In order for you to reach your fullest potential, you need to shed that way of thinking. It will only hold you back."

"I just miss him so much and regret the choices I made back then."

"Have you ever explored this in therapy?"

"No," I replied. In a true testament to how hypocritical life is, I eschewed therapy for myself, choosing instead to carry the burden of Tyler's death on my shoulders rather than try to embrace a potential path to healing.

"And the failure of your marriage?"

I shook my head.

"You can't move forward in life until you address these wounds, Michael."

"I don't think these wounds will ever heal," I admitted. The truth is, I grew up believing suffering was a good thing.

"You said something interesting in your FLP, something about offering suffering up for the souls of Purgatory. What does that mean?"

I laughed a little at that. "You aren't Catholic, are you?"

She shook her head. "Anglican."

"Catholic light," my mother would say.

"My father would call us Catholics with money," she joked.

"Well, we poor Catholics believe in this concept called Purgatory, where souls go for more spiritual cleansing after they die. It's believed that we here on earth can help these souls in Purgatory get their heavenly reward if we offer up our suffering for their benefit."

"So, subconsciously, you feel as if the burden of your son's death and your failed marriage are weights you should carry so that a bunch of people who are already dead, and who you never knew, could get into heaven?"

"Something like that." The way she said it sounded so crazy. "But there's more to it than that. Maybe I don't want to heal because I feel that I deserve to suffer."

"Listen to me, no one deserves to suffer. Look, you will always carry scars from these tragedies, and you will never be the same as you were before experiencing a trauma as severe as what you experienced, but those wounds can heal if you let them."

I gave her a puzzled look.

"Let me give you a quick example. Imagine that you've got a hammer, a nail, and a block of wood. You bang the nail into the wood. That's trauma. Now, you remove the nail and what is left?"

"A hole," I replied.

"Yes, the trauma is gone, but its effects remain. Now, you can repair that hole, can't you?"

"I suppose, you can Spackle it."

"Very good. Now the wood will never be exactly what it was before the nail was beaten into it, but it won't be as bad as it was when the nail was still in it. Understand?"

I nodded.

"Now, another thing that was clear; you were a person of religious faith before and that is something you wrestle with now. Your subconscious characterized you as St. Michael the archangel after all."

She was right, I was a person of faith at one point, but the sexual abuse scandal put a nail in the coffin of my faith.

"They preyed on children and others covered it up," I protested.

"I'm not blaming you, but your subconscious is clearly hungry for something more. You need to find a way to reconcile your anger at the Church and your desire for something spiritual in your life."

St. Thomas Aquinas was the church on campus and was run by the Jesuits, a religious order that's very academic in nature and one that I have a lot of respect for as they can be considered change makers in the Church. I'd passed by it countless times and debated going in, but always held back. Perhaps it was time to explore Ignatian spirituality.

"Another thing, and it's somewhat embarrassing to bring up, but you are very lonely, aren't you?"

Over the past five years, I'd buried myself in the pursuit of my degree and didn't make any time for romantic relationships.

"Yes." I nodded.

"And it's clear that you don't have much confidence in yourself sexually. I mean, that much was pretty clear in your story."

Now I knew what she meant when she said something would be embarrassing. I visualized a pretty intense sex scene with her, thereby betraying my attraction to her.

"What is it with men and anxiety around sex? You are always so worried about how good you are that you can never enjoy the moment."

"In my defense, I don't have a lot of experience in that area. I only had one lover before meeting my ex-wife, and she wasn't exactly what you would call a practitioner of the sexual arts."

"Fair enough, but you are only what, forty-six?"

I nodded.

"You also fantasized about changing your appearance including your face and also your body. Where does that come from?"

"I've always been self-conscious about my body type. No matter how much I diet and exercise, I never look the way I want."

"Believe it or not, a lot of my male clients have this same problem. They lack confidence because their bodies do not reflect what culture says a male body should look like. First off, you are fine. Second, it really is all about attitude. An objectively handsome man could walk into a room and wouldn't turn any heads if he kept telling himself he wasn't good looking enough. Conversely, a mediocre-looking guy with an abundance of confidence can land a supermodel. Focus your energy on what you can control, such as your attitude and your inner dialogue. So, put yourself out there, fall in love, have some good sex. You are a good-looking guy, just believe in yourself."

Engaging in a fulfilling, loving relationship was one of Frankl's keys to living a fulfilling life. It all gets back to Frankl!

"I only have a few more points to make. It's clear that you crave adventure in life, I mean you just envisioned being what amounts to a spy after all. Did you ever feel as if you had adventure in your life?"

In truth, I did, particularly in the early days of my career when I was helping invent the interactive marketing industry. "Yeah, at one point, but that kind of decayed once I hit a certain point in tech. I realized the technology I was developing was turning people into nothing but eyeballs to get ads and messages in front of."

"And what about now? How will you find adventure as Michael Corrigan, Ph.D.?"

I laughed a little. That's a similar question as to the one Sam had challenged me with over dinner.

"I'm still working on that."

"Good!" she said emphatically. "I didn't expect you to have a firm answer, but the fact that you are conscious of it is a good thing. You have to find meaning in work."

Frankl again.

"Now, one last point. All of what I am suggesting to you including addressing your wounds and the resentment lingering from them, finding love, and building a meaningful career is going to take courage. It's not easy to examine your life the way you need to do so and you may be scared of what you find. But, to paraphrase JFK, don't do it because it is easy, do it because it is hard. You can have an unbelievably fulfilling life if you just let yourself. What's key to that is allowing yourself to have everything you've ever wanted.

"You know, that's been one of my biggest challenges," I

said.

"What's that?"

"Being able to verbalize what I want in life. I've never been able to do it."

"Why do you think that is?"

"I never wanted to disappoint anyone. I always told people what I think they wanted to hear, even when I knew it wasn't right for me."

"And by always attempting to not disappoint others, who did you always wind up disappointing?"

I closed my eyes and admitted, "Me."

Somewhere along the way, and I can't really pinpoint where, I wound up losing myself. When I was younger, I had dreams and aspirations but as I got older, I made too many compromises and, through a dangerous defense mechanism called rationalization, kept telling myself it was okay because I was getting something else in return. At forty-six, I made a vow to start putting myself first more often. To start living for me.

"Then I, the great Madame Charcot, who does not have a butterfly tattoo above my hip, a private jet, or ties to a secretive American intelligence agency, absolve you of your sins. Go forth and sin no more."

CHAPTER THIRTY-SIX

Redemption

I walked out of the green room and exited Jorgensen though a back door, presumably one that performers use when arriving and departing. It was well after midnight, and the center of campus was dead, though I could hear some loud voices coming from the direction of the bars located just off campus.

I walked back to Hale Hall where my car was parked and was thankful that it had not erupted in flames. I spotted a note that rested under one of my windshield wipers, removed it from its rubber prison, and read it. It was from Gianna.

"Well you have quite the imagination, Agent Avellino. My grandfather is going to get a kick out of your thinking he was mobbed up. I hoped you enjoyed your night. Great job today —G."

I smiled and then drove back to my house on Lake Coventry and found that, while my day was an emotional roller coaster, I wasn't the least bit tired.

I hadn't looked at my phone since before the show and, finding nothing of interest on the television, decided to see if I had any missed calls and noticed one from Anna. I never did get back to her to let her know that I successfully defended my dissertation earlier.

"I know you don't text so I'm just calling to see how it went. I'll be up late because Philip is away. Give me a call." Instinctively, I hit redial and regretted it immediately after Anna picked up and said, "Hello," with the groggy voice of someone who'd clearly just been awoken.

"Mike, what time is it?"

"12:45. You said you were going to be up late."

"Yeah, but up late to me means *The Tonight Show*, not *The Late Show*."

"I'm sorry. I just wanted you to know that things went well today, that's all."

"Good," she said. "I'm happy for you. Really."

"Thanks," I replied and then paused.

"What is it?"

I thought about all the things Marie illuminated for me tonight and figured there was no better time than the present to address some of my lingering emotions with Anna.

"I need you to listen to what I have to say, I mean really listen."

"Sounds serious," she quipped.

"Look, I know I wasn't the best husband and that I worked too much and wasn't attentive to your needs. I also know that I was too passive with you even after suspecting that you were having an affair. You needed a few things that I couldn't provide, and I just wanted you to know that I'm sorry for all of that."

I could tell that this caught her off guard because I remained silent for a few moments before speaking.

"You weren't always a bad husband, Mike. Our dynamic was flawed from the beginning. I knew that I was taking advantage of you and that, in many ways, I wasn't giving you what you needed, and you found that in your work. But I did love you."

I've had to counsel couples through the clinic on campus and have come to realize that when relationships go into crisis, it's not the fault of any one person but rather something in the dynamic that needs to be addressed. If both parties are willing to own up to their contributions to that dynamic, they have a chance at repairing the relationship. If not, then it's off to Splitsville.

"Thank you for saying that," I replied. "Are you happy with Philip?" In the past, I'll admit to wanting to hear her say that she was falling out of love with the guy, but at that moment I honestly cared about her wellbeing.

"I am, Mike, and I hope one day that you can find someone who deserves all that you have to offer."

"Thank you for saying that," I replied. "I'll let you get back to bed."

At some point I'd have to tell her about the role she and Philip played in my future-life progression, but tonight wasn't the time.

After hanging up, I was still wide awake and remembered that there was still a cipher included in the back of the book that Sam had given me earlier in the evening.

After retrieving it from my car, I poured myself a glass of wine and cracked the book open. The first thing I had to do was identify a six-letter code word to build the cipher key. Knowing how powerful the subconscious is, I tried using the word that I dreamt up in the FLP that Marie walked me through on stage—Frankl.

After building the cipher key, I went to work decoding the message and, sure enough, it wasn't gobbledygook. What I had deciphered was an email address. Donald dot Witryol at cia dot gov.

Clearly, Sam was suggesting that I reach out to someone he

knew at the CIA, but why? There's only one way to find out so I opened my computer and typed an email.

Dear Mr. Witryol,

My name is Michael Corrigan and, recently, I successfully defended my doctoral dissertation in clinical psychology. My dissertation advisor, Sam Shoah, suggested I reach out to you as I consider what the future holds for me. If you are amenable, I'd love to have a conversation at your earliest convenience.

Regards,

Michael Corrigan

I hit send, poured another glass of wine, and switched on the TV. The opening credits of *The Thomas Crown Affair* had not finished rolling when a bing emanating from my laptop announced an email came in. I was shocked to see that it was from Don Witryol.

Dear Mr. Corrigan,

Thank you for reaching out. Sam speaks very highly of you and took the liberty of forwarding us your written dissertation. We at the agency are putting together a new digital division and could use someone with your background and skillset to help develop cutting-edge cyber tradecraft to support our missions in the digital age. We feel that someone who understands how both computers and people work would be a valuable asset to our organization. I'm based in Washington but can meet you at our field office in New York City tomorrow afternoon at lunch.

If not interested, simply don't reply. This message will self-destruct.

Regards,

Don Witryol

PS. This message won't really self-destruct. Who said government spooks can't have a sense of humor?

I had to reread the message five times to make sure I understood it correctly. The Central Intelligence Agency, an organization I wanted to work for since I was a kid, was interested in talking to me about helping them build a new capability. I had given up on a dream of adventure in the world of spy craft years ago and now an opportunity to follow that dream was staring at me in the face.

It was a scary proposition. A future life in academia would be comfortable and intellectually fulfilling, but boring as hell. Life as a therapist would be personally fulfilling, but could I really see myself counseling unhappy people all day? Life at the agency, on the other hand, would be challenging. I imagined there would be some intense training and I'd be thrust into dangerous situations where perhaps the safety of our nation would hang in the balance.

Who was I kidding? This was a no brainer. I went back to my computer and tapped out a reply.

Mr. Witryol,

I'll meet you in New York. I'll be wearing a dark suit, and a monocle.

Regards,
Michael Corrigan

Michael the Archangel appears multiple times in the Bible as protector and defender. In the book of Daniel, Michael the Archangel appears in Daniel's vision as "the great prince" who defends Israel against its enemies. In the Book of Revelation, he leads God's armies to final victory over the forces of evil. Devotion to Michael the Archangel is the oldest angelic devotion. The Church in the West began to observe a feast honoring Michael and the angels in the fifth century. Today, St. Michael is invoked for protection from evil and from enemies.

In 2018, the bishop of our diocese, the Most Reverend Frank Caggiano, asked each parish to recite the prayer to St. Michael at the conclusion of every mass. In his words, "Christ has conquered sin and death, but we are still in the midst of a spiritual battle. For that reason, I would like the Prayer to St. Michael the Archangel recited at the end of every Mass in the Diocese. I believe that the Church is facing a moment of crisis that demands honesty and repentance from the bishops and decisive action to ensure that these failures will never happen again."

I often receive inspiration for stories in mass and once I heard the phrase, "seeking the ruin of souls," I knew I had a title on my hands. The story, though, took two years to develop and, as much as it was inspired by the line from a prayer, it was also inspired by someone who had a profound impact on my life, the late Sam Witryol, Ph.D.

Dr. Witryol was a professor emeritus at the University of Connecticut, where I earned an undergraduate degree in psychology. He was my professor for Psychological Tests and Measurements and I took a shining to him right away, so much so that I'd meet him in his office before class and carry his canvas bag of books from the psych building to Monteith —a brick building located just behind it. While we walked, Sam always enjoyed a pipe as well as giving me unsolicited advice. He died at the age of 93 on August 3rd 2015—twenty-eight years to the day I lost my grandfather, who also inspired a character in this novel.

Patsy Mazzone's house is located at 90 Chatsworth Avenue in Larchmont. That's the same address my grandparents lived back in the 1950s. My grandfather, Peter Fauci (yes, he's related to Dr. Anthony Fauci) did have an office in that home and my mother would work there doing the books. She still tells the story about how he would accept locally grown produce from patients who struggled to pay his fee with money. Grandpa Peter was a World War II vet involved in the invasion of Normandy and was, like the character inspired in this novel, forced to perform surgery at gunpoint on German officers. I've been looking for a way to weave that family fact into a storyline, and The Ruin of Souls provided a perfect opportunity.

Another address in this book holds some significant family meaning. When my parents were first married, they lived in New Rochelle at 55 Interlaken Avenue and my father always refers to that house as the one he should never have sold. I drove my mother and him by it recently and I explained how much he loved the home and I wanted to memorialize it in this story.

Two of my three children are studying at the University of Connecticut right now and that inspired me to make that a key setting for this novel. Since they started school, I've often dreamt about going back and pursuing the Ph.D. I put off for twenty-five years and, while a boy can always dream, it's highly unlikely I'll be able to check that off of my bucket list. That said, it was fun living vicariously through Michael Corrigan as he was able to accomplish something I always wanted to.

Speaking of which, as an undergraduate at UConn, one thing I did do was wind up on stage my freshman year at a hypnotist's show. James Mapes came to UConn every year and during the fall of 1992, I was put in state and made part of his show. When I initially outlined this novel, I thought having the lead character attend a similar show would be a fun way to walk down memory lane, but it wasn't until I was writing the end that I decided to make it a much more important plot point.

Lastly, while the name of this novel came to me a few years ago, the story itself was written in the middle of the COVID-19 pandemic. You, no doubt, noticed some parallels to the virus mentioned in the book and the novel coronavirus that is impacting our world. To be clear, I do not believe this virus is part of a conspiracy to bring down the global economy, but the creative in me couldn't help but indulge in a little fantasy while writing this story.

I'd like to thank the meticulous Sue Oates for helping proofread this novel as well as my editor Eagle for her keen eye and helpful suggestions.

I hope you enjoyed this book and look forward to dreaming up another story for you again.

—Michael Carlon, December, 2020

www.ingramcontent.com/pod-product-compliance
Lightning Source LLC
Chambersburg PA
CBHW060245100726
47907CB00003B/768